Race the ATLANTIC WIND

OISÍN McGANN is a best-selling and award-winning writer-illustrator. He has produced dozens of books and short stories for all ages of reader, including twelve novels, in genres ranging from comedy horror to conspiracy thriller, from science fiction and fantasy to historical fiction. These include the *Mad Grandad* series, *Headbomz: Wreckin' Yer Head*, and novels such as *The Gods and Their Machines*, *Rat Runners* and *The Wildenstern Saga*. He is married with three children, two dogs and a cat, and lives somewhere in the Irish countryside, where he won't be heard shouting at his computer.

Race the ATLANTIC WIND

The Flight of Alcock and Brown

Oisín McGann

THE O'BRIEN PRESS
DUBLIN

First published 2019 by The O'Brien Press Ltd,
12 Terenure Road East, Rathgar, Dublin 6, D06 HD27, Ireland.
Tel: +353 1 4923333; Fax: +353 1 4922777
E-mail: books@obrien.ie
Website: www.obrien.ie
The O'Brien Press is a member of Publishing Ireland.

ISBN: 978-1-78849-101-3

7 6 5 4 3 2 1
22 21 20 19

Printed and bound by CPI Group (UK) Ltd, Croydon, CR0 4YY.
The paper in this book is produced using pulp from managed forests.

Published in:

DUBLIN

UNESCO
City of Literature

Race the Atlantic Wind receives financial
assistance from the Arts Council

DEDICATION

For my father, Dr Brendan McGann,
who explored the world and the mind
and passed that curiosity on to his children

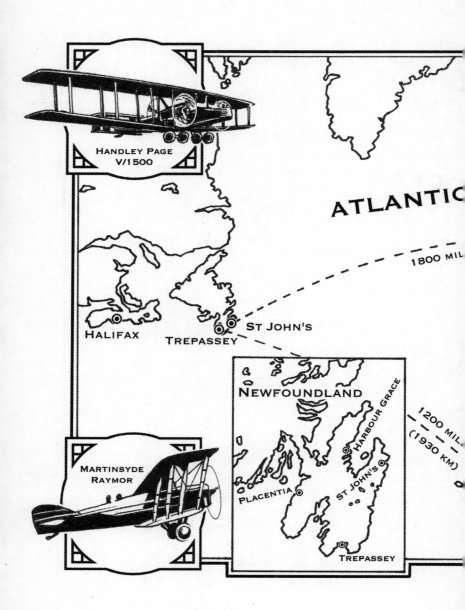

HANDLEY PAGE
V/1500

ATLANTIC

1800 MIL

HALIFAX   TREPASSEY   ST JOHN'S

NEWFOUNDLAND

HARBOUR GRACE

1200 MIL
(1930 KM)

PLACENTIA   ST JOHN'S

MARTINSYDE
RAYMOR

TREPASSEY

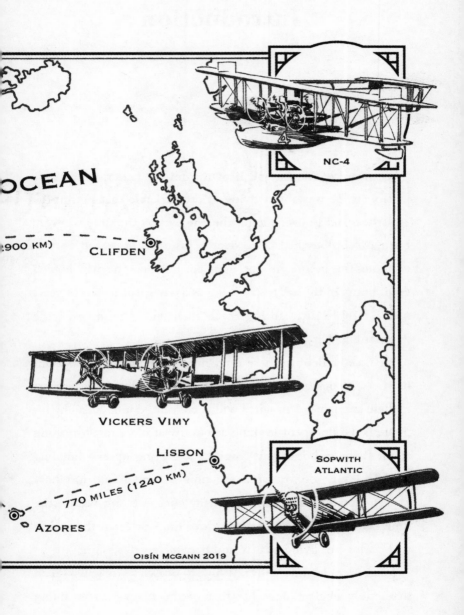

OCEAN

(900 KM)

CLIFDEN

NC-4

VICKERS VIMY

LISBON

770 MILES (1240 KM)

AZORES

SOPWITH
ATLANTIC

OISÍN MCGANN 2019

Introduction

I first heard of Alcock and Brown from my father. Given how passionate he was about flying, it's remarkable that my brothers, sisters and I never caught the bug, but by the time we were born, psychology had taken over as his main obsession. In that previous life before he got married, however, he had logged 6000 hours in the air, first serving as a navigator for eight years in the Royal Canadian Air Force, then with Canadian Pacific Airlines and Aer Lingus.

He owed a debt to those early fliers – we all do. The Wright brothers, Alcock and Brown, Charles Lindbergh, Amelia Earhart ... these are names I associate with a childhood influenced by his interests. Hours spent looking at photos of old aircraft, reading about them in books and comics and staying up late building models. I was too young at the time to understand just how experimental – and downright dangerous – flying was in the time of these pioneers, but I did love the stories. In the end, it was stories, not flying, that would become *my* obsession.

John Alcock and Arthur Whitten Brown's story has been shamefully neglected, as has that of the Navy-Curtiss flying boats, both overshadowed by Lindbergh's solo flight. The huge risk they took is really only appreciated now by historians and by flying enthusiasts like my dad. And yet the story of the flights from Newfoundland is an absolute thriller of a tale. Alcock and Brown, and others like them, were to make an all-or-nothing attempt at something many at the time believed to be impossible: to fly non-stop across the Atlantic Ocean.

Let me lay out how insanely difficult this challenge was.

I've flown across the North Atlantic four times. Like millions of others who make the trip each year, I was a passenger in an airliner. Apart from the take-offs and landings, and the odd bit of turbulence that knock the plane around, it's like riding in a bus – safe and comfortable, a smooth ride. These birds can fly higher than 30,000 feet, above the worst of the winds. You're riding in a craft whose internal air pressure and temperature is carefully controlled, a vehicle built with space-age materials and carried through the sky by powerful jet engines. You can read, sleep, play games or watch films while you fly.

The pilots have computers to help control the plane and plot their course. They use radio beacons and satellites to keep track of their position. Modern communications keep them in contact with air traffic control all over the world. Their mind-boggling array of instruments tell them everything they need to know about the state of their aircraft, how fast they are flying and at what altitude, what weather they are flying into, and what other aircraft are in the skies around them.

Now let's move more than half a century back through time. When my dad started flying in 1958, many of these technologies didn't exist, or were only being developed. He made regular flights between North America and Europe, serving as a navigator in planes like the Lockheed Hercules, the Douglas DC-8 and the Boeing 720 and 707. Aircraft from that era would be considered antiques now, but compared to the craft that Alcock and Brown flew in, they were like spaceships.

Navigation, however, was a different matter. Though they had far better instruments than the first pioneers of flight, Dad's generation flew without the help of computers or satellites, often using a technique known as 'dead reckoning', just as those early fliers did. With scant information about weather out over the oceans, often flying blind through cloud or over a featureless expanse of water, he still had to use basic instruments like paper charts and a compass. He'd use a drift sight to look down at the sea to judge how much they were being blown off course, and a bubble sextant to judge their position using the stars.

Imagine flying in a jet aircraft, and yet still having to peer through an eyepiece at the stars to find your route – essentially *the same technique used by sailors centuries before*. Even at this stage in the development of flight, bad weather, poor visibility or a simple miscalculation could easily cause you to lose your way over the ocean.

But at least you were in an enclosed, protected cockpit, you had a good radio, accurate instruments, a sturdy aircraft and powerful, reliable engines. In 1919, when the teams of aviators gathered in Newfoundland to attempt the first non-stop crossing of the Atlantic, their aircraft were utterly different. The Wright brothers had achieved the first ever powered flight less than sixteen years before. The two brothers made their living from manufacturing *bicycles*. The development of flying machines had progressed quickly during the First World War, but apart from the engines, aircraft were constructed with thin metal frames, wood, fabric and wire. Their cockpits had no roofs or canopies, so the crew were exposed to the elements.

The flight from Newfoundland to Ireland was over 1800 miles; no airplane had ever flown this distance over land, never mind over the ocean. Few could even carry the amount of fuel needed for such a journey. Aerial navigation, for the most part, still relied on being able to see the ground, following the roads, rivers and railway lines marked on maps. It was very common for fliers to get lost in cloud or fog, even over familiar territory. Very few pilots were experienced at flying at night. To fly over the sea, the first aerial navigators like Arthur Whitten Brown were having to learn their skills from sailors.

The development of engines was still in its early stages. Aircraft fell from the skies on a fairly regular basis, due to engine failure or fires. Any fire would spread quickly across the wooden and highly flammable, doped fabric structures. Early wireless could provide communication, but these radios were heavy, bulky, unreliable, used Morse Code and demanded that the flier trail a long wire from their aircraft as an aerial. Flying instruments were incredibly basic, typically measuring only height, speed, fuel and oil. A compass for direction, and perhaps a spirit level, in case the pilot couldn't see their horizon to keep the machine level.

The route Alcock and Brown and the other teams planned to take, from Newfoundland to Ireland, was the shortest one possible, but it was over freezing water dotted with icebergs in a region not known for its good weather. There was no reliable way of forecasting that weather. They were not prepared for the violence of the cold and winds they could face over the Atlantic, conditions their machines couldn't fly high enough to escape.

This flight would be an all-or-nothing attempt. Once they passed the point in the journey where they didn't have enough fuel to return, they would have to reach land or come down in the sea. Bad weather, mechanical failure, pilot error or a small mistake in navigation could doom their flight.

This was a dark time. Most of these fliers were veterans who had survived the horrors of the First World War. The Spanish flu had claimed even more lives than that terrible conflict. Whole nations were recovering from trauma, grief and financial ruin. People needed hope for a better future. Those pioneer pilots were like astronauts in the early days of space-flight, glamorous figures, going where no one had gone before. Instead of seeking out a safer existence after the war, they chose to take on an awe-inspiring challenge, one that would change the lives of future generations. And yet we learn very little about them these days. For a long time after my dad first told me about the fliers who took on the Atlantic, I heard next to nothing about them from anywhere else. I have vague memories of the basic facts of Alcock and Brown's flight, an image of that most famous photograph – of the crashed plane.

When the O'Brien Press asked me to take on this project, it lit a spark, bringing to mind that thrilling story, one which demands to be told again; a tale of hope, courage, intelligence, tragedy, a spirit of adventure, and a belief in a more open, more united world.

I hope you'll enjoy it as much as I have.

1

They were going to crash into the sea, and there was nothing he could do about it. Lieutenant John Alcock's frozen fingers gripped the wheel, his hands cramping as the aircraft wallowed clumsily through the sky, wrestling with him for control. His eyes flicked constantly between the faint horizon bordering the night sky and the compass situated behind and to the left of the wheel, illuminated by a dim electric light. The muscles of his arms and back ached and his clothes beneath the heavy leather flying suit were soaked in sweat.

The Handley Page O/100 bomber had two engines for a reason: an aircraft this size couldn't fly on just one. He glanced bitterly past his companion at the port engine, the broken remains of its four-bladed propellor spinning uselessly in the wind, no longer under power.

Aird, the navigator, sat to Alcock's left in their cramped, exposed cockpit. The two men's only protection from the slipstream was the low Pyralin windscreen, and between the noise of the starboard engine and the wind, conversation had to be shouted back and forth. Not that there was much to say. In the gunner's cockpit, right out on the nose in front of them, Wise was huddled behind his twin Lewis machine guns. Even more exposed to the wind, the engineer and gunner was unable to communicate with the two men behind him without standing up and bellowing over the windscreen. They had passed over the coast just minutes earlier, and Wise was desperately scanning the darkness of the open sea for a glimpse of a British ship. It was their one hope of escaping the enemy, who might be hunting this wounded bird even now.

The wind hummed through the wires and struts that held the upper and lower wings together, the aircraft rocking and bouncing in the turbulence. The big Handley Page was normally more stable than the smaller scout aircraft that Alcock also flew for the Navy, but now she was barely going fast enough to stay aloft. Her light wood-and-metal frame, covered in green painted fabric and plywood, trembled like a weakened, dying beast. Alcock could feel the vibrations through his hands and feet and back. She didn't have much left in her.

How many times had this craft flown successfully over the anti-aircraft batteries that protected the Turkish coast, as the shells exploded around them? Just recently, Alcock had flown a record 600 miles on one raiding flight.

This was the most advanced aircraft of its day, the British Navy's secret weapon. It was the 'The Bloody Paralyser', the first long-range bomber to operate over the Aegean Sea. The Turks and the German Navy had been taken completely by surprise by the first attacks, in September 1917. They had sent out their own aircraft to find the bomber's base, but they didn't suspect it was all the way out on the Greek island of Lemnos, far off the coast of Gallipoli. Here was proof that the Royal Naval Air Service was a new and powerful force of war.

And now Alcock and his crew were about to fall from the sky because of a busted bloody propeller.

Aird's lean face was partially covered by his goggles and leather flying helmet, and yet there was no hiding his fear. He glanced at Alcock every now and then, waiting for the decision that only the pilot could make. Their mission was over before it had properly begun; they had already dropped all their bombs to lighten their load. It only remained to be seen if they would survive the night.

'You've done your best, old chap!' Aird called out. 'But she's had it! We'll have to ditch!'

Alcock shook his head, his teeth bared as he worked his feet on the rudder bar and hauled on the wheel to pull the port wing up yet again. They had managed to fly sixty miles back towards home. Not enough. Not nearly enough.

'Not yet!' he barked back. 'We can get closer still!'

The responsibility he felt for his crew weighed on him like the heaving motion of the aircraft. It was his job to see them home safely.

'Archie', the anti-aircraft guns, had got them over Gallipoli, on the Turkish coast. They had only been ninety minutes out from their aerodrome at Mudros, the port on the island of Lemnos – still a long way from the railway stations they were supposed to bomb near Constantinople. An Archie battery had taken pot shots at them. Though it was unlikely they could be seen in the dark sky, the gunners had probably heard the engines. Most of the fire had been hopelessly wide, harmless-looking puffs of smoke in the gloom. Then one stray shell had burst ahead of them, close enough that they could feel it in the air, and shrapnel had struck the port propeller, splintering the blades.

Alcock had cut power to the port engine to prevent further damage. He managed to keep the machine in the air, and turned her about to head for home. But the biplane was one of the largest aircraft ever built – over 9,000 pounds of sprawling frame, with a wingspan of a hundred feet. As the engine between the wings to his right struggled to maintain the craft's speed, the motor on the left was dead weight. That whole half of the aircraft dragged, trying to pull them into a spin that would send them spiralling into the sea. It was taking all his skill and strength to keep them in the air, but they were losing height and speed the whole time.

Any minute now, they'd slow to stalling speed, the wings would lose their grip on the air and that would be that. A tumbling plunge to their deaths. He had to put her in the drink while he could still control their descent, and yet he put it off for another minute … and another.

This had been a good day – one of his best. That morning, three seaplanes had appeared over the aerodrome at Mudros. Thankfully, the Handley Page was out of sight, under the cover of its hangar. Alcock had been the first to take off, in his Sopwith Camel, the first to engage the enemy. The dogfight had been brief and ruthless, the Ottoman Navy aircraft unable to match the Sopwith's agility. Within minutes, two of them had smashed into the sea, and the appearance of his fellow fliers had scared the other one off. Alcock had been sure he'd escaped death for the day.

The aeroplane lurched and he almost lost control of it, levelling it out with all the strength he had left. They were very close to stalling. If their speed dropped any further, the wings would slip down through the air instead of gliding across it, and they'd be done for. He had to put her down now, while the decision was still his to make.

He motioned to Aird, who unbuckled, stood up and reached out to slap the wooden side of the cockpit. Wise looked around and Aird pointed downwards. Wise gave a grim thumbs up and nodded, then braced himself in his own small cubbyhole, readying himself for what was to come. As Aird sat down again, he checked on the flare pistol clipped to the wall near his knee. They'd need the Very lights to signal for help.

The three men loosened their seatbelts, for fear of being dragged under the water if the machine should start sinking as soon as they were down. Alcock turned into the wind, got the aircraft as level as he could and throttled back, cutting the starboard engine. Thankfully, the sky was clear enough that they had a bit of moon and some starlight. There was enough of a breeze at sea level that he could see the ruffled white caps of the waves, but no major swell. That would help. Now routine took over, as he tilted the nose down into a glide, the strain on the aircraft easing as gravity added speed. Actually *landing* would be another matter entirely.

He watched his height on the altimeter until he was too low for it to be accurate. Then he looked out to the dark horizon and down, trying to gauge exactly where the sea's rippled surface was in the blackness below. Alcock's timing would have to be perfect. If he misjudged the moment they hit the water, he could smash in too hard or dig the nose in – or drop the tail in first – and flip the whole machine over. If he didn't keep the wings level, he could gouge the surface with a wingtip and send them spinning.

As the sea's surface rose to meet them, he pulled the nose up for those last few moments and felt that floating sensation as the wings caught more air, trying to soften the blow. His technique was good, he had timed it well …

The water was rougher than it had appeared. They hit the top of a wave, and the first impact was a shocking jolt that tore off the undercarriage.

Spray smacked against the windscreen as the aircraft bounced violently, and Alcock jammed his feet hard against the rudder bar and locked his arms to hold himself in place. There was a crack of wood and the sharp, guitar twang of wires snapping. The machine came down again, this time smashing full force into the water, snapping off the lower left wing, which took the port engine went with it. Beside Alcock, the starboard engine wrenched free with a scream from its mounts. Thrown upwards, it caught on some wire and punched a hole in the leading edge of the upper wing. The propellor shattered as the engine swung back down and gouged a wound in the wall near Alcock's feet, some of the prop's fragments shooting through the cockpit like shrapnel, one piece narrowly missing his face. The aircraft's nose plunged into the water, drowning Wise's cockpit. The tail came apart, and a section of the rudder flew overhead, the broken pieces of spruce and linen catching on the upper wing and spinning crazily off to the side. The aircraft ploughed to a halt, the force of its sudden deceleration buckling the fuselage, splitting its frame and skin. The cold sea rushed in around Alcock's legs, rising quickly to his waist.

With frantic movements, he pulled himself up over the seat onto the leather-padded back edge of the cockpit. Aird clambered up beside him with the flare pistol. Their eyes were already casting forwards to Wise's cockpit, where they could see the bulge of his head in the flooded hollow of the nose. Then he burst upwards, sucking in a desperate breath with a chest tightened by the chill of the water. He scrambled up the nose, over the windscreen and into their cockpit, their hands then grasping him and hauling him up onto the flat top of the fuselage.

The aircraft was slumped low in the water, but she wasn't sinking. She'd held together enough that the fuel tanks, even though they were mostly full, were keeping her afloat. The machine was a wreck, but they were alive.

The three men looked all around, hoping for some sign of a British ship they could signal to with the Very lights. There was nothing. Aird fired one off anyway, on the slim chance some unseen, blacked-out vessel might see it. There was no response from the darkness. They pulled off their goggles, flying helmets and boots.

Torn between wanting to keep their leather flying suits on for warmth and knowing they'd have difficulty swimming in them, they struggled out of the bulky garments, but stayed wrapped in them for as long as they could remain on top of the fuselage. The machine wouldn't stay afloat forever.

Despite the suntans they'd picked up from their time on Lemnos, they all looked pale and shaken. Wise had blood running down his craggy face from a shallow wound on the forehead. He'd injured his ribs too – cracked, perhaps broken. He cursed and flexed a sore knee.

'Where are we?' he asked. 'Close enough to the coast, I think?'

'Further north than I'd like,' Aird replied. 'The Gulf of Xeros, a few miles from Suvla Bay. Though we're still within reach of our destroyers, I'd say.'

'Only if they come out this way,' said Alcock, stroking water from his ginger-brown hair, his usual good humour finding its way back to his broad, blunt features. 'Otherwise, we're sunk. I say we swim for it. It's southeast to the nearest bit of coast. Any idea which way the current is flowing?'

'Towards the coast, I think,' Aird told them. 'Let's hold on here. Help might come yet.'

Help did not come. Though Alcock did his best to keep the others' spirits up, chatting and cracking jokes, they all knew they were in a tight spot. Alcock thought of the strangeness of their situation. He had started out as a mechanic in Manchester, working on bicycles, cars and motorcycles – and eventually working his way up to the races in Brooklands in Surrey. At that time, the purpose-built race track was already being used as an aerodrome by those early aviators in their experimental aeroplanes. His skill had led to work on aircraft engines, and then to becoming a pilot himself – not something that would ever have been expected of a Mancunian working-class lad.

Now here he was, only a few years later, in the middle of a war, floating on a wrecked aeroplane off the coast of Turkey.

After nearly two hours, having fired off their few flares, the three men finally decided to swim for the coast. They were shivering with the cold and aching from the crash, now that the adrenaline had worn off, but there was nothing else for it. Alcock was nervous. The difficult flight had worn him out. Land was just in sight, a black sliver against the horizon when they were lifted higher by the waves. But there was a fair swell and he wasn't much of a swimmer. Apart from larking around in Manchester's canals as a lad, he'd spent much of his youth in garages and workshops; there hadn't been much call for swimming long distances.

Still in their tunics and trousers, the men slipped into the chilly water, thankful that this was the Aegean, and not the freezing waters of the Atlantic or the North Sea. Aird led the way, the strongest swimmer and the one with the best idea of where they were. Alcock cast one last look at the sinking bomber and then turned and struck out for the shore.

It seemed to take forever, and there were times when they felt the current was pulling them backwards faster than they could swim forwards. Eventually, however, they dragged themselves onto the beach. Alcock groaned as he felt solid ground under his feet, sand between his fingers. He stood on wobbling legs and waded the last few yards to the shore, exhausted but relieved. Dropping to his hands and knees, he gazed around him. There were high banks of grass ahead, bordering the beach, and the first of the dawn light was beginning to pick out the gold of the sand.

Their relief didn't last long. A group of figures was running along the beach to their right. Turkish soldiers in light-brown uniforms and German-style helmets. One stopped, raised a rifle and fired. Now the others did the same, and the three British fliers, in bare feet and still dressed in their uniform tunics and trousers, ran for cover as bullets threw up gouts of sand around their legs. They ducked down behind some rocks, the whine of rounds flying over their heads, with more smacking the rocks around them.

The shooting stopped, and Alcock cautiously peered out. The men were Arabic looking, rugged and hardened by combat. One, who appeared to be an officer, called out to the fliers. He was calm, a man who knew he was in control. And though he spoke Turkish, his meaning was clear: 'If you make us come in there, we'll come in shooting.' They would need little excuse to kill the men who had bombed their towns and cities.

Alcock looked to his companions, and with sour resignation, they came to the decision together. He raised his hands and stood up, and they followed suit.

This was it. The war was over for Lieutenant John Alcock.

2

Arthur Whitten Brown screamed in his sleep. The confusion of battle surrounded him; some part of his brain tried to make sense of it, while another part knew this could not be real. He was in the trenches during a bombardment, crouched shin-deep in mud, artillery shells detonating around him like God roaring in his ears, trying to make his head burst. Where was he – Ypres? The Somme? He couldn't even remember any more. The world was filled with the noise of bombs and the screeches of the dying around him, men bursting apart. The dust and debris of the pulverised British defences assaulted his eyes and nose and ears, mingling with the stench of smoke.

Then a cool wind blew across his face and, lifting his head in puzzlement, he realised he could look over the top of the trench without climbing a ladder. He was sitting down, the mud was gone and there was a leather-covered, wooden rim around him at shoulder height, a tiny rectangle of windshield in front of him. This was wrong ... this was nearly a year later, after he'd transferred to the Royal Flying Corps. He was in the observer's cockpit of a BE2C. They were flying over the enemy trenches, photographing them, as he had done so many times. The pilot behind him – Lewis? No, Henry Medlicott – was struggling to keep them on their course, the light biplane lurching awkwardly in strong winds and the shockwaves of anti-aircraft blasts; Archie was piling it on. Despite the fact that it made them an easier target, they had to fly in a straight line so that Brown could get accurate pictures of the enemy trenches below.

His body worked on reflex. He peered down through the eye-piece at the cratered landscape, snapped another photograph and went to change the plate. Archie's shells were bursting around them, machine gun rounds zipping past. A line of bullets drilled the fuselage; one punctured the fuel tank. He knew what was coming. No … Oh no. Not this again. The engine failed as Medlicott threw them into a banking turn away from the enemy fire. The machine stalled and they began to fall. As they spiralled madly, Brown was pressed back and to the side by the force of the motion. Medlicott fought desperately to bring the aircraft under control. He managed to straighten out, and level them off, but they were coming down too hard, too fast – and straight towards the enemy positions. The nose crunched into the ground, break-ing the machine's back, and Brown's cockpit folded in on him, crushing his left leg. Blood sprayed across his face as broken bone split the top of his thigh. He shrieked, fighting with the hands that gripped him, shaking him, shaking him. He opened his eyes, but it was dark now. Half-awake, he saw the faces of the dead again, some talking or laughing, some grey-skinned, disfigured by wounds. What was happening? Why couldn't he think? His leg was in such intense pain it felt as if it was being *burned off* ...

'*Arthur, you must wake up!*' the voice was saying. 'Arthur ... Teddy, wake up! It's all right, you're having the nightmares again. Wake up!'

As he rose into a befuddled consciousness, the agony of his leg was still there, but muted, hurting because he'd been thrashing around on the hard bed again. It had been nearly two years now, since he'd been injured.

'Henry?' he croaked, blinking in the gloom, the face above him in deep shadow.

'No, Teddy, it's Marchand. You're having a nightmare.'

Not Henry Medlicott ... of course not. This man had a French accent. Arthur Whitten Brown, known to his friends as 'Teddy', finally remembered where he was. He was a prisoner in Germany. Henry was here too, though he was currently locked away in solitary after another escape attempt. A French pilot named Marchand was clutching his hand now, trying to bring him back to his senses.

Brown groaned, rubbing the old wound in his thigh with his free hand. He and Henry had been shot down over Valenciennes, near Lille. Henry had done well to get the machine to the ground in one piece, for it was full of holes, the petrol tank ruptured. Brown's left leg had been shattered in the crash, which had also dislocated his hip and both his knees, and knocked out a few of his teeth.

Though the doctors at the hospital in Aix-le-Chapelle had done their best, his leg was as healed as it would ever get. He had been months recovering from his injuries, his pain eased with blessed morphine, before they'd transferred him to the prisoner-of-war camp in Germany. He would be walking with the help of a cane for the rest of his life. Lying here now, he felt so utterly exhausted. He never seemed to be able to sleep through the night any more.

Teddy looked around the shed where the officers were held. A few others peered blearily at him before turning over and going back to sleep. The officers had better quarters than the enlisted men – even a decent stove – but the place was still a hovel, with beds that were little more than wooden racks, musty straw mattresses and threadbare blankets. Despite the cold, the skin of his face, back and chest were coated in sweat. He shivered, wiped a sleeve across his brow, and tucked his blanket tighter around him.

'I'm all right, thank you,' he said to Marchand. His own accent was that of an educated Manchester man, with a hint of his parents' American twang. 'Sorry I woke you. Heaven knows, it's hard enough to sleep in this place without me raising a ruckus.'

'You're not the only one who gets nightmares, Teddy,' Marchand replied softly.

Taking a slim silver hip flask from his pocket, Marchand offered it to Brown, who gratefully unscrewed the cap. It was brandy, warm and soothing. He only had a few sips, for he could tell there wasn't much left. It was precious stuff in here.

The French pilot had also been captured after being shot down.

Like Brown, he had served in the trenches before becoming an aviator – transferring to the Aéronautique Militaire, the French army's flying corps. Like Brown, he considered himself a lucky man. They had made it out alive, when many had not.

Marchand squeezed Brown's hand, patted his shoulder and returned to his own bunk. Looking at his watch, Teddy saw that it was four o'clock in the morning. There would be no more sleep for him now, so he took a small tunneler's torch from under the jacket he used as a pillow and switched it on. There was a pile of books under his bed, and he pulled out the one on the top. Most of these had come into the camp in Red Cross parcels, sent to the prisoners, which he'd traded for, though he'd managed to do some deals with the guards too.

All of the books in his little library dealt with navigation. Opening this latest one at the page he'd marked, he began reading.

The war had gone on long enough for doctors across Europe to recognise what was happening to those involved in the fighting for any length of time. What had once been considered 'a lack of moral fibre' was now understood as shell shock – a man could be physically unharmed, but emotionally and mentally destroyed by the brutality of war. Brown was a highly intelligent man, who valued his keen mind. He was determined not to lose it to the horrors he'd seen. The nightmares were a constant reminder that he might well be up and walking, but he was far from recovered.

Distractions helped. He needed something to occupy him, to challenge him. He was disabled now. His gammy leg meant that, even if he managed to get back to the Royal Flying Corps, he could not train as a pilot as he'd intended. He was confident he could fly any of the machines he'd been up in, but the Corps demanded that its pilots be in peak physical condition.

The sky had become a crucial battlefield. Some of the other chaps in the hut with him, who had been captured more recently, told him that new pilots in the Royal Flying Corps were being thrown into action after only a few hours' flight training. It was madness. Being able to control your aircraft was only the half of it. A fresh recruit lasted an average of three weeks, easy meat for any ace flier who caught them in the air.

Brown was an engineer by education, and had been a competent mechanic by the age of seventeen. He understood these flying machines, and yet he was looking further into the future. When you flew across the lines of battle, you needed to know the landscape below you. But the features pilots relied on to find their way – roads, buildings, railway lines – could be there one day, obliterated by shelling the next. And that was assuming you didn't have fog or cloud obscuring your vision, which was often the case, or that you weren't being thrown around in bad weather.

It made a man humble, to gaze down on the ground far below and realise how insignificant humans were in that vast land. How many lives had been taken so cruelly for a few yards of ground this way or that?

War was an absurd waste, but it had transformed aircraft engineering. Once an oddball pursuit, confined to a few innovators, it was now an industrial process. As aircraft flew faster and farther, they were beginning to outpace their pilots' ability to navigate this new, wider world. Finding your path along roads as a car did, or plotting a course across the sea, at the plodding pace of a ship, could not compare with the speed and unpredictability of flight. Humans had found their way into the sky. Now they had to learn to find their way *through* it.

Huddled in his bed in that miserable prison camp, Brown leafed through the pages, continuing his study of the stars. He had seen the world from the air, had seen how much bigger it was out there, and it had changed him.

And he wanted more of it.

3

Maggie McRory was ready to do a deal. What she was not ready for, was the four crates of seal skins sitting in front of her on the cobblestones of the dock. She was just sixteen years old, but she was nobody's fool.

'What am I supposed to do with these?' she asked.

'Sell them,' Alistair Finch replied, his weathered sailor's face adopting an innocent expression.

He was native Newfoundlander, with that accent that still sounded more English than Canadian or American. Though he was a fit man in his thirties, a life spent sailing the North Atlantic had beaten on his skin and greying beard, making him look at least ten years older. He was a good-hearted sort though – not every man was happy to do business with a girl like her.

'What do I know about seal skins?' Maggie protested, brushing a stray brown lock of hair from her freckled face. 'Apart from they belong on the backs of seals. Are they good quality?'

'The best,' he said.

'Yer havin' me on!' Her skeptical grunt came out as a puff of vapour in the cold air.

Living on a farm, Maggie was not sentimental about animals, but she liked seals. An Irish girl, she'd only moved here to Newfoundland a couple of years before, and the wildlife was her favourite thing about this rough, cold island. Finch was a fisherman though, not a hunter. She wondered how he'd come upon this particular haul, and why he was so eager to get rid of it. There must be a few hundred dollars' worth of merchandise here. Why was he trying to offload it on her?

'My brother gave them to me to sell,' Finch continued, as if reading her thoughts. 'But I can't get back to St John's until the ice clears from the harbour. Besides, I haven't time for wheeling and dealing. I'll give you twenty percent of the price if you take them to town and sell them for me.'

'Would Crocker Bellamy not do it for you?'

'He's back in St John's, and you're here. And he's looking for thirty percent, and he's not getting it. This is easy money for someone, lass.'

Maggie scrunched up her impish face. She knew that this meant Crocker was looking for fifty percent at least. And she suspected that this money wouldn't be all that easy. There were plenty of traders selling seal skins.

Now, at the end of March, the weather was finally warming, as spring found this wild place. Even so, a brisk and chilly breeze was blowing in across the harbour. Well-wrapped as they were in boots and thick socks, her toes were going numb from standing there on the icy cobbles. She stamped her feet to keep the blood flowing.

Winters in Newfoundland were like nothing she had experienced back in Ireland. Here she was, in Placentia harbour, many miles from her home, because the mouth of St John's harbour was blocked by ice. In March. Ships bound for St John's, the island's capital, were having to dock here instead.

Maggie had been delighted to come across Alistair, the skipper of a fishing boat, who she knew from the docks at home. She had been hoping to do a bit of trading while she was here.

'I'll have to think about it,' she said, pulling her cap down tighter on her head. 'Now, do you want some eggs or not?'

'I'll take a dozen,' Finch said. He was sitting on one of the crates, and had some paper packages with him. He opened one to show her its contents. 'I'll give you two mackerel.'

'Only two? They're very small.' She squinted at the silver-and-blue fish, striped with black, as if she found them hard to see.

'The cheek of you, lass! Perhaps you should tell your hens to lay bigger eggs, and they'd be worth something more,' Finch snorted, pushing back his cap to give her the eye. 'A dozen eggs for two mackerel, and you take the skins to sell.'

'Make it three mackerel, and you keep your skins,' she threw back. 'My Uncle Patrick's coming home today. Anyway, what do I know about selling seal skins?'

'Nothing, I'm sure, but how else are you going to learn?' he replied.

He took a fish from another package, adding it to the two he'd shown her. They'd be good quality, she knew. His main business

33

was cod, and the rest of his catch would already be on its way to the fish market, so these would be the fish he'd kept for dinner for his crew. Less for them now, but the war had caused food shortages, and they'd be glad of a few eggs.

She tucked the wrapped fish into the satchel hanging by her thigh. Her eggs were in a box of straw held under her arm, and she counted out the dozen and handed them to Finch. He put them gently into the pockets of his big coat. Aunt Gretchen was making a roast dinner tonight, as it was a special occasion, with uncle Patrick coming home from the war, but the mackerel would make a good meal for tomorrow.

The freighter *Digby* was now drawing close to the wharf, the much smaller trawlers and tug boats put-putting out of its way as it crawled across the slate-grey water. The honk of the ship's horn carried through the pungent smell of coal smoke and seawater, and Maggie regarded the ship with nervous excitement. Watching the ship manoeuvre towards the docks, she wondered why Patrick was coming home on a freighter, instead of on the passenger ship the *SS Corsican*, like most of the other soldiers.

She hardly knew her uncle; he had left Ireland when she was only little, and had left Newfoundland to fight in the war before she'd arrived here. She had been living with his wife, Gretchen, for the last two years, helping out on the small farm and in the garage Patrick had set up, and though they struggled for money, she thought it was a good life. Now, everything was about to change.

She was somewhat intimidated too; Patrick was a *pilot*. He'd actually flown *real aeroplanes* in the war. Maggie had never seen an aircraft in real life. You'd never see the like in her hometown of Longford, and there were none here in Newfoundland either. It made Patrick seem as if he was a being from another world, like something from a Jules Verne science fiction novel. Gretchen, however, had assured her that her uncle was very much a human being, and a good man. It would all be fine. Different, but fine.

'The war changes them, y'know,' Finch said quietly, as they gazed out at the approaching ship.

'What do you mean?' Maggie asked.

'The ones who come back. They're changed by it. You'll see. Take good care of your aunt, Maggie. She'll be needing you. And your uncle too.'

Maggie jumped as a horn tooted behind her. There was Gretchen, all done up in her best dress, coat and hat, behind the wheel of their muddy Ford Model T. She was a few yards away, half-hidden behind some stacks of barrels and crates. Maggie waved, said goodbye to Finch and hurried over.

'The ship's almost in, hurry up!' Gretchen called. 'Did you sell any of those eggs?'

'I got some mackerel from Finch.' Maggie laid the egg box on the floor in the back.

'Good girl. Come on now, we don't want to keep Patrick waiting!'

For Gretchen, it was always 'Patrick'; never 'Pat' or 'Paddy'. Her family was German, and you could hear it in her accent. Gretchen

35

was tall, with a face that had some early lines on its long, flat, but attractive features. Still in her twenties, she behaved like someone older. She was so different from Maggie's mother, so strict about being civilised and having good manners, and yet so much kinder than Ma had ever been. As far as Maggie could see, she was kind and civil to everyone, and yet her German background had caused some people to turn against her because of the war.

Some were also offended by the fact that she was Jewish, and by the fact that she had converted to Catholicism to marry Patrick. It was little wonder that she was so tolerant of her unconventional niece.

Despite her devotion to propriety, Gretchen was almost breathless with excitement with the thought of seeing her husband again. Her voice betrayed a hint of anxiety too. Maggie touched her hand briefly, trying to reassure her.

Patrick's last letter had said he'd been injured when his aeroplane had crashed. It was clear from the letter, written in someone else's handwriting, that he didn't want to give details, but felt he had to prepare his wife. His legs had been broken, and he had been burned. He had said he looked different now, and he hoped it would not come as too great a shock to her.

The car ground its gears as Gretchen pulled away, her nerves rattled. That gearbox needed some work, Maggie reminded herself. She had kept the car running, and helped some of the neighbours with theirs too, but she had never taken a gearbox apart before. Still, there was a first time for everything. Perhaps she and Patrick could do it together.

As they drove along the wharf, getting as close as they could before the crowd blocked the way, they could see the gangway being set up to let passengers off the ship. A crane was swinging into position to start unloading cargo.

Gretchen swung down from the car and strode quickly into the crowd, striding forwards so fast that Maggie had to trot after her, her short legs no match for her aunt's long paces. It was strange; there wasn't usually much of a crowd when freighters were docking – they didn't carry many passengers. But today, dozens of people swarmed around the end of the gangway, including some reporters and even a few photographers.

A man appeared at the top of the gangway and gave a modest wave. He was small and young, with boyish good looks and a friendly face, dressed in a smart suit and cap. It was immediately clear that this was who everyone was waiting for. The reporters started clamouring for his attention, each wanting to be the first to ask questions. Maggie was about to ask her aunt who this might be, but Gretchen had eyes for only one man in the crowd.

'Patrick! Oh, Patrick, over here, my love!'

And Maggie turned to set eyes on her uncle for the first time in years. She expected to see the rangy, rugged Irishman with the roguish smile that she knew from photographs framed on the walls and on the mantelpiece at home.

This man, however, was something altogether different.

4

Patrick McRory had his back to the crowd and to the ship, and everything about him gave the impression of a man alone and closed off. He was thinner than in the photographs, and more hunched. His hat was low on his head, his head low on his chest, the collar of his dark grey coat pulled up around his cheeks. In his gloved left hand he carried a plain, boxy suitcase. He wore wire-framed spectacles, which Maggie hadn't expected, and there was something about his face that wasn't right.

Only when she and Gretchen drew closer did Maggie realise that Patrick was wearing a mask.

It wasn't a full mask, and it wasn't immediately obvious when you first looked at him; it was the same colour as his skin and covered nearly half his face, from just under his right eye to the right side of his chin. It almost looked natural. Almost. Maggie tried not to stare. The mask sat perfectly flat against his cheek, so there must be some kind of hollow beneath it. He was missing flesh. His right eye did not move like the left, and did not match exactly. Maggie had seen this in war veterans before – Patrick had a glass eye.

She looked to her aunt, unsure how she should react.

Gretchen's face was frozen, and tears were welling in her eyes. She went to embrace her husband and he raised his free hand, shaking his head and walking past them.

'It's good to be home,' he said hoarsely. 'You must be Maggie. Look at you, all grown up and all the way from Longford, eh? That's the car, isn't it? Looks like it's been well run in. I could do with a drink.'

He shuffled through the stragglers at the edge of the crowd, opened the passenger side door of the Model T and got in, dropping his suitcase on the back seat. Gretchen had one hand to her mouth, the other clasping Maggie's hand just a little too tightly.

Disturbed by Patrick's frosty behaviour, Maggie glanced back at the fellow who was coming down the gangway. Another man followed close behind him, older and taller, dressed in a Royal Navy uniform. Both of them greeted the reporters. Beyond them, a harbour crane was lifting a massive crate, long and narrow, from the ship's hold. This, too, excited the crowd. Photographers were standing back to take shots of it. Maggie wanted to stay, to find out what was going on, but her first duty was to her aunt and uncle. This was their day, and she had to be there for them.

Nobody said a word as Gretchen drove them through the small town of Placentia and onto the road towards St John's. The stony landscape was desolate in this area, especially towards the end of winter, with drifts of snow still lying in many places. It was cold in the open-sided car too, which would make the long journey all the more uncomfortable. Any attempt to talk to Patrick was met with a grunt of a reply.

'How long have you been wearing spectacles?' Gretchen tried at one point.

'I can see perfectly well,' he replied, touching them. 'They are part of the mask. They help to keep it on.'

This answer seemed to upset Gretchen so much, she didn't ask any more questions. Maggie, however, was still thinking about the scene at the harbour, and eventually, she couldn't contain her curiosity any longer.

'Do you know who that man was, that everyone was looking at?' she asked Patrick.

Sitting on the left side of the bench seat, he turned to look over at her.

'The small man was Harry Hawker, the famous pilot. The other one was his navigator, Lieutenant Commander Kenneth Mackenzie Grieve. They're here to try and fly the Atlantic.'

Maggie's jaw dropped. She couldn't believe they had just driven away from that.

'Did they have an *aeroplane* on that ship?'

'Yes, the Sopwith *Atlantic*,' he snorted. 'A presumptuous name.'

Maggie almost whimpered. There was an aeroplane in Newfoundland, and she wasn't going to see it! She had heard that aviators might be coming to the island, but that had just been rumours. A few weeks before, the local newspaper had said that Lord Northcliffe, the owner of London's *Daily Mail* newspaper, had offered £10,000 to the first fliers to cross the Atlantic. Some pilots would start their journeys here, it had said. It hadn't seemed real at the time. Some other British papers had made fun of Northcliffe's offer, saying they'd give similar prizes to anyone who flew to the moon, or to Mars.

'Could we go back and look at it?' she exclaimed. 'Will they be flying it today?'

'Maggie, we're going home!' Gretchen told her sharply, her voice a little too shrill.

'There's nothing to see yet. It's in pieces, and has to be assembled,' Patrick told them. 'It will take a team of workers several days to do. And they won't be the only ones to come. There's another pair, Raynham and Morgan, due in a week or so, with another aeroplane. I've heard that there could be as many as seventeen teams coming. One from Shorts, others from Handley Page and Vickers … It'll be an invasion. I wish the swines would all just stay away.'

It seemed such a strange thing to say. Nothing this exciting had ever happened in Newfoundland. Why would Patrick wish it away?

'I think it's wonderful,' Maggie said. 'I'd give anything to see an aeroplane.'

'It's not the machines, it's what they *mean*,' Patrick rasped. 'It's what they *bring*. The British Army, the Navy, they never cared about this place. Now we've got their attention because this is a jumping-off point, the shortest route across the Atlantic to Ireland. The Americans are coming too, I hear, with flying boats and a whole fleet of ships. If any of them actually succeed, then more will come. You watch, it will ruin this place. *They* will ruin it. They are a *scourge*, like locusts, these great armies and their bloody war machines …

His voice trailed off, and his hand went up to touch the flesh-coloured mask.

'I should never have gone there,' he muttered. 'God help me, I should never have gone.'

It was a long drive, on rough roads, back to Patrick and Gretchen's farm on the outskirts of St John's. They hardly spoke again. Finch had been right – the war changed people. Maggie had heard about other men who'd come home, how they'd been … damaged.

It would be all right. She and Gretchen would take care of Patrick. They would help put back in whatever the war had taken out of him.

They turned onto the slush-covered, hard-packed mud of the driveway, and pulled up in front of the house. It was a weather-beaten, wooden, single-storey building with small windows. It had a picket fence around it to keep the animals out of the house and the garden at the back. A shed on one side was for the hens, and a slightly bigger shed on the other side was for the tools and the pigs, and sometimes the goats. The few fields they had with decent soil were planted with potatoes, turnips and carrots. It wasn't much, but it was better than what Maggie had left behind in Ireland.

They had no proper barn, but off to the left of the drive was another, much bigger shed. This was one of Maggie's favourite places in the world – the garage where Patrick had set himself up as a mechanic before the start of the war. This, not the farm, had been his and Gretchen's main source of income. Gretchen had not grown up on a farm, and was still finding her way. When her family had arrived in Newfoundland, a generation before, they had made a meagre living trading in salt fish and *shmattes*, rags, before they'd become landowners. Whenever Maggie had time to herself, she would be in the garage, tinkering and fixing things.

Maggie was first out of the car, greeting the five goats who gathered round her, wearing the wide wooden collars that kept them from getting through the fence to the garden. She took Patrick's case before he could get hold of it and brought it inside. She was trying not to look at him.

It was so frustrating; there was no way of getting more news until she went into town. She worked in the evenings in Cochrane's Hotel, washing dishes to earn some extra money, but she would have to sit through dinner first. It would be hours before she could get any gossip from the hotel staff; Agnes Dooley, in particular, always knew what was going on.

Patrick was still outside; he hadn't made it up the three steps to the porch. He stood there, crying, and Gretchen was a few paces behind, afraid to touch him, looking visibly distraught. Maggie thought it was the saddest thing she'd ever seen.

'There are so many people waiting to see you,' Gretchen said. 'John and Mick and Mary and … the boys from the motorcycle club … We're all so happy to have you home, Patrick. We were going to meet up in Cochrane's tomorrow. Would you like that?'

'How could I want to meet anyone, looking like this?' he asked. 'Can't I see your face when you look at me? And Cochrane's? Christ, it'll be packed. The fliers will be staying there. The *reporters* will be there, for pity's sake. Everyone will. God, there's not a worse place I could think of going. No, Gretchen. I'm just glad to be home. I'm sorry for crying. It's just … it's all a bit much for me.'

He slumped down on the damp step, and his wife sat beside him and put a hand on his knee, disregarding the dirty slush that soiled the hem of her dress. Maggie hovered nearby, still on the porch. She didn't want to crowd them, but she was desperate to hear more about the fliers.

'They're staying at Cochrane's?' she said, breathlessly. 'Did you meet Mr Hawker on the ship? I mean, you're both pilots after all. What's he like? What does the other man do in the aeroplane? There's no aerodrome on the island. Are they going to build one? Where are they going to –'

'I'm done with all that!' Patrick snapped, turning round to glare up at her, the strangeness of the mask and his dull glass eye giving him a menacing appearance. Then he lowered his head again. 'I wanted to leave all that behind me. Just to get back to working in the garage and being with you, Gretchen, and … and there they are on the bloody ship, and more of them coming here too. It was madness over there, in France. Good God, the things I saw … Put a man in a uniform and make him part of a mob and you can make him do anything, commit any horror. *And look what it did to me!*'

He touched his mask again, tenderly, as if it was real skin. Maggie, who prided herself on being good with her hands, could only marvel at how well it was crafted, the paint matched so closely to the colour of his real skin.

'An American woman made this for me in Paris,' he told them. 'Anna Coleman Ladd, her name was; she crafted it from copper. An extraordinary woman. If I didn't have this, I'd be unbearable to look at. And there are thousands of others like me, many of them more damaged than this.' He turned to gaze up at Maggie again. 'I'm sorry for snapping at you. I … I used to be like you, y'know. I can see it in yeh. I was so taken by the glamour of it all; the *adventure*. And I *loved* the flying. But I saw what men did with those machines too, their aircraft and ships and their artillery … It wasn't just soldiers being killed on the front lines. Towns and cities were attacked – old people, women and children, dying or horribly injured. And the further those machines can fly, the more harm they can do.

'Seeing them here, it's like … it's like Hell has followed me home.'

5

The Vickers Vimy was a fine aircraft, a two-engined biplane designed as a long-range bomber, and at the age of twenty-six, Captain John Alcock was already a masterful pilot. Jack, as everyone called him, seemed to become one with the machine, once he'd settled behind the controls. He was a thoroughly decent sort too, his warm spirit and positivity infecting all those he worked with. Sitting close on Alcock's left side, Arthur Whitten Brown felt completely at ease with this man. He thought they might have a shot at success, though their chances of being first to fly across the Atlantic were looking increasingly slim.

They had a good machine, a good plan, and the engineers and resources of Vickers at their disposal. Teddy Brown felt he was where he belonged, sitting up here in an open cockpit with the raw wind rushing over him, a roaring engine on either side and the land stretching out beneath him.

It was Saturday, the 5th of April, and this was the Vimy's third test flight, and the first one at night. Fresh from the factory, the machine was tight and clean, though it needed a good run in. Teddy could still detect that new cockpit smell of castor oil, fabric dope and varnish.

They'd been flying for hours; Jack was testing the aircraft's limits, throwing her around in the air as if she was a fighter scout half the size, challenging Teddy to try to get readings on the stars in the brief moments that he kept her level. The night sky was clear above them, but the horizon was obscured by mist. Without the horizon to line his sextant up to, Teddy was forced to use an Abney spirit level – a bubble in a framed glass tube of liquid – to keep the sextant level. The sextant looked like pieces of a small telescope had been mounted on a quarter of a steering wheel. Taking a sight on the pole star was a ticklish matter, but Teddy was satisfied that his readings were good.

They had to be. Travelling these short distances over land offered little challenge to a navigator, so long as they had decent weather. Out over the featureless expanse of the Atlantic Ocean, it would be an entirely different matter. One small mistake in his pathfinding could cost them everything.

Jack pitched the aeroplane into a dive, then banked hard to the right, and Teddy gave up on trying to follow the line on his chart until they'd righted themselves again. They shared a four-foot-wide padded bench in the small cockpit, and Teddy was thrown against Jack's shoulder.

'Hell's bells! You won't be ducking Archie out there, you know!' Teddy shouted over the racket of the engines.

'One thousand eight hundred miles of ocean, Teddy! Who knows what we'll come across!' Jack called back, grinning. 'Besides, we might as well have a bit of fun now … She'll be a pig to fly once she's all loaded up!'

This was true. The big, pale grey Vimy was a good choice for the marathon journey, and not just because it was an advanced but stable design. With its new Rolls Royce Eagle VIII engines and the extra fuel tanks that now filled the bomb-bay and the observer's cockpit, it was also capable of carrying the 865 gallons of petrol they'd need to get across the ocean. Most aircraft could not. They would also need close to fifty gallons of oil to lubricate the engines and sixty-four gallons of water for the radiators to cool them. The Vimy was a large machine, fifteen feet high, forty-three feet long and with a wingspan of sixty-eight feet. Fully loaded, it weighed 13,000 pounds, as much as a fully grown African elephant.

Flying was all about balancing weight and lift. The more weight you added, the more strain you were putting on your engines and on your wings. Once it was loaded up for their epic flight, the Vickers Vimy would struggle to get off the ground.

Still, this was a great machine. Weight was not their problem – their problem was *time*. Work on building the Vimy, and altering its design for the task at hand, had started about two months earlier. Jack had been chosen as the pilot not long afterwards. When asked if he was willing to take on the Atlantic, he had answered with typical aplomb: 'I'm on it any old time!' Teddy smiled at the thought of it. Jack's ambition and drive had helped motivate the Vickers team to finish the aircraft in record time. Though Teddy Brown had only been involved for a few weeks, he and Jack had quickly become firm friends.

But they were latecomers to this competition. Harry Hawker and Kenneth Mackenzie Grieve, with their Sopwith machine, the *Atlantic*, were already in Newfoundland. Raynham and Morgan and their Martinsyde *Raymor* were well on their way. Two other aviators, a Major Wood and Captain Wylie, were planning to attempt the crossing from east to west, against the prevailing wind, in a machine built by the Short brothers. They would start from Limerick, in Ireland, and their single-engine biplane, the *Shamrock*, was apparently ready to go.

There was a Handley Page team too, with a giant V/1500, a larger and more advanced version of the bomber in which Jack had achieved his record bombing run across Turkey. Rumours of at least five American teams circulated among the fliers at Brooklands, including the well-known aviatrix Katherine Stinson, an endurance record holder. Like Wood and Wylie, Stinson intended to fly east to west, from Europe to her native United States, though no one knew who was providing her with an aircraft. Ruth Law was throwing her hat in the ring too; the first woman to fly at night, she intended to make her attempt in a new twin-engine Curtiss biplane. Others believed one of the new British or American hydrogen-filled airships had the best chance of making the crossing.

Germany had some of the most formidable pilots and machines in Europe, but they were all grounded while the treaty was being negotiated in Paris, to pull Germany's teeth after the end of the war. By all accounts, the Kaiser's people were to pay a painful price for his pride and aggression. Their military was being pulled apart. There would be no challenge from that quarter.

And then there was the United States Navy.

Unlike the other challengers, they were not competing for Lord Northcliffe's *Daily Mail* prize of £10,000 for crossing in a single aircraft in one journey. They were treating it as a full-scale military operation, with four newly designed flying boats and a fleet of ships to provide support. America was keen to prove itself as the world's greatest military power, and this operation would be part of that proof.

Compared to the best of these contenders, Jack and Teddy were considered rank outsiders … by those who were even aware of them at all.

'That's long enough, I think,' Jack said, looking at the clock on the dashboard. 'She's proved her worth. Let's take her back. Where are we headed?'

Teddy had already plotted the course back to the Brooklands aerodrome in Weybridge, where Vickers had its factory. He shone his torch on the map for his friend, who cast his eyes over the course, nodded and brought the machine around to its new bearing. Cloud was rolling in, creeping westward across the land below them, but they'd beat it home. After half an hour, they could see the paraffin flares below them that marked the airfield in the darkness. Jack took them down, landing the Vimy with no more than a soft thump of the undercarriage, as if he'd done it a hundred times before; no mean feat with a machine this size in the darkness.

Even as they taxied towards the lights of the hangar, they could see Percy Maxwell Muller and some of the other Vickers men coming out to greet them.

As they trundled across the flat stretch of beaten earth, Teddy thought back to the day he and Jack had met. After fourteen months as a prisoner in Germany, he'd been released to Switzerland, where he'd spent another nine months. He finally returned home in 1918, not long before the end of the war. Unable to resume active service, his engineering skills had been put to use for the Ministry of Munitions, in the manufacture of aircraft engines. The war had a voracious appetite for men and machines, and consumed both at a horrendous rate, ensuring plenty of work for the factories.

It was there he'd met the woman who would claim his heart, Marguerite Kathleen Kennedy – and he had asked her to be his wife. The plans he and Kathleen began making for their future together, however, suffered a blow when he lost his job.

The defeat of Germany had ended the need for most of that manufacturing almost overnight, and suddenly there were a lot of men out of the war and out of work. These factories were laying off hundreds of employees – and Brown was one of them. Britain and her allies had triumphed, but the war had left her economy in ruins.

After finally getting his pilot's license, Teddy had heard that some of the companies were making plans to take on the Atlantic, an unprecedented challenge for aerial navigators. He had sought interviews with one firm after another, hoping to get involved. Time after time, he was turned down. His visit to Vickers had been a complete fluke; he'd been accompanying a friend who had a meeting there to discuss aircraft radiators. Teddy had been unaware that this firm were also intent on crossing the ocean. He'd been sitting having tea with Percy, the works superintendent, while he waited for his friend, when Percy mentioned Vickers' plans for the transatlantic operation.

The talk turned to navigation, and it wasn't long before Teddy was offering opinions on the matter. Impressed with what he was hearing, Percy led him out to show him the Vimy and meet the pilot, Captain John Alcock. The two men took a liking to each other immediately. They discovered that they had grown up not far from each other too, in Manchester, and had friends in common.

Kneeling on the floor near the machine, they began sketching on the ground with chalk. Jack was an expert pilot and mechanic, who knew every inch of his aircraft. He was a competent enough navigator over land, but controlling the machine on this flight would take all his effort. Besides, he knew his skills were not up to crossing an ocean, though they were good enough for him to appreciate Teddy's, who had a better grasp of the theory, the science of it all. As well as the advanced mathematics involved, he was capable of picturing the world beneath him in his imagination when there was nothing around to guide his way. After a curt nod from Percy, Jack had, in characteristic fashion, made a prompt decision.

'Lieutenant Brown, would you care to fly the Atlantic?' he had asked.

'Captain Alcock, I'd be delighted to,' Teddy had replied with a smile.

The Vimy now pulled onto the apron in front of the hangar and Jack cut the power, immediately unbuckling his belt and jumping to his feet. He flexed his legs after the long flight, and then swung himself over the side of the cockpit and onto the lower right wing with easy agility. The four-bladed, ten-foot propellors had hardly stopped spinning before his boots hit the ground.

Teddy got up with considerably less ease. His gammy leg, stiffened further by hours of sitting in one position in the cold, made the climb out of the cockpit slow and awkward. Percy held out his cane to him as he clambered down to the ground. Teddy could feel the heat off the port engine behind him, and hear the ticking sounds as it cooled. He took off his fur-lined helmet and gloves and raised his eyebrows, seeing from the Scotsman's manner that he had news for them. Jack came around the nose of the machine to join them.

'Raynham just arrived in Newfoundland, and Hawker's had his first test flight there in the Sopwith already. Unless the machine gives him any problems, I'd say he could leave as soon as he gets some decent weather.'

'Well that's cheery,' Jack grunted, his Manchester accent coming out strong. 'We'd best get a move on then, eh?'

Hawker, an Australian, along with his navigator Lieutenant Commander Mackenzie Grieve, was the favourite to succeed.

Hawker was a hugely accomplished pilot, probably the best known in Britain. Grieve, a sailor rather than an aviator, was a highly experienced navigator, a man who had spent his career crossing oceans. The Sopwith aircraft was lighter and considered less sturdy than many of its competitors, but Sopwith were famous for the quality and reliability of their aeroplanes. The Sopwith Camel had been one of the most successful machines in the war.

'How's she flying?' Percy slapped the nose of the Vimy.

'I think we could do with reinforcing the undercarriage,' Jack replied. 'And she's leaning forward a bit. When you finish fitting the extra fuel tanks, the weight will be distributed differently. I can already feel the difference with the tank in the nose when I land. Perhaps we should lose the front skid, and the tail-skid too. Any extra ounce of weight we can find. And I'm still worried we're going to get air locks in the new petrol pipes. I want another look at those valves. But it's all fine tuning now – a couple more flights and she'll be set to go.'

'All right then.' Percy turned and gestured to his men, who started to pull the aircraft into the hangar for yet more work. He faced the two fliers again: 'It looks like we're on course. Listen, there's talk of strikes on the docks in London, which could hold us up, so if you're agreeable, I'll book you on the *Mauretania,* leaving Southampton on the fourth of May. That'll get you to Newfoundland around the thirteenth. Bob, Monty and Ernie will travel with you, and Bob Lyons from Rolls Royce. We'll crate up the Vimy and she'll sail on the *Glendevon* later, with the rest of the team.

There's no aerodrome anywhere in Newfoundland, and I've heard the whole place is like the bloody Yorkshire moors, so you'll need some time to find a suitable airfield before the machine arrives.'

Though Percy didn't say it, some of the Vickers men and women were getting anxious. With the war over, there were too many aircraft manufacturers and not enough demand for aeroplanes. Britain was in crisis; aviation was no longer a priority. The country had burned away its wealth, and the economy was also reeling from losing a shocking proportion of the population in a few short years.

As if the war's death toll had not been enough, the end of the conflict had contributed to another catastrophe. The movement of millions of troops across Europe in 1918, along with refugees and former prisoners, had created a perfect storm of circumstances for the spread of a disease that would end up killing more people than the war itself.

The Spanish flu had swept through Britain, wiping out over 200,000 people in that country alone. It was thought that soldiers returning home after the Armistice had brought the virus with them. All across Europe, hundreds of thousands of people had been travelling, spreading the illness as they went. It was thought that the disease had claimed almost fifty million lives worldwide. The worst affected by the epidemic were people in their twenties and thirties, so many of whom had already been lost to the war. Britain, like dozens of other nations, had been hit with this new disaster when it was least able to cope.

Hundreds of aeroplanes left over from the conflict were being scrapped, now that they were no longer needed. To stay in business in this devastated world, aircraft manufacturers were going to have to prove that they were still needed, that there was a future in air travel. Whoever was first to conquer the Atlantic would help shape that future. Vickers was in trouble, and the company badly needed this win.

'This race could be over before we even get to the starting line,' Percy observed quietly.

'Winter's slow to pass over there,' Teddy said, tapping his cane against the ground. The child of American parents, he understood just how different North America's climate was from Britain's temperate one. 'Having your machine ready is one thing. But then there's *everything else* to consider. Let's wait and see what Newfoundland has in store for us.'

6

J oey Smallwood, the young journalist with St John's local paper, the *Evening Telegram*, leaned forward in his leather armchair, notebook and pen in hand, his eyes fixed earnestly on the famous pilot, Harry Hawker.

'Tell me about your rival, Freddie Raynham. You've known him since before the war, is that right?'

Maggie, who was gathering the dishes from the tables in the lounge, took her time. She worked in Cochrane's Hotel as a dishwasher, but was dawdling out near the guests as often as she could. Her entire attention was focussed on learning as much about the aviators as possible.

Hawker leaned back in his chair, sipping on a cup of coffee as he considered the question. A blacksmith's son, born in Melbourne in Australia, he was small, shorter even than Maggie. His slim build and dark curly hair made him almost boyish looking, and a handsome boy at that. There was age around those eyes though, experience and loss. He was an odd sort, with a brash confidence around his fellow aviators, and a quick smile, yet shy and quiet around others.

'Freddie's a first rate test pilot,' he said at last, his Australian accent strange to Maggie's Irish ears. 'One of the best in Europe, I'd say. And he's a top bloke, an absolute gent. When I showed up at Hendon, near London ... back in 1912 it was, looking for work as a mechanic, I didn't know a soul, but Freddie was one of the few boys who took me seriously. He was –'

'What does that mean, a "test pilot"?' Maggie blurted out, unable to contain herself. 'Sorry, Mr Hawker, but if he's so good, why is he still doing tests?'

Smallwood scowled at being interrupted, and was about to give her a piece of his mind, before Hawker answered with a smile:

'To be a test pilot means you work for a manufacturer, testing their new aircraft. Freddie's only ... what, twenty-six? And he's logged more hours doing it than anyone I know. It's a dangerous job; only the best pilots can take it on. When a machine comes off the line, someone has to fly it for the first time, to make sure it works right. And not all of them do, of course. Some'll try and turn on you.'

'You have to fly aeroplanes *that don't work properly*?' Maggie said in amazement.

'Well, the only way to find out if it doesn't, is by *flying* it,' Hawker said, shrugging modestly. He brought his attention back to Smallwood. 'There's only so much you can learn by looking at a new machine on the ground. It's our job to put any new bird through its paces, to see if there's anything wrong with it ... And if there *is* something wrong with it, then it's our job to make it back to the ground alive, so you can tell the blokes on the shop floor what to fix. Freddie Raynham is one of the very best; that's how he's lasted this long, when so many others haven't. He was the first pilot ever to get caught in a tail-spin and come out alive. He could never say how he managed it, but it gave the rest of us hope, I can tell you, to know it could be done.'

'And yet, you've beaten him every time you've competed against him,' Smallwood said helpfully. 'Does that make you the better pilot?'

'Haw! It makes me *luckier*, anyway. Engine failure has dropped him in it more than once. For all his skill, Freddie has always had a problem with Lady Luck,' Hawker replied. With a reluctant grin, he looked out the window at the light fall of sleet drifting out of the overcast sky and added: 'Though for once, she seems to have taken his side.'

Maggie had been paying close attention to conversations that she heard in the hotel; it was a great place for gathering gossip. The four-storeyed building was the only proper hotel in the town, and it was a pleasant place to work. The sprawling hallway and lounge were wood-panelled and furnished with leather armchairs and sofas, polished wooden tables and a scattering of potted plants. The walls were adorned with cut-glass mirrors and framed nautical prints. Local musicians played in the evenings, and the place had a welcoming atmosphere.

Harry Hawker and his team had been in Newfoundland for nearly two weeks now. They had taken a site for their airfield on Glendenning's farm, near Mount Pearl, about six miles away. In that time, they'd erected a wooden hangar and workshops, and assembled their aircraft, the Sopwith *Atlantic*. They had flown their aeroplane for the first time on Thursday, the 10th of April.

It seemed as if they had a good head-start. Raynham and his team had only arrived on Friday the eleventh, though they hadn't wasted any time, setting up their operation out on the flats beside Quidi Vidi Lake, just on the edge of town.

Hawker and his navigator, Kenneth Mackenzie Grieve, were in a hurry to leave while they still had the advantage, before Raynham could get his machine ready. If it came to a neck-and-neck race across the ocean, the Martinsyde *Raymor* was a faster machine than the *Atlantic*. There were rumours of other teams on their way too. The Sopwith fliers had intended to leave on Saturday, the 12th of April, but the moody Newfoundland weather had closed in around the island. It was now Wednesday the 16th, and Raynham's team had been working away on their aeroplane this whole time. Word was, they almost had it finished.

Maggie had cycled out to the Sopwith airfield a couple of times, only to find the aeroplane hidden away in its hangar. Now, days later, she had missed the test flights because she could never find out what was going on in time, or couldn't reach the airfield fast enough when she *did* hear about something happening. She had been unable even to get a look at the Martinsyde machine either. The frustration was eating away at her, so desperate was she to see a real aeroplane fly. The way things were going, she was going to miss *everything*.

'How soon do you think you'll be able to leave?' Smallwood asked.

Hawker grunted and finished the last of his coffee. Maggie took the empty cup on its saucer, and hung there, conscious that she was being rude, but needing to hear the answer.

'We're at the mercy of the weather,' the pilot said. 'Right now, we're having to empty our machine's radiators any time the engine's going to be sitting cold, because the water will freeze. We can fly in these temperatures, but there's always the threat of the machine's controls icing up, and with the wind and cloud …' He gestured towards the window again. 'Nobody's going to be flying out over the ocean in that.'

The front door was thrown open and another man walked in, brushing sleet from his shoulders and knocking his cap against the doorframe to clear it off. He came through the hallway to the lounge and caught Hawker's eye.

This was Grieve, the Australian's partner. A striking contrast to Hawker, Grieve was tall and skinny with a large nose and sunken cheeks that give him a gaunt appearance. At the age of thirty-nine, the quiet Scotsman was nearly ten years older than the Aussie, and unlike the others involved in the transatlantic challenge, he had almost no aviation experience. He had been trained and qualified as a pilot purely for this operation, and did not consider himself an 'aviator'. He was, however, a lieutenant commander in the Royal Navy, and a highly experienced navigator. He had met Hawker during the war, while the Navy had been experimenting with landing aeroplanes on the decks of ships.

Maggie was starting to grasp the fact that, up until quite recently, aeroplanes had been unable to fly long distances. Ever-longer flights now demanded the kinds of pathfinding skills that sailors had needed for centuries.

'Freddie's ready for a test flight,' Grieve said simply. 'They're taking off in a few minutes, I'd say. The weather's expected to clear for a bit.'

'Are you sure?' Hawker jumped to his feet and strode over to the coat stand to grab his jacket.

'Aye, I was watching from the tea house near the cricket club,' Grieve told him, already turning back toward the door. 'Saw them pull the machine out into the field. They've been warming the engine up, and haven't pegged her down, so it can't be long now. We'd best get a move on if we're to catch the take off.'

With that, the two men were out the door, and the young reporter followed a moment later. Maggie was left gazing after them. It didn't surprise her that Grieve had been spying on their rivals. Though the men were all friends and treated each other with genuine camaraderie and respect, they were also fiercely competitive. The first team to set out for Ireland would set the terms of the race. Maggie hesitated for a couple of seconds, then rushed into the warm, scent-filled kitchen, still holding the cup and saucer. Agnes Dooley, the matriarch of Cochrane's Hotel, had just opened the door of one of the ovens and was inspecting a joint of roast beef.

'Agnes, can I go and see the aeroplane take off?' Maggie begged, the words nearly bursting out of her. 'It's goin' right now in a minute! I'll come back as soon as it's done, I promise!'

Agnes, a strong, stout woman of indeterminate age, regarded the Irish girl for a moment, an eyebrow raised in mock disapproval. She glanced at the clock on the wall, then folded her arms and pursed her lips.

'All right then, my little tearaway,' she said at last. 'But you just make sure you're back within the hour, for we've a full house and I'll need the dishes doin' if we're to have enough for everyone.'

'Thanks Agnes, you're a saint!' Maggie tore her apron off and threw it over the back of a chair.

'Just you be sure and be back before I serve dinner!' Agnes called after her as she raced out the door. 'Or you'll find out how much of a saint I'm not!'

Maggie nearly forgot to take her coat, and she was glad of it as she stepped out of the kitchen and into the bitter chill of the breeze that blew against the back of the building. The hotel was on a hill, on the corner of two streets, one of them sweeping down to the harbour and offering a view of the town and some of the bay. She was pulling her bicycle through the gate when she saw Gretchen and Patrick drawing up across the street in the Model T. Frowning, Maggie left the bike in the yard and strode across to the car.

'Hello, Maggie, darling,' Gretchen said, as Maggie opened the door and jumped in the back seat. From the tightness of her voice, Maggie could tell they'd been arguing. 'We were out at the doctor, and I thought we might come in to the hotel for a cup of tea, but Patrick doesn't want to.'

Gretchen had caught that bad flu over the winter, and though it hadn't taken her life, as it had taken so many others, it had left her with a niggling cough that she couldn't seem to shake. Dr Gerszel could ease her discomfort, but nothing seemed to get rid of the cough.

'We should just go home,' Patrick muttered from the passenger seat. 'This was a waste of my time.'

'And what else are you doing with your time?' Gretchen retorted sharply. 'Sitting in all day, doing nothing? The doctor is a resourceful man. I thought he might help you. He's been a great boon to so many of the men who've come home …'

'What do you know of the man? What's he even doing here? He's Polish!' Patrick growled. 'And a *Jew*!'

'*I* am a Jew, Patrick!' Gretchen said in bitter exasperation. 'Or perhaps you're unhappy with *that* too, as you are with *everything* now!'

'That's different, it's not the same.' Patrick turned his masked face towards her, one eye staring intently at her, the right one, the glass one, dull and cold. 'All I'm saying is –'

'Raynham's going to fly the Martinsyde aeroplane!' Maggie cut across them. 'Any time now, I heard. They're down by the flats near the lake. Why don't we go down and watch? It'd be marvellous, don't you think?'

'No, we'll do no such thing,' Patrick declared.

'It sounds marvellous,' Gretchen said. 'That's exactly what we'll do.'

With a quick glare across at her husband, she put the car in gear and pulled away down the road. Even as she did, they heard a buzzing whine and something large and dark flew low over the buildings. Maggie pressed against the window, craning her neck, and caught a glimpse of a winged shape swooping out to the south. It disappeared behind the looming bulk of the hotel.

The Martinsyde machine was already in the air.

7

Maggie had never told anyone that she wanted to be an explorer, not even Gretchen. She had grown up reading the stories of Jules Verne and HG Wells, and the exploits of adventurers like Nellie Bly. Her ambition seemed so unlikely, so unrealistic, and Maggie was sure she would be laughed at if her friends found out. The kinds of people who became explorers either had lots of money or had the support of people with lots of money, and Maggie had neither. But she did have a dream.

When she was little, living in Longford, Patrick had been her favourite uncle, always there with his jokes and tickles, always encouraging when she talked about the imaginary worlds she played in. He ran the garage with her father, and when her dad had died, Patrick had left for Newfoundland, to start a new life. He married a German woman over there, who took to writing to her husband's favourite niece in the following years, as they had a shared interest in books.

Not long after the war started, Maggie had received a letter from Gretchen, this aunt she had never met, who talked about being lonely.

Patrick was serving on the front in France, and Gretchen was finding life hard. His pay from the army did not make up for what he had once earned from his garage, and the farm did not earn enough to keep up with the payments on the land they had bought. There were a lot of shortages on the island; everything was more expensive, harder to get. Some of Gretchen's neighbours had turned away from her, because she came from a German family, and Germany was the enemy now.

Maggie's life at home was not a happy one; her mother was an unhappy woman, prone to using her fists against her daughter any time Maggie defied her – and Maggie was a defiant girl who did not care for the life that was being laid out for her in the parish. Ireland was becoming a violent place. Already affected by the conflict in Europe, the population was rising in angry rebellion against Britain, and many said an all-out war for independence was coming.

Apart from her books, these letters from her aunt were Maggie's only window into a bigger world. And so, on reading about Gretchen's loneliness, and at the tender age of thirteen, Maggie decided to run away from home – from her abusive mother, from the memories of her dead father, from the priest and his 'special' talks about sin, and from everything else that she knew.

Most children who run away don't get very far. Maggie made it all the way to Dublin, walking and hitching lifts, stealing food and doing odd jobs for money until she reached the port. A few days later, she stowed away on a ship bound for Newfoundland; by the time she was discovered, thirsty and starving, they were halfway across the ocean. Escaping from the bemused ship's crew when they docked in St John's, she had eventually found Gretchen. Her aunt greeted her with absolute astonishment, but then welcomed her in and told her that this could be her home if that was what she wanted.

Since then, they had become very close. Maggie quickly decided she liked the island and its people, whom she found to be very like the Irish in nature – indeed, many of them *were* Irish, or descended from Irish people. It was somewhat bigger than her home country, though its population was far smaller, probably due to the harsh weather. You had to be the hardy type to want to stay here. Gretchen found Maggie's industrious nature a huge help on the farm, and told her niece the money she made at Cochrane's, she should keep for herself.

Now, with aviators arriving in Newfoundland, Maggie's dreams of being an explorer began to seem just that little less like a fantasy. If you could fly, you could go *anywhere*, and though the aircraft were incredibly expensive, some of these pilots were not rich or upper-class. Harry Hawker was the son of a blacksmith, Freddie Raynham the son of a farmer. These were real people, here in this town, who had been born into ordinary lives and were now famous adventurers flying these wondrous machines. Even Patrick, who had started as a mechanic like *her* father, had become a pilot. She felt like she could almost reach out and touch the possibility of being one herself.

The sleet had stopped falling by the time she, Gretchen and Patrick reached Quidi Vidi Lake, about a mile from town. A crowd had gathered near the canvas-and-wood hangar that stood on the flats beyond the cricket ground. Drifts of snow still lay in some places, and the ground was littered with stones, with shoulders of rock protruding through the still-frozen earth.

Newfoundland was not a landscape that lent itself to easy cultivation. With only a thin soil laid across rock, it could be a forbidding place, especially after the winter when the grass was all dead and pale yellow. Flattening a large section of land out of this had been a challenge, but Raynham's team had managed it, with the help of a few locals. It was only a couple of hundred yards long, and very narrow, but it was enough for this aeroplane, apparently, which needed less of a run than its competitors.

As of yet, there was no sign of the aircraft. Patrick sat in the car as Maggie and Gretchen joined the crowd near the hanger, gazing up into the sky, hoping for some sight of the flying machine.

Hawker and Grieve were standing nearby, shadowed by Smallwood and a gang of other reporters. There were journalists from London's *Daily Mail*, as well as from the *New York Times* and the *New York World*, among others. There were more from American newspapers than from British ones, even though most of the aviators preparing to take on the challenge were British. Despite a biting breeze that was already making her fingers numb, Maggie could sense the excitement in the crowd, like being at the horse racing back in Ireland.

Then people started pointing, as a dot appeared from out of the clouds. It grew quickly, taking shape as it circled, the aeroplane getting closer and swinging round to line up with the field. Like the Sopwith *Atlantic*, this was a single-engine biplane, but with brighter colours, crimson and silver, with yellow wings. It looked slightly sleeker than the pictures Maggie had seen of the Sopwith aeroplane, though perhaps a little smaller too.

'Bit of a crosswind,' she heard Hawker mumble. 'He'll want to watch that.'

As the Martinsyde *Raymor*, named for its pilot and navigator, Raynham and Morgan, approached the end of the airfield, Maggie could see what Hawker meant. The breeze didn't feel that strong, but far down the field, gusts of wind were jolting the machine to the side, causing it to swerve in the air, its course being corrected constantly by the pilot. Raynham cut his engine and glided down, flying in a strange, S-shaped path as he drew close to the ground. At the last moment, the nose lifted, and the aircraft touched down, bouncing and tilting over slightly as another gust caught it while the tail was still up. Then it settled onto the ground and decelerated, the engine given just a touch of power to turn the machine and drive it in the direction of the hangar.

'Good show,' Hawker said, nodding in approval.

'What an extraordinary thing!' Gretchen breathed.

The crowd cheered, and immediately started pushing forwards, eager to greet and congratulate the fliers after this successful test of their machine. Maggie was pushed along with them, and she found herself near the front as the machine came in close and the propellor stuttered to a stop. Freddie Raynham was in the rear cockpit, his navigator, Captain Fairfax Morgan – known to the other fliers as 'Fax', in the front. Raynham was first out, and Morgan was slower, on account of his false leg, which was made of cork. His left leg had been amputated after a crash, when he'd been shot down over France.

Fax Morgan was popular with the press, loud and outspoken and fond of telling war stories. He claimed to be a descendent of the famous pirate Henry Morgan, and played up the part. Still in his flying helmet and goggles, he waved to everyone as he dismounted and the reporters started shouting questions at him. Raynham left his friend to deal with the press, preferring to talk to the team of riggers and mechanics about the test flight. Like Hawker, he looked younger than he was, with his long, smooth-skinned face and slight build. It was hard to believe he was old enough to have been a test pilot before the war.

But it wasn't the fliers that seized her attention. Maggie gazed at the aeroplane as if hypnotised. Members of the Martinsyde team were trying to keep people back, as the crowd closed in around them like a slow tide, hands reaching out to touch this magical machine. Maggie had assumed that aeroplanes were solid and heavy, like cars. But although this machine was about forty feet wide and twenty-five feet long, it only took a few people brushing up against the aircraft to move it; one man leaning on the tip of the lower left wing made it dip. The wing was painted yellow, but when Maggie put her hand on its surface, she felt a thin, taut skin, like that of a drum, held in shape by narrow wooden ribs. Thin enough for light to show through. She had heard that aeroplanes were made of some kind of lacquered Irish linen, with only parts of the fuselage constructed of plywood, but she hadn't truly understood how fragile these machines were. No wonder that light breeze had shunted it around so easily as it came in to land.

It was as though someone had put an engine onto a very large kite.

The men who were trying to protect the aircraft called out, asking people to stand back. It was proving difficult to keep the crowd from touching and prodding its delicate skin. One man, standing just next to Maggie, went to press the lit end of a cigar against the surface of the wing.

'What are you doing, you fool?!' a voice barked. 'Do you want to set fire to the bloody thing?'

It was Patrick. Maggie hadn't realised he'd even got out of the car. He was hauling the offender away, and snatching the cigar off him. As he barged through the dense crowd, the cigar was struck from his hand, spraying burning ash into his face, and another blow knocked off his mask. For the first time, Maggie saw the terrible state of his disfigured face, the burn scars like melted wax, the sagging cheek and mottled pink and yellow skin. Some-one cursed in shock; a woman let out a shriek. Patrick put a hand up to cover his face, stooping at the feet of the milling crowd to search frantically for the fallen mask. Maggie spotted it just as someone stood on it, squashing it into the ground. She rushed forward, pushed the woman aside, and snatched it up. It was bent out of shape, but she thought it could be fixed. The copper was flexible, and the flesh-coloured paint had not cracked.

'Patrick, Patrick, it's all right!' Gretchen was saying, her hands up to reassure him.

He was distraught, his breath coming in short wheezes, casting his eyes around at the expressions of all the people staring at him, ranging from sympathy to horror. He ran back to the car, his movements awkward as his damaged right arm fumbled weakly at the handle.

By the time Maggie reached the car, Patrick had thrown himself into the back. He was lying on the floor, his arms up around his head, as if taking cover from an explosion. He was crying like a child, in terrified moans. She stared at him, deeply disturbed by the sight. She'd never seen a grown man behave this way. What was wrong with him?

'Maggie, get in the car!' her aunt said firmly, as she climbed into the driver's seat. 'Don't tarry now, we need to get him home.'

'But … but, Gretchen, what's the matter with him?'

'We can talk about it later. You have his mask, yes? Good. Get in the car now, that's my girl, and I'll drop you back to the hotel.'

Maggie did what she was told, hopping into the passenger seat, and they drove off around Quidi Vidi Lake towards town, with her uncle sobbing on the floor behind her.

8

Jack Alcock was on his feet, hands up in front of him, totally absorbed in the boxing match, willing the fighters in the ring to up their game. He had money on Murphy, who had taken a great deal of punishment over the previous rounds and was showing the strain. Dabral, the Indian, was younger, lighter and faster on his feet, and was being careful to avoid the London Irishman's famous right hook. Murphy was wearing down, but he had strength, reach and experience on his side. One good blow could still floor his opponent.

'Watch his left, watch his left!' Jack shouted, though there was no chance of being heard over the clamour of the crowd in the hall. He ducked and rocked his shoulders as if he was in the ring himself. 'Come on, lad, keep that guard up!'

His bluff, big-featured face was flushed with excitement, his red hair a mess as he glanced down at Teddy, sitting grinning beside him. The navigator was getting as much entertainment from his friend's antics as he was from the fight. That was fine, Jack thought. They'd been to a musical comedy the previous night, in the West End – Teddy's choice. Theatre was all right; Jack and the other boys in the prison in Turkey had kept their sanity by setting up their own amateur productions to let off steam, but give him a good fight over a play any day of the week.

'Head back, *head back, Murph*! Stop leading with your face, you fool! Get in and lamp 'im, for God's sake!'

Dabral came in too close and took an uppercut to the chin that knocked him back against the ropes. If that had happened in an earlier round, it would have ended the fight, but Murphy was out of breath and flagging. Dabral came back off the ropes, nearly walking into a lumbering right hook. He ducked under it and threw a couple of jabs to Murphy's ribs. Murphy struck the Indian an illegal blow across the back of his head and Dabral lost his temper, snapping an elbow into the Irishman's cheek. Murphy's head bounced back and he dropped to one knee, dazed. Snorting like a bull, he lunged into Dabral, and they both went down. When the referee finally parted them, Murphy was flopping on the floor, unable to get back on his feet, and the referee called the fight for Dabral. Few in the hall were happy with the result, though it couldn't be argued with.

Jack tore up his betting slip in disgust as he and Teddy strode out of the hall. Teddy was tapping along with his cane, and they both blinked in the bright daylight as they stepped out into the street from the smoky gloom of the hall. It was a clear April day, warm and sunny for the time of year. Both men could only hope that the weather was far less pleasant in Newfoundland, and would keep their rivals grounded for the time being.

Across the street, the ruined remains of a large building loomed over them. There were empty voids where the windows had once been, the walls within scorched by fire, the floors gone, and all that remained of the roof were some charred rafters at one end. The building next to it was hardly more than a pile of bricks, and the next one along had been damaged by fire too.

It was a stark reminder that, by the last year of the war, Germany had built aeroplanes that could bring the war to London. First came the Gothas, which could fly higher than any British plane of the time. They were faster, more accurate and less vulnerable than the airships that had come before. Then, towards the end of the war, came the Giants, whose wings were almost the width of a football field. The horrors of the battlefield had been visited upon innocent civilians, far from the front lines. No Giant had ever been shot down over Britain – more machines were lost to mechanical failure than enemy fire.

The Allies, of course, had responded in kind, sending their own bombers out over the enemy cities. If the war had gone for much longer, there was no telling how far the devastation might have spread on either side.

Jack had never seen the results of his own bombing runs across Turkey – flying high above the enemy, he'd always been removed from the destruction he'd caused. It wasn't the first bomb damage he'd seen, of course. He'd witnessed enough men dying in his time, seen the broken and burned bodies left after aeroplane crashes and at the motor racing at Brooklands. But as a pilot, the war had been fought at a distance, far from the bitter struggles that had gone on down in the mud of the battlefields.

Seeing things at ground level made it far more real. He gazed up at the tragic scene now; the general sense of depression in London was casting a sombre mood over him after the exhilaration of the boxing match. They turned and walked on, and Teddy stopped to buy a newspaper from a boy on the corner. The front page was about the goings-on in Paris, as was so often the case these days. The diplomats and generals were negotiating the terms of surrender for Germany and its allies, carving up the winnings. There was to be a complete clampdown on the development of Germany's air force. Jack wondered if he would ever get the chance to fly some of those wonderful German machines.

A ragged, mop-haired beggar sat with his back to the wall of a closed-down bakery. A roughly scrawled sign propped up beside him read: 'BLINDED BY GAS AT HULLUCH. NO HOME. CANNOT SPEAK. PLEASE HELP.' His face and hands bore the scarring from the kind of chemical burns you got from mustard gas, the worst of it around his nose and mouth. It was a crime, Jack thought, to leave a man in this state after his service to his country, and yet it had become a common sight, crippled veterans reduced to begging in the streets. He dropped a couple of coins into the tin can at the beggar's feet, and Teddy did the same. The man waved a feeble thanks.

'Poor devil,' Teddy muttered as they walked on. 'Did you hear his breathing? One bad winter will put an end to him. What a life to be left with.'

There came the whining drone of distant aero engines. The two men looked up, as a wide shadow passed over them. High above them, an airship floated across the gap between buildings. The huge, hydrogen gas-filled shape, silvery grey in colour, was almost silhouetted against the bright sky, and they couldn't make out its markings. Jack caught the expression on his friend's face, and it made him smile. Teddy was like a boy watching a magic trick. Here was a professional aviator, whose experience of flying was entirely coloured by war, and that rubber cloud still gave him a sense of wonder. Jack was reminded that, under a logical and rational exterior, Arthur Whitten Brown was something of a dreamer.

To some, Teddy might have seemed a soft intellectual, with his gentle, easy-going manner, his love of poetry and theatre, and his eagerness to talk of scientific research. Jack had no such illusions. Here was a man who had survived fighting on the front lines, a level of violence Jack could only imagine. Then there had been hundreds of hours flying above those battlefields, enduring anti-aircraft fire, including two serious crashes and crippling injuries.

Teddy was engaged to be married, but instead of settling into a safer life, he had postponed his wedding to sign on for an under-taking that many people believed to be impossible. Jack found great reassurance in his partner's unassuming steel and intelligence.

'They'll carry passengers across the Atlantic some day,' Teddy said, as the airship disappeared beyond the rooftops. 'That's the future, Jack. They can carry far more cargo and passengers than an aeroplane ever will. They can't be matched for range – so long as nobody's trying to shoot them down, of course.'

'Not much fun though, are they?' Jack chirped. 'Imagine trying to do a loop in one. Here, fancy a pint before you head off?'

'Yes, why not?'

Teddy was meeting his fiancé, Kathleen, later in Wimbledon. They were to spend a few days together before he and Teddy took the train to Southampton, to board the ship to Newfoundland. The two men were free for the afternoon, having visited Burberry's that morning to try on the electrically heated suits they would wear on the flight.

The day before, they'd made an appearance at the Royal Aero Club, which was responsible for running the transatlantic challenge. The organisation would ensure that anyone competing for Lord Northcliffe's £10,000 would follow the rules he had set out. Jack and Teddy had also chatted to the press again. This was important for Vickers, who were putting up all the money for the endeavour. If their team succeeded, the prize money would go to the aviators, not the company – which would already have spent far more on the operation. All Vickers would get was publicity for their aircraft. For this reason, the fliers had to hold as many press conferences and give as many interviews as they could – a job neither man relished.

'Damn it, this ruddy waiting's killing me!' Jack said abruptly. It was almost unbearable to be here, waiting to leave and unable to do anything, while hearing news of the other teams who were on the verge of making their flights. Teddy, with his wide range of interests, always seemed to be able to find something to occupy his mind. Jack, on the other hand, had a low boredom threshold. If he wasn't flying or racing, he needed to be fixing something or making something he could fly or race in.

'It's torture!' Jack continued. '"Hurry up and stop! Hurry up and stop!" I'd give anything to just get going and be at it. You know Wood and Wylie could start any day now?' He gestured at the clear sky. 'They're flying the other way; I'm sure they have this same jolly weather in Ireland. They could easily take off in this.'

'Yes, and fly right into the weather that's keeping everyone on the ground in Newfoundland,' Teddy reminded him. 'I must say, I don't understand their thinking. It has the whiff of poor planning about it. Why choose to push *against* the prevailing wind? They'll fly slower, burn more fuel – it makes no sense.'

'At least they'd be *flying* instead of talking to bloody reporters all day. Here, the Irish nationalists are raising a ruckus now, ain't they? Maybe they'll decide they need an aeroplane! They might steal it, when it arrives in Limerick.'

'Jack!' Teddy thumped his arm.

'It's just a joke, mate.'

They stopped, waiting to cross a road, and Teddy took the chance to glance at his paper.

'Bolsheviks still stirring things up in Russia …' he murmured. Then he added, sourly: 'Oh, blast it.'

'What is it?'

'The Handley Page team have left for Newfoundland. They set sail on the *Digby* on the fifteenth.'

'Well, that's just dandy, ain't it?' Jack said, with a dry chuckle. 'Perhaps we could leave it a bit longer and wait for some of them French lads to shoot on by too. One of 'em's bound to have a go. At this rate, we'll be sailing across just in time to see everyone else flying past in the other direction.'

'You know the pilot, Brackley, don't you?'

'Yes, from Eastchurch. I taught him to fly.'

This was a sore point with Jack, that he had spent the first part of the war as a flying instructor, instead of serving at the front. The Navy felt he was more valuable helping to train more pilots than out there flying himself. Granted, being an instructor had offered its own unique thrills. Jack would give a novice flier control of an aircraft, let him muck it up and leave it to the very last second to see if he was going to sort it out before taking back control and saving both their lives. It could be hair-raising stuff, but it didn't give him much of a crack at the enemy. He'd always regretted being late to the conflict.

'Brackley was a journalist before the war. A solid man ... ended up commander of a bomber squadron, I believe. A real aviator, not like this fellow who's "commanding" the aircraft, Admiral Kerr. He's a very different animal. He's qualified as a pilot all right, but he's a Navy man through and through. Getting on a bit though, he's fifty-five. He's spent most of his career commanding ships, and was in Greece around the same time I was, but he was brass by that point, and didn't see much action. Still, a formidable type, or so I hear. Gets things done. Their navigator is a Norwegian, I think. I don't know him.'

'It's Tryggve Gran,' Teddy said. 'First man to take an aeroplane across the North Sea. Flew from Scotland to Norway.'

'Oh, *that* fellow,' Jack grunted, wincing. 'Bloody hell. He was on Scott's Antarctic expedition as well, wasn't he?'

'Yes. A very resourceful man.'

Neither man spoke for a few minutes as they continued walking. This was another impressive team, already two weeks ahead of them, with the Handley Page V/1500, a larger, more powerful machine than the Vimy. Jack wasn't the type to brood much, but he felt a powerful wish to be away from London, with its poverty and choking smog and closed-down businesses. He wanted to be back in the Blue Bird Restaurant having a laugh with some of the boys at Brooklands, or warming up an aeroplane, ready to take to the sky, or feeling the madness in a car or on a motorcycle, tearing around the track at breakneck speed.

But the truth was, times were tough there too. Vickers was up against it, along with many others. From what he was hearing, Sopwith might even have to close down. Thousands of their well-built aircraft were being sold off cheap by the military, meaning there was little demand for new machines that they might build.

'Who would you put your money on, if you had to?' Teddy asked in a subdued voice.

Jack considered the question, much as he disliked thinking about it. He stopped and lit a cigarette, and took a long drag.

'Hawker,' he said at last. 'With Sopwith in trouble, Harry will want to succeed for them. And he never got to serve in the war because of his bad back – too many crashes from flights and racing. He'll be powerfully motivated. He may be an Aussie, but he'll want to do it for Sopwith and for Britain. Though Freddie Raynham has a point to prove too – he'll want to beat Hawker, since he never has. There's nowt between them, really. Frankly, Teddy, there are already too many people ahead of us who want this as much as we do.'

'Well, nobody's tried it yet.'

Jack smirked.

'Yes, but really … how long do you think that rubbish weather can last?'

9

The rain lashed down, drenching Maggie before she was even halfway home, cycling miserably along on a road that was quickly turning to gritty mud. It was nearly six miles from Cochrane's to the farm, most of it uphill, and she'd had a long day. The worn-out chain on her bicycle was also starting to slip when she leaned into it too much, meaning she couldn't stand up for the steepest parts.

She was walking the bicycle up to the crest of the latest hill, with about two miles to go to the farm, when the rain finally eased off. Now there was just the breeze, and up here, exposed as she was, it turned her skin to ice, blowing through her soaked clothes. What must it be like if it rained on you when you were high up in the sky, in an open cockpit, with the wind rushing past you? No wonder they needed that bulky leather flying gear.

It was two days after the Martinsyde test flight, which Raynham and Morgan had declared a complete success. The Martinsyde team and the Sopwith team were both determined to set out across the Atlantic at the first break in the weather, but a thick fog had rolled in from the sea, with a storm forecast to be close on its heels. There would be no flying for the next few days.

The aviators' impatience was infecting the journalists staying at the hotel, creating an atmosphere of nervy anticipation. Alcock and Brown with their Vickers machine, and the Handley Page team with their giant bomber, would both be leaving Britain soon, though they would both surely be too late to catch Hawker and Raynham. Other adventurers would be coming before long too, if these early teams failed in their attempts.

However, every day that passed meant a chance that those first teams might take off. Maggie's slow progress on the bicycle was another reminder that, even if she did hear that they were leaving, she had no easy way of getting to either of the airfields in time to watch them take off.

And once they were gone, that would be it. The challenge was a one-off; once somebody had done it, the aviators would head away somewhere else, looking for a new impossible journey. Perhaps more aircraft might come later, but Newfoundland would never again be the centre of the world's attention as it was now, bringing all these exciting people to their shores. Gretchen was too busy with the farm to drive her around all the time, and would not spare the money for all the petrol they'd burn. Maggie could well end up missing everything if she couldn't find a faster way to get around. She couldn't afford a motorcycle, let alone a car.

The trees that lined the hillside, balsam fir and black spruce, did not extend to the top of the hill, an open, flat stretch of grass and stones and scrub. Maggie saw a car parked at the side of the road, with a woman leaning against the fender. A pallid, stern-looking yet handsome woman, she wore the navy frock coat of the Women's Royal Naval Service, the 'Wrens', with the diamond markings on the cuffs and the stripes of an assistant principal. She wore heavy boots, well suited to the rough terrain, and a pudding-basin-style hat. Maggie had considered joining the Wrens herself. Though she'd heard they didn't actually serve on ships, they could be stationed abroad, and it seemed like a good way to start seeing the world. But there was talk of them being disbanded now that the war was over. The woman was reading a magazine, and paying little attention to her companion.

Not far off the road, a man in dark blue uniform trousers and a warm overcoat, but without a hat, was holding up a large, pale yellow balloon, about a yard in diameter. He released the balloon, which had a piece of red cloth dangling from a string at the bottom, and then he leaned in to study its ascent through a scope he had mounted on a tripod. Maggie watched with interest, her eyes following the balloon as it rose quickly, at a slight slant. Then, when it was several hundred feet up, and only just visible, she saw it suddenly change direction, whisked away by what must be a much stronger wind higher up in the atmosphere.

'Hello there,' she called. 'Can I ask what you're doing?'

Both the man and woman looked up in surprise, caught by the girl's quiet approach. The Wren waved.

'I'm Assistant Principal Sulley of the Admiralty Wireless Station in Mount Pearl,' she said, flashing Maggie a friendly smile. 'This is Captain Daniel Hobbes, of the United States Navy. Captain Hobbes is –'

'Pardon me, Miss Sulley, I must attend to this first.'

The man held up his finger for them to wait a moment, and the woman went quiet, adopting a far less good-natured expression for her colleague than she had for the girl. So that is how things are here, Maggie thought, lifting an eyebrow. Sulley caught it and gave the tiniest roll of her eyes. The man, a balding fellow with a round face and wire-rimmed spectacles, continued to watch the balloon through his scope, and then made some notes in a book he took from his pocket.

'And there we have it,' he said, as if the notes explained everything. He had the accent of a New Englander, an educated man, with a mildly superior tone. 'Sorry about that, young lady. I had to ensure I noted the correct velocity. Now, good afternoon, miss. What can we do for you?'

'Hello, I'm Maggie McRory. I live near here. What's the balloon for?'

If her blunt question bothered either of the two, it didn't show.

'We're measuring —' Sulley began, but Hobbes cut across her.

'I'm an aerologist,' he said, as he began to fold up the legs of the tripod. 'Do you know what that is?'

Maggie had never heard the term, but in her experience, an 'ologist' studied the thing in front of the 'ology'.

'You study ... the air?' she tried after some hesitation.

'That's right, more or less,' he said, giving her an approving nod, as if she was a dull student who had said something surprisingly perceptive. 'I study the *atmosphere*. Thanks to the cooperation of the Royal Navy, I have Miss Sulley, a telegraphist, as my guide and driver for the week. Do you have an interest in science?'

'Not really,' Maggie replied. 'Although … it depends what I can do with it.'

'Well,' he smirked, 'what *we're* doing is taking readings of the winds around Newfoundland ahead of the Navy's operation to cross the Atlantic. Have you heard of it?'

'You want to cross the ocean in a flying boat … a seaplane,' Maggie said.

'*Three* of them, actually,' Hobbes said. 'The NC one, three and four. Yes, they're setting out next month, with support from our fleet as they fly across. My colleagues and I are trying to gather information on the kinds of winds they'll be flying in.'

To Maggie, it seemed impossible to figure out what way the wind was going to blow. She knew the big winds blew west to east for most of the year, but other than that, the island's air just seemed to go all over the place.

'Is there much to find out?' she inquired doubtfully.

'More than we'll ever understand in my lifetime!' Hobbes chuckled. 'But we have to start somewhere. The flyboys will need all the help they can get. Your Newfoundland sailors have very accurate knowledge of the winds and currents in the seas they travel across; they know how they change through the year, but up there?' He pointed into the sky: 'Why, we're only starting to understand what the pilots will be facing.'

'The wind is different up there?' Maggie remembered the balloon's sudden change of direction. 'Does it go in different directions to the wind down here?'

'Different directions, different speeds,' he said, as he put the tripod and scope into the boot of the car. 'An aircraft rides the winds. A treacherous wind can throw it miles off course without the crew even realising it. Add in clouds and fog to block your view of the sky and sea, and an aviator can become utterly lost, tossed around without any way of knowing which way to steer his aeroplane. A knowledge of the winds will be essential for flying across the ocean.'

'The British fliers aren't letting off any balloons,' Maggie said.

'Yes, they're being very adventurous,' Hobbes grunted. 'They're intent on hurling themselves across in one all-or-nothing dash, throwing caution to the wind ... quite literally.'

The men Maggie had met in Cochrane's did not seem all that foolhardy, and they certainly paid attention to the weather. For all their daring, they struck her as very intelligent and deliberate fellows.

'The United States Navy is not competing for a prize,' the aerologist continued. 'Apart from the honour of being first to cross the Atlantic, of course. We intend to give our aviators all the support we can, and that includes providing them with the most accurate information possible. It's a perilous undertaking under the best of circumstances, and we don't want to endanger our men any more than necessary.'

'When do the flying boats get here?' Maggie inquired, her eyes wide. Three aeroplanes – and seaplanes at that! Imagine an aeroplane taking off from the water!

'Well, they're not coming to St John's –' Sulley began, before Hobbes interrupted her again.

'The NCs will depart from Trepassey,' he said. 'These are very large aircraft. They have to take off from the water, and St John's harbour is too small for the run they'll need, so Trepassey was chosen. I'm not sure when the NCs will arrive, but some of the support ships are already on their way. They'll be anchoring there in the next week or two.'

Maggie felt a sickening, sinking sensation. She had never been to Trepassey Bay; it was sixty or seventy miles away, on the south of the island. A train ticket would be very expensive, and she had no other way of getting there unless Gretchen and Patrick let her take the car. There was little chance of that. Though the US Navy operation would be an amazing spectacle, she doubted that Gretchen would spare the money for petrol. Maggie's mind was already scrambling for alternatives. Three flying boats and a convoy of Navy ships. She *couldn't* miss this.

'A week or two for the ships, you say?' she repeated. 'But the seaplanes will be here next month?'

'They're brand new, only just built,' Hobbes told her. 'I believe the crews are still ironing out some mechanical problems.'

'It's already cost them one seaplane – they started with four, but they had to cannibalise one for parts,' Sulley said, folding her arms and twitching a smile. 'They'll set out soon enough, I think. America's pride is at stake. The operation is enormous; I'd say they'd call it off if one of the British teams managed to make the crossing first, and without all that support.'

'Not necessarily,' Hobbes said, pursing his lips in annoyance. 'There's a great deal of scientific data to be gathered on this mission.

The endeavour has already been of immense value. It's providing a marvellous focus on the importance of meteorology. It's not true to say it would all be called off if we couldn't be the first across.'

'I'm sure you're right, Captain,' Sulley said, giving Maggie a wink. 'The US Navy would be happy to dedicate all those ships, those aircraft and all the costs involved … to achieve second place.'

Maggie was already mulling this over. If the US Navy, who knew quite a bit about the sea, had decided it would take such a huge effort to fly across the Atlantic, what chance did the aviators in Cochrane's have?

'I think we should move on to the next site, if you're quite ready, Miss Sulley,' Hobbes muttered. He favoured Maggie with a condescending smile. 'Needs must, I'm afraid. But it's been a pleasure meeting you.'

Maggie nodded, said goodbye and wished them luck in their work. She would have liked to learn more from them, despite Hobbes's irritating manner, and the tension between him and Miss Sulley. He seemed to know a great deal about the journey the fliers would make.

But her mind was whirring as she set off on her bicycle again, coasting down the other side of the hill and making for home. The transatlantic challenge was the most exciting thing ever to happen in Newfoundland, the most exciting thing to happen *in her life* … so far, at least. And there was the chance she might miss it all because of a lack of transport.

She was going to have to do something about that.

10

When Maggie cycled into the yard, it was raining again, and she left the bicycle standing in the porch. Shivering, she hurried inside, threw off her coat and went into her tiny bedroom to change clothes. She'd once had the second biggest room, but Patrick was in there now. He had trouble sleeping, so he and Gretchen had taken to sleeping in separate rooms. Maggie was left in what had once been used as a store room, where she slept on a camp bed.

Maggie had hardly spoken to Patrick since the episode at the airfield. She didn't know what to say to him; she'd been so embarrassed, partly out of sympathy and partly because he'd made such a fool of himself – and her and Gretchen – in public. She could hear him in his room now, the rocking chair creaking back and forth. He would sit there for hours at a time, smoking and reading or just staring into space. Occasionally, he would go out for a walk around the farm. They needed him to return to work, now that he was back. He was no longer receiving pay from the Army, and they were missing that money already. As far as Maggie knew, Patrick hadn't even stepped inside the garage since he'd been home.

Maggie left the house and strode through the rain to the large shed that had once housed Patrick's business. Letting herself in, she lit the oil lamps. The farm did not have electricity yet – it was too far out from St John's. Then she stood in front of the carcass of the big motor car, standing on blocks, which took up nearly half the space in the garage.

It was a 1912 Buick tourer, a dull blue, where you could still see the colour of the paint on the battered bodywork. She had spent days sanding the worst of the rust off it. It had been a good car once, and might have been considered valuable, if the farmer who'd owned it had kept it maintained. Instead, he'd driven it around the salty, rocky Newfoundland coastline until it was little more than a piece of junk. Patrick had bought it before the war, intending to fix it up, but he had hardly started on it before he enlisted. For the last two years, Maggie had worked on it, experimenting and learning and doing her best with her limited skills and even more limited budget. She had grown up tinkering in her father's garage before her mother had sold off most of the tools. Maggie hoped Patrick would help her finish the Buick off now that he was back, but she had decided he was a hopeless case. Besides, she reckoned the car needed a new engine, and they had no money for that.

'My God, did you not sell that thing?'

The voice made her jump, and she turned to see her uncle standing in the doorway, staring at the machine. She had fixed his mask for him, after it had been trodden on, and though he was wearing it again, the sight of his ruined face had left a lasting image in her mind. It was something she could never unsee.

'I've been working on it,' she said timidly. 'I thought we could make more money off it if I could get it running. Or … or perhaps I could keep it and use it myself, for going to work.'

She wasn't sure how he'd take that; it was his car after all. Stepping back, she let him examine the vehicle. He shuffled in a circle around it, leaning in here and there to take a closer look at one thing or another. Maggie put her hands behind her back, feeling like a school pupil waiting for an exam result. He stood back and scratched at the skin around the edge of his mask.

'You've not done a bad job,' he admitted gruffly. 'The springs look in better shape, you've replaced the flooring and got most of the rust off the body – though you'll need to paint it or it'll rust right up again. Some of these fittings on the doors are new, aren't they?'

'Got them off Crocker Bellamy, secondhand,' she said. 'Payment for fixing the steering on his Oakland. He doesn't know one end of a car from another, but he's good for finding spare parts, if you tell him what to look for. And he'll trade for eggs, sometimes.'

'He'll take your hand and sell it back to yeh, that fella,' Patrick snorted. 'Still, you've made some progress, though it's a long way from done.'

He had a strange look on his face, as if he had come to some decision that still troubled him.

'I'm sorry for my behaviour,' he said hoarsely, then cleared his throat. 'At the airfield, I mean. I suppose it must have been … shocking. There are times when my memories feel very … very real. Almost like visions. It's like seeing terrible things right there in front of you, when they actually happened years ago.'

Maggie felt suddenly awkward, unsure how to respond.

'Was it the crash?' she asked gently. 'Is that what you saw?'

'Not so much the crash as the fire,' he told her. He took in a long breath and touched his mask. 'The worst ones are always the fire.'

She didn't say anything. Perhaps it was best just to let him speak, if that was what he needed.

'I flew a Morane Parasol for most of my time over there,' he said, staring at the motor car rather than at her. 'A French mono-plane – a terror to fly, but I loved her. They were one of the few machines that could match the agility of the Germans' birds back in the first year or two. She was pretty patched up at that point; we were going to be getting new machines that month.

'I was out on patrol when I got caught by anti-aircraft fire – blew my rudder off, and I went into a spin. The corps had parachutes by that stage, of course, but the brass didn't want us wearing them. They thought a flyer might be too inclined to abandon his machine rather than try to save it. I made it down alive, but the crash smashed the rudder bar up into my shins, breaking both of them. I was trapped in the cockpit.'

Patrick rubbed his hands together, and Maggie saw the burn scars on his right one, which still did not work properly. Though he could grip with it, the fingers could barely move separately. The hand was more like a stiff claw.

'I was lucky that the fire didn't start while I was still in the air,' he continued. 'Those machines can burn up so quickly, you can fall from the sky like a bloody meteor. The cellulose dope painted on the aeroplane's fabric pulls it as tight as a drum, and makes it waterproof. But it's highly flammable. Add in varnished wooden struts, a plywood body and a fuel tank, and an aeroplane is a bonfire waiting to happen.

'Fuel was leaking out after the crash. It was ignited by the hot engine, and in seconds … in seconds, the machine was on fire, there was petrol dripping down the wall of the cockpit and I couldn't get out. *I couldn't get out.*'

He paused for a moment, the silence almost painful in its intensity.

'I was starting to burn when two French farmers pulled me from the wreckage. I would certainly have died if they hadn't appeared at that moment. They chopped the side of the cockpit away with an axe and got me out, rolled me in the wet grass to douse the flames. Those seconds before they came to my rescue … those are the moments I live through, over and over again.

'And every time it comes back at me, I find myself thinking: "What am I doing here? Why am I going to die like *this*?" I'm an Irishman who's travelled from Newfoundland to die in a French field, fighting for the British against a bunch of Germans I've never met.'

'It is … strange, I suppose, when you think of it,' Maggie agreed, hesitantly.

'Strange? *Strange*? It's an obscenity!' Patrick exclaimed, spit flying from his mouth. 'What were *any* of us doing there? Have you any idea how far some men travelled to die in that mud? How many different countries were involved in this … this … cataclysm? Men from all over Europe, from all over the *world*. *None* of us should have been there!'

'But it had to be fought, didn't it?' Maggie said. 'To stop the Kaiser and all that?'

'The Kaiser! A sulky man–child with an empire as his toy,' Patrick snarled, the grimace shifting the mask on his face so that some of the scarred flesh was visible. 'Empires, that's what started all the trouble. Countries trying to take what isn't theirs! Look at what's happened to us, because of the British. Is it any wonder there's a rebellion going on back home?

'Any time you have people showing up where they've no right to be, it upsets the natural order of things. If everyone just stayed put, things would ... would ... would be all right. Everyone in their place. And now we have these British fliers drawing the world's attention to *this* place, and the American Navy coming here. It won't end well, I'll tell you that! They should leave us in peace.'

'But *we* came here from another country,' Maggie said, frowning. 'This is a British colony, like Ireland. You married a German Jew! And sure, weren't you a pilot? It was the British who taught you to fly, and you could go all over the place in an aeroplane. Why would you want to give that up?'

'Look at me, girl,' Patrick rasped, bringing his face in close to hers. 'You think I ever want to fly again? Aeroplanes and airships are the future, I know that. I know it better than most. There's no stopping them now. And I tell you, if there's ever another war like this last one, no place on Earth will be safe from them.'

He was breathing heavily now, strain showing on his face, and Maggie thought he might be in some pain from his injuries. He was clutching his right arm with his left hand and sweat had broken out on his brow. They looked away from each other, both feeling an urgent need to change the subject.

'Can we … talk about the car?' Maggie asked.

'All right then,' he said, in a grudging tone.

'I've never got it to start. I think the engine's seized, but I can't do engines. I'm stuck.'

'It's not seized,' her uncle told her, shaking his head. He walked around to the side and lifted the bonnet. 'At least, it wasn't when I left. It's probably just a rotten gasket. The petrol can eat away the rubber, or oil can turn it to jelly. You get bits clogging up the carburettor. You have to clean it out regularly or it chokes on them. I'll show you how to do it.'

'You could get twice the price for it, if it was up and working,' Maggie said.

He turned to gaze down at her again, the living eye and the glass one both directed at her. Blinking slowly, he looked back at the car.

'No,' he said. 'No, I think it's yours now. You've put the work in, and … and you've been very good to Gretchen while I've been away. I know she struggled before you came here, and some of our … our *neighbours* didn't treat her well, what with her coming from a German family, an' all that. No, I think you've earned this car, and we'll get it finished for you, one way or another. It's hard to get around out here, and this'll be easier than keeping a horse.'

Maggie's mouth dropped open; she was almost afraid to believe what she was hearing.

'You mean it? You'll let me keep the car?'

'You'll have to get your licence, when you're old enough to take it out on the road. And you'll pay for all the petrol yourself.'

'That's ... oh my God, that's ... thank you, Patrick. It's so kind, I can't believe it ...'

'Don't go all to pieces on me, girl. If I'm to get this garage back in business, I'll need an extra pair of hands, so I'll be putting you to work.' He patted his damaged arm. 'This is healing, but it's slow. Now, how's about we take a look at this engine?'

'Here Patrick, do you think we could have it running by next week?'

'Next wee– Good lord, girl, what's your rush?'

'I want to drive to Trepassey to see the American flying boats.'

Patrick gave her the look of a man gazing at a lost cause.

'And how would you do that, when you don't even have a driving licence?'

'It's country road all the way – sure, who'd be lookin'?' she said brightly.

'"Sure, who'd be lookin'?"' he sighed and shook his head. 'You haven't heard a damned word that I've said, have you? God help me, it's like your father come back to life. All right then, young Margaret, let's see if this old banger will get you as far as Trepassey.'

11

Maggie gazed at the two photographs in the London *Times*, an edition that was more than a week old by the time it reached St John's by ship, where it was delivered to the lounge in Cochrane's Hotel. The first picture showed the aeroplane to be used by John 'Jack' Alcock and Arthur 'Teddy' Whitten Brown for their flight across the Atlantic – assuming they ever got started. Their Vickers Vimy had two engines, and it was bigger than the Sopwith and Martinsyde machines – built as a long-range bomber.

The second photograph showed a stack of huge crates sitting on a dock – the same aircraft, in pieces, packed up and ready to be loaded on a ship. Word was, in the week that had passed since the printing of the newspaper, the aeroplane had still *not* been loaded on a ship. Nor had the article been given much prominence – it was buried in the back pages, under the headline: 'Alcock and Brown Set for Transatlantic Attempt'.

They would want to pick up the pace a bit, Maggie thought, if they're to have any chance at all.

A thick fog had blanketed the town, ruling out any thought of flying for the time being. It was hard even to see the far side of the street through the windows of the lounge. Being cooped up was proving to be a challenge for the aviators, and their restlessness was manifesting in high jinks and pranks.

As Maggie cleared the tables after lunch, Freddie Raynham was waving a New York reporter into one of the leather armchairs, distracting him by showing him a photograph as he sat down.

'Larry, come in, have a seat! I don't think you've seen this picture of the girls at the Armistice party last year?'

With his attention diverted, the reporter did not notice the water pooled in the seat of the chair, poured there moments before he'd come in.

'What the blazes?!' he yelped in shock as he felt the water soaking through to his backside.

Jumping back up again, he scowled as Freddie burst out laughing, joined by Hawker and Morgan, who were watching from seats at the window.

'Chrissakes, Freddie! What a thing to do!' the newspaperman growled in disgust and hurried off towards the stairs to change his trousers.

'Serves him right,' Raynham said to Maggie when he caught her look as she mopped up the water with a towel. His youthful, oval face lost some of its innocence when it broke into that roguish smile. 'The rotter's in the room next to mine – he sits up till all hours, clattering away on his typewriter, keeping me awake. Perhaps he'll listen, next time I tell him to stop.'

Maggie thought it unlikely; reporters were exceedingly stubborn by nature. This was just the latest in a long string of pranks. The fliers mostly played them on each other, though they sometimes found other victims. Hawker had got Raynham yesterday with a bucket of water propped on top of a half-open door. This was in response to Raynham's letting the air out of the tyres on Hawker and Grieve's car the day before. At another point, Grieve had been napping in the lounge, when Hawker crept up behind him with a car horn and nearly lifted him out of the chair with a loud blast. A few days ago, someone had rolled an empty garbage can down the hill on the street outside, nearly knocking Morgan over. Raynham was considered the worst prankster, but they were all at it.

Grieve, who'd gone up to his room for a few minutes, came into the lounge and headed for his chair. The paper he'd been reading, folded back to the article on Alcock and Brown, was on the table next to his cup of tea. He picked it up and started to unfold it, when the wad of inner pages fell out, all cut to shreds. The pieces littered the floor at his feet.

'Oh, for God's sake!' the Scotsman roared as Morgan creased up in shrieks of laughter, waving a scissors. 'You have the mind of a bloody twelve-year-old! Go find yourself a train set to play with!'

His reaction got an even bigger laugh, and he grinned despite himself, throwing the remains of the paper at the other navigator.

'Any more of this nonsense and I'll pull that wooden leg off you and carve a ruddy boat out of it, you tosser!'

Maggie shook her head and walked back into the kitchen. Agnes was sitting down for a break and a cup of tea at the worn, sturdy table after the rush of activity at lunch. Maggie put this last stack of dishes on the sideboard by the deep sink and got stuck into the washing.

'Dear Lord,' Agnes sighed, swilling the tea leaves in the near-empty cup. 'I know I'll miss them when they're gone, but I do wish the weather would clear and give these boys something to do. They're flapping about like bats in an attic. And the *language* out of them! They're almost as bad as the sailors.' She shook her head again. 'Here, how's that uncle of yours doing, Maggie?'

Maggie was deep in thought, her hands moving automatically as she worked through the dishes, stacking the clean ones on the draining board. She and Patrick had spent three days working on the Buick, but if she was to have any hope of seeing the flying boats in Trepassey, it looked like she might have to spend some of her savings on spare parts and petrol. It was a miserable thought.

It had taken nearly two years to save what little she had, and her plan was to use it to leave in a few more years and explore Canada and America. It was also *her* money, the little independence she had. Though she was incredibly grateful to Patrick for what he'd done, years of conflict with her unpredictable mother had taught her never to depend on anyone's favour. Her experience of running away from Longford, with almost nothing in her pockets, had also left her determined never again to be without the means to strike out on her own.

'Maggie?'

'Sorry, what?' she said, blinking and snapping back to the present.

'I said, how's your uncle?'

'Oh. He's a bit better, thanks, Agnes. He's started doing some work again, and I think it's helping him.'

'That's good. I'm glad to hear it. Work's a great tonic, I always say.'

'Yes … Agnes, have you heard about the US Navy coming to Trepassey?' Maggie asked. 'There'll be ships and three flying boats, all anchoring in the bay. It's awful exciting!'

'What, in *Trepassey*?' Agnes laughed. 'That'll be a sight to see! Where will the sailors find their entertainment in that godforsaken place, I wonder? They'll be bringin' rocks and moss home as souvenirs, will they?'

'What do you mean, "souvenirs"?'

'You know, things to bring home, to remember a place by. You ever see a Navy ship come into St John's?' Agnes asked, standing up to hand her cup and saucer to Maggie. 'The sailors flood off those boats on shore leave, wanting to spend their pay and have a good time. They'll be hard pressed to do that in Trepassey.'

'Why?'

'There's hardly anything there, girl! A church and a general store, I think, and little else. Some farms and fishermen, and not much of either. It's the back of beyond. Those folks in Trepassey will think the whole world's turned up on their doorstep.'

And right then, Maggie knew what she was going to do.

12

Under Prohibition law, the drinking of alcohol was banned in Newfoundland. That was not to say that people on the island stopped drinking alcohol altogether; it just became harder to get, and you had to avoid being caught with it.

In a town with more than its fair share of fishermen and sailors to do the smuggling, and many miles of unguarded coastline, there were places you could go if you wanted a drink. And Maggie, who made it her business to know everything that went on in St John's, knew where to find most of them.

Alistair Finch, captain of the fishing trawler *Orca*, was in the third place she tried. A basement beneath a guesthouse served as a speakeasy, where fishermen gathered to indulge in a drink or two. The landlord, a lump-faced man with some kind of rash on his left cheek and neck, opened the door and his eyes went wide in surprise when he saw who was outside. This was no place for young girls.

'What do you want?' he demanded.

'I have a message for Finch,' she replied.

'Well, give it here.'

'I have to deliver it in person. He'll want to hear it, believe me. Don't act the innocent, Mr Arkwright, I know what goes on here. I won't tell a soul.'

He muttered something guttural under his breath and opened the door, letting her pass before casting a furtive glance out past her and then slamming it shut. There were eight other men in the room; no women. Finch was sitting at a table with two other fishermen. He saw her coming and groaned into his small glass, which contained an amber-brown liquid. From the faint scent in the air of spicy brown sugar and vanilla, she could tell it was screech, a kind of rum that was a traditional drink in Newfoundland. That was fine, a few drinks in him would help her strike a good deal.

'Hello, Alistair, how are yeh?'

'Do we have to do this here?' he asked.

'Do you still have those seal skins?' she put to him.

'I might.'

'You have them, so. I'll sell them for you. But I want forty percent.'

'You can *want* all you like, you're not having it.'

'I can get higher prices for them than you'll get in St John's.'

'Where can you do that?' he snorted.

'Trepassey Bay.'

'Trepassey?!' Finch laughed, and his two mates joined in. 'Who's going to buy them there? They've more seals than fish down there! Or should I be trying to sell them *fish* too?'

'Maybe you haven't heard, but half the US Navy's going to be sailing into Trepassey Bay next week. Their flying boats are going to leave from there to cross the Atlantic,' she said. 'And I'll be there to meet them.'

Maggie knew Finch could take the pelts down to Trepassey himself – he had his boat after all. But she also knew he was a lazy man at heart, with no appetite for any kind of work except sailing and fishing.

'Why are they coming to that godforsaken place?' Finch wondered aloud. 'Surely St John's would be better?'

'It's too small for the seaplanes to take off from,' she told him.

'Anchorage is good in Trepassey,' the man beside Finch said. Jeremiah was an old black man with grey hair and beard; something of a blow-in, having come over from Maine only thirty years before. 'Placentia is not sheltered enough from the big waves, and St Mary's Bay is too deep. Loose rock along the bottom of both of them as well, makes for bad anchorage. Trepassey's a sound choice. The ice has completely cleared there too.'

'We should go down there ourselves,' the third man said. This was Jeremiah's son, Matthew, a leaner, paler version of his father, who also worked on the family's boat. 'That would be something, to see those flying boats.'

'I think it's madness, taking on the ocean in those little kites,' Finch declared, shaking his head. 'Have you seen that one out by the lake? It's like someone stuck wings on a canoe! One bad wind out over the Grand Banks will fold that thing up and feed it to the sea.'

'I think they're a modern miracle,' Matthew said firmly. 'Imagine what it's like to *fly*, Alistair!'

'Imagine what it's like to fall from a great height and crash, Matthew!'

'Do we have a deal?' Maggie asked Finch impatiently.

'You can have twenty percent,' he said to her.

'Don't be fooling yourself. I'll take thirty-five.'

'Twenty-five,' he said, grimacing as if he was cutting off his own hand. 'And I'll throw in some fish.'

'Thirty-five, and I'll throw them back at you. I'll have my own goods to sell. Sure, you can have a hundred percent if I don't take those skins at all, but what good is a hundred percent of nothing? You know I'll get them sold.'

'I suppose I do,' he sighed wearily. 'Thirty percent then?'

'Thirty percent, and you pay for my petrol to Trepassey.'

'God save us from this wolf of a girl! She'll want to take *my* skin along with the seals'! All right then, petrol to get you there. You can pay your own way back.'

'I can accept those terms,' she said solemnly.

They spat on their hands and shook on it, and the deal was done. Maggie was going to Trepassey Bay.

13

J ack woke with a shock to the sound of shouting. He sat bolt upright in the darkness, utterly disoriented, trying to make sense of what was going on. There was a lamp on the bedside locker next to him and he fumbled around until he found the switch, and then had to cover his eyes against the light. It was Teddy, who was still asleep in the other bed, crying out in fear and pain.

Jack's awareness of his surroundings came to him quickly now. It was the 4th of May, and they were in a hotel in Southampton. They were boarding a ship for Newfoundland that day. Throwing his covers off, he lunged out of bed, not knowing what to do. Teddy looked all right, but he sounded tormented. Like Jack, he was in pyjamas, and he had kicked off his covers, his hand clutching his left thigh, his brown hair pasted across his pallid, sweating face.

This wasn't the first time Jack had seen someone in this state. War ground you down, and the constant stress of flying in combat wore holes in you the way cloth thinned and tore over time. Jack remembered the empty chairs in the mess tent back on Lemnos, marking each man who didn't come back from a mission – but there were other men whose nerves ended up in shreds, who became hollow shells of what they had once been. They were still showing up to fly, but they were a mess inside. Teddy wasn't one of those poor creatures, though after his experiences on the front lines, he might have been close to it before his injuries put him out of the war.

Jack leaned over his friend and shook him gently.

'Teddy? Teddy, man, it's all right. You're all right! Come on now, wake up! You're dreaming, lad. Wake up!'

Teddy's eyes snapped open, his hand grabbing Jack's wrist. Slowly, he relaxed and looked around him, as he gradually realised where he was. He nodded to show he was all right, then sat up in the bed.

'I'm sorry, I must have woken you,' he said croakily, then cleared his throat. 'I get nightmares sometimes … beastly ones.'

Jack tilted his head in acknowledgement, relieved to see his friend's head was clear. There was a knock on the door, and Bob Dicker called in a low voice:

'Everything all right there, Jack?'

'Just bad dreams,' Jack answered, trying to sound as casual as possible. 'Nothing to be bothered about.'

'A'right then,' the Vickers man replied, and went back to his room next door.

Teddy looked shaken, but flushed with embarrassment too. He sagged back against the wall and picked up his book of Yeats poetry, clutching it to his chest with one hand. Jack sat back on his own bed, and neither man spoke for a minute, as if they needed the space that silence could give them. It was an awkward moment, neither of them knowing if he should say anything. Jack wanted to offer some kind of comfort to his friend, but was unsure how to go about it. Most men did not want to talk about the things that terrified them.

It was a concern though; if Teddy's nerves were already scraped raw, were they close to snapping? It was not something Jack wanted to find out halfway across the Atlantic, when he was relying on this man to keep them pointed in the right direction. Jack shook his head. They were committed now, and he reminded himself that, while he would be trusting Arthur Whitten Brown with his life, Arthur had placed his own life in Jack's hands. That was not the act of a faint-hearted man.

'I won't sleep now. I might read for a bit, if you don't mind the light,' Teddy said at last. He didn't open the book, but just kept his gaze on the cover. 'I'm sorry for waking you. Do you ... do you ever have nightmares?'

'Sometimes, though I sleep pretty well for the most part,' Jack admitted. His mind went back to the bomb damage he'd seen in London, and to the many times he'd dropped bombs on complete strangers in other cities. The room suddenly felt a little colder. 'I've known other lads who get nightmares, though. I do sometimes ... sometimes think about, well ... how I was a nightmare for *other* people, you know? I think of that from time to time.'

Teddy nodded. Jack looked away, and his eyes fell on his watch, which lay beneath the lamp.

'Here, they'll be serving breakfast soon,' he said. 'A good cup of tea is what we need. And some grub. There's nowt like a bacon butty to sort you right out. What do you say?'

He paused for a moment, then added:

'Oh! And we must show the lads your pussycat!'

By the time they were cleaned up, shaved and dressed, breakfast was indeed being served, though it was still very early, and the ship did not leave until late morning. Teddy's spirits had lifted, and apart from the bags under his eyes, there was no lingering sign of the visions that had troubled his sleep.

They chose a table by the window, from where they could see the passenger liner *Mauretania*, docked a couple of hundred yards away. Sipping on his tea, Jack felt butterflies in the pit of his stomach. Strange that it should be this ship that would bring him to Newfoundland. The liner had served as a troopship in the Aegean Sea during the war. The last time he'd seen it in port, he'd been flying over it in the Handley Page machine that he would later crash into the sea.

Putting that morbid thought out of his mind, he opened the newspaper he'd picked up from the rack on the way into the room. A photograph of another aeroplane caught his eye – a single-engined Short Shirl, renamed the *Shamrock*. Alongside was an article about Major Wood and Captain Wylie. They too had gone down in the water – engine failure over the Irish Sea on the way to Limerick.

This was old news; the *Shamrock*'s forced landing had happened on the 18th of April, about two weeks ago, but Wood had now confirmed that, even though the aircraft was still in one piece, salt water damage to its lower wings meant they were out of the transatlantic race for the time being. Well, that's one less competitor to worry about, Jack thought, though he was glad the fliers were unharmed.

'You lads are up with the lark and no mistake!' Bob Dicker said to them, as he came over.

Bob was a rigger, responsible for the Vimy's flight controls. He was an old friend of Jack's from before the war, when they had both raced motorcycles. Bob, an athletic man with a long, flat-boned face, was still a champion racer, and as methodical and steady in his work as he was a demon on the track.

The other three men with him would also be shipping out with the fliers on the *Mauretania*. There was head erector Gordon 'Monty' Montgomery, head carpenter Ernie Pitman, and the Rolls Royce engineer Bob Lyons, who would be looking after the Vimy's engines. All four men were intelligent professionals with considerable expertise in their fields – good lads to have on your side. They sat down at the table next to Jack and Teddy.

'Bit of bad luck for them, eh?' Bob remarked, gesturing to the article Jack was reading. 'You know, there's a logic to what the Americans are doing, when you think about it. Using flying boats, I mean. Look at them gulls out there, that's how nature does it. At least you can put her down in the water if there's a problem. You might even be able to do a repair there and then.'

'I don't care for the idea,' Jack said, sniffing. 'At least not for our purposes. If you make a craft that's half aeroplane and half boat, then you'll not have enough of either, in my view. They have their uses, I suppose, but we'll need every inch of air the machine can give us.' He motioned with his hand, thrusting it across the table. 'Straight across, without getting our feet wet. That's how it has to be done.'

The *Shamrock* article was a stark reminder of the scale of the challenge they faced. The Irish Sea was a tiny hop compared to the Atlantic, a flight of about fifty miles over water, and yet it was still a risky endeavour. The first successful crossing by aeroplane had only been achieved in 1912, less than seven years earlier. Robert Loraine had tried it in 1910 in a Farman biplane, and had ended up in the water towards the end. He'd swum the last few hundred yards.

Engine failure again.

Three other men made the attempt two years later, Damer Leslie Allen, Denys Corbett Wilson and Captain Vivian Hewitt, all using Bleriot XI monoplanes. Allen disappeared without trace, but the other two made it. Corbett Wilson was the first, landing in Wexford, while Hewitt made it to Dublin, his machine nearly flipping over in the wind when he landed in Phoenix Park.

Wood and Wylie, both experienced military aviators with a more advanced aircraft and a more reliable engine, had still failed to fly those fifty miles across the Irish Sea.

The shortest distance across the Atlantic was one thousand eight hundred miles.

'Never mind all that now,' Jack said to the other men. 'Gentlemen, we have a far more serious matter to discuss. Arthur, if you please?'

Teddy reached under his chair and placed a stuffed toy on the table for them all to see. It was a black cat, little bigger than his fist, with a yellow scarf around its neck and a benign, slightly surprised expression on its face.

'Aw, that's *adorable*!' Bob exclaimed. 'Where'd it come from?'

'It's a "her". Kathleen gave her to me,' Teddy said proudly. 'For luck.'

'What's 'er name?' Monty asked.

'Twinkletoe,' Teddy replied.

'Suits her,' Ernie said, in his usual doleful tone. 'She looks like a Twinkletoe. A black cat. It's a good thing, we'll need all the luck we can get.'

'That's why she's going on the flight with us,' Jack told them. 'Only now I think the luck's not balanced. How can Teddy fly with a mascot when I've none? It's not right. Something has to be done.'

'She can be the mascot for both of you,' Monty told him. 'Potent enough, I think, even if she's just a wee thing.'

As it often did, his gravelly Scottish accent had the effect of making his declaration absolute.

'Yes, she's more than enough for the two of us,' Teddy said with earnest reassurance, clutching Jack's forearm. 'Kathleen would wish you every bit of luck … what with me sitting beside you the whole way. Our fates our intertwined, remember.'

'I appreciate your generosity, Teddy,' Jack said. 'But we don't want to place too great a burden on Twinkletoe's little shoulders. No, she needs a partner, I think. Someone to help carry the weight.'

'Don't you worry none,' Monty replied. 'Me and the boys'll see to it. We wouldnae send you out over the ocean without the necessary support.'

'Oh, absolutely,' Bob added, slapping Jack on the shoulder. 'Just look at that American lot with all their ships. No … No, I think another stuffed toy is the least we can do.'

14

Maggie stood on the porch with Gretchen, the two of them watching as Patrick split logs, swinging the axe one-handed because his grip with his right hand was still weak. The yard was freezing cold, the ground all slushy mud, and yet his pale torso was only covered by a thin shirt. He rarely wore his mask when he was at home now. It wasn't all that comfortable, and his wife and niece were becoming used to his disfigured features. When his face was twisted in fury, as it was now, he was extraordinarily ugly. His movements were angry and sloppy, and Maggie thought he might hurt himself if he kept swinging the blade the way he was.

'I don't want to bring him,' she repeated. 'You saw what he was like with Albert.'

'Yes, I saw,' Gretchen replied with a heavy sigh. 'Heavens girl, I've never been so embarrassed in all my life. The way he was roaring ... and the *language* he used! Albert was so good about it, but I could see how offended he was.'

When Patrick had found their neighbour's cattle on their land early that morning, he'd confronted him out in the field, and threatened to take his axe to Albert, calling him foul names and telling him to 'go back to bloody Africa'. Albert, whose family had been in North America for three generations, had stood his ground and asked Patrick if he could repeat himself, as he found the Irish accent hard to understand.

'He's been using that pasture for his cattle for years now, and Patrick knows it,' Gretchen said. 'It's the quickest to drain in the spring, and too stony for crops. We won't be using it until we get our own livestock. Albert's always been a good neighbour to us. I wouldn't have got through the first winter of the war without him. I'll wait until you're gone and then go see him and apologise properly. I'll bake him a pie, I think.'

'*I'm not bringin' Patrick!*' Maggie insisted. 'He'll make a fool of me!'

'No, Maggie. *He's* bringing *you*. You're sixteen years old! You don't even have a licence! Do you seriously think I'd let you drive off all the way to Trepassey on your own, especially when it will be swarming with sailors? Get a hold of yourself, girl! I thought you had more sense. You're going together, and that's all there is to it. It will give me some peace for a couple of days.'

Her last comment was meant to hide how worried she was, but Maggie knew she was not comfortable with the plan. At the same time, Gretchen knew her niece was not be stopped when she had her mind set on a course, so all she could do was try and keep Maggie as safe as possible.

'I don't know why you're so obsessed with these fliers,' her aunt said in a softer voice. 'They'll be here while it suits them and then they'll be gone. That's the way of those … racy types. I think you're blinded by the glamour of it.'

'I'll be one of them, some day,' Maggie told her, gazing evenly at her uncle, who had stopped to snarl at a particularly resilient log. 'You wait and see. I'll get out of here and see the world.'

'What?' Gretchen said, blinking at her in surprise. 'But this is your home, Maggie love. I always thought you'd stay here.'

'Here? Why would I want to stay *here* for the rest of my life?' Maggie snorted.

And because she was staring at her uncle, she did not see the sharp grimace of hurt on her aunt's face.

'Well then … you should go and see your aeroplanes,' came the flat reply. 'But you're not going alone.'

And that was how Maggie ended up behind the wheel of the battered, rusting blue Buick, hauling her cargo down the rough dirt road to Trepassey, with her surly uncle sitting beside her. They were both wrapped up against the cold, Maggie in trousers instead of a dress, the legs tucked into her thick socks. The car had a roof that could fold back, but no shelter on the sides. Alistair Finch's four crates of seal pelts were tied down on the back seat. And stuffed into every spare corner of the motor car were packages – all the candy, gum and cigarettes her savings could buy. She had taken a big gamble, spending everything she'd had left after fixing up the car.

She'd also brought eggs, because their hens had been busy, and there were still food shortages on the island. Wherever she went, Maggie knew she could sell eggs.

They would be staying with Gretchen's cousin Judith, who lived in Trepassey village, right beside the harbour.

Patrick had not protested much about the trip. Perhaps he knew that he had tried his wife's patience and needed to give her some time on her own. He wasn't the most pleasant of company that day, but Maggie was glad to have him with her after the first ten miles, when the weather turned again and the Newfoundland rain set in. They had to take turns twisting the lever above the two-piece windshield to work the little wiper so that she could see where she was going.

Sixty miles was a long way on these roads. The rough surface bucked and bounced the car. The Buick had once been a luxury vehicle, a big beast riding on thirty-six-inch wooden-spoked wheels with four-inch-wide tires. It had carbide headlamps on the front, between the curving black fenders, and acetylene lamps mounted off the corners of the windshield. The lights hardly pierced the grey gloom of the rain.

Her inexperience showed during the drive. Three times, she stalled the car, and Patrick had to climb out with the crank handle to get it started again. He let her continue driving though, even when she stalled for a fourth time and they couldn't get it started again, and he had to inspect the engine and fix a loose hose. Gazing around at the wild, hilly, wooded landscape, still scattered with drifts of melting snow, Maggie was struck by how far they were from any help. This was a thinly populated country, and they hadn't seen a house for miles. At that moment, she was grateful to have her uncle there. Without his skills, she might have been stuck, helpless. Maggie resolved that if she was to succeed as an explorer, she would have to master the workings of engines.

At least it was only a motor car, and not an aeroplane. They could stop on the road and fix the problem, instead of falling from the sky.

If anything, Patrick seemed happier than he'd been in days. He always found peace when he was tinkering with an engine, and though he was capable of driving, it wasn't easy for him with his weak right arm, so he was content to let Maggie carry on.

The rain cleared, though the clouds did not, and a brisk wind still blew through the car. As the road curved round the top of a hill, Maggie got her first view of Trepassey Bay and the fishing village. Now she understood Agnes Dooley's amusement at the idea of hundreds of sailors landing there. The harbour was five miles long, but about half a mile wide at its narrowest. Around its edges lived a community of about 1,000 people, in houses scattered thinly across the rough, grassy terrain that sloped down to the rocky harbour.

It was Wednesday, the 7th of May, and the earliest American ships had arrived five days earlier. A thin fog lay on the bay, but Maggie could see three naval destroyers, along with what looked like a fuel tanker and two other ships. She drove down into the village, stopping not far from the general store.

Three sailors in dark blue US Navy uniforms, complete with the flat hats worn by the enlisted men, were walking past. Maggie stood up from her seat, leaned out and waved them over.

'Are you boys here for the flying boats? Have they arrived yet?'

'No, miss,' one replied politely, tipping the brim of his hat. He had a pushed-in face like a bulldog, and small ears that stuck straight out, and he spoke with a drawling accent from one of those southern American states. 'They've been expected for a few days now, but there've been delays ... at least, that's what we've been told. Have you come far, little lady?'

'From St John's,' she said, wincing in disappointment. 'Here, I've good stuff to sell, if you're interested. American dollars accepted. Tell your friends too. I've got candy, gum, cigarettes.'

The sailors' faces brightened at this announcement.

'Good timing, miss,' the bulldog-faced man said. 'They only got one general store here and it's been cleared out – twice actually, after they'd ordered in more stock an' all. We came in on the *Aroostook* on Saturday, and by the time we got to shore, there was hardly a thing left. Why, we'll take some smokes off your hands right now. And some gum.'

'Right you are,' Maggie said, grinning. She opened the door and jumped down from the car. 'I've got some fine souvenir furs too, genuine Newfoundland product, for those who want to spend a bit more.'

Patrick remained seated, saying nothing, his hat low on his head and his collar turned up, so that little of his face could be seen.

'Furs, you say?' one of the other sailors asked, a man with a bass voice and deep brown, square features. 'What kind?'

'Seal skins, from harp seals,' she told him, opening the back door to lift a lid from one of the crates and pull out a silvery-grey pelt to show them. 'They're soaked in Newfoundland magic, guaranteed to cure all your ills, give you great strength and make you more attractive to women.'

'Hell, I'll take *all* of 'em!' the bulldog-faced man said, and his friends laughed. 'Seriously though, young lady, what you askin' for 'em?'

'Five dollars each.'

'I ain't payin' five dollars, but you're such a spirited child, I'd give you four and no more.'

'And you'll be wanting the teeth from my head an' all, will yeh? How about you give me four seventy-five?'

'My mother wouldn't pay four seventy-five, and she has the heart of a saint. I tell you what, make it twelve fifty for three and you got yourself a deal. One each for my dear old momma and my sisters.'

'Twelve fifty for three it is, then,' Maggie spat on her hand and they shook on it.

She let him pick them from the crate himself, while the other two men took a pelt each at four seventy-five, on the condition that they didn't tell anyone else of the ridiculous bargain they were getting, as it was like Maggie was cutting off her own hand, selling them for so little. Weren't they lucky lads to be getting in early on a deal like this?

Word spread quickly, and the Americans came from all around. It was amazing how many had infiltrated the landscape – they came from walks or visits to the Catholic church or from fishing in the streams. Patrick went off to find the house where he and Maggie would be staying that night, while she stood on the running board of the car, doing deals. Most of these lads weren't much older than her, and the more outrageous her claims about the seal skins, the more the sailors laughed. And the more they laughed, the more they bought.

Every chance she got, Maggie asked what the men knew about the flying boats – what was happening and when they were coming. Some of the Trepassey residents even came to buy her candy and cigarettes, since their store had been emptied by the visitors, though they scoffed at the prices she'd been charging the sailors.

There were reporters in the village too. With no hotel facilities, they had leased a railway carriage, a dining car, for accommodation. Maggie decided to make her way down there as soon as she'd finished her business. She'd learned from the crowd in Cochrane's that journalists were the nosiest people in the world – if there was information to be had, those hounds would dig it up. For the time being though, she was happy here, pitching her wares, taking money and shooting the breeze with the sailors. And the village of Trepassey, a sheltered and isolated place, buzzed with an excitement it had never known before.

15

The game was called 'baseball', and Maggie did not understand the rules. She was trying to distract herself from her disappointment; everyone who knew anything about the giant flying boats had said they would not be arriving for a few days. They hadn't yet left Rockaway Beach Naval Air Station in New York, and they would be stopping off at Nova Scotia first; it would take them at least two days to fly to Trepassey. She wouldn't get to see them before she had to leave.

And so she relaxed and tried to get her head around this strange game. On a rise looking over the harbour, four old car tyres had been used to mark the corners of a large square. A man in the middle had to throw a ball past a man in one corner, who had to use a bat to hit it out into the field beyond the square. Everyone else had other, less specific things to do. The game wasn't remotely like hurling, which Maggie's father had played. In hurling, everyone had a stick and you could run all over the field. She thought it might be more like cricket, which she didn't understand either.

The sailors were mad for it though, and the locals, or 'Newfies' as the Americans called them, were having a great old time taking it all in. Crew members of the *USS Aroostook* were playing a team from the *USS Prairie*. There was a friendly rivalry, and bets being taken. It was early evening, and Maggie was exhausted after her epic drive and her frantic market stall experience. It was a pleasure to sprawl out on her coat on a soft patch of mossy ground and watch the game. There was still no sign of Patrick, who was avoiding the Navy men, but she was fine with that.

In the days spent waiting for the flying boats to arrive, the Americans had been welcomed by the people of Trepassey, who provided them with home-cooked meals and guides to the best places to fish for trout in the local streams. The Navy had been keen to show their appreciation for that welcome. The medical officer and the dentist aboard the *Prairie* were providing treatment for the Newfies – a diet that consisted mainly of fish left the locals with notoriously poor teeth – and the ship's band had been putting on musical concerts. Gifts of copper and brass rings, bracelets and other trinkets were given to the children.

The Newfies were fascinated by the aerologists, who launched their pilot balloons from various places offshore. Fishermen with intimate knowledge of the winds at sea level watched in astonishment as a balloon rose up, carried on a southeast wind, and then, at 1,000 feet, suddenly blew off eastwards. As Captain Daniel Hobbes had said, back on the hilltop near St John's, there was still so much that was unknown about the sky.

The first sailor Maggie had met, the one with the sticky-out ears and the pushed-in face, chatted with her as they watched the baseball game. His name was Bob Lee Olsen, Seaman First Class. Actually, Bob Lee had hardly stopped chatting since he'd run into her. Maggie had the impression that he'd already talked his way through all of his shipmates, and some of the men from the other ships too. Bob Lee had the gift of the gab.

'... and then the NC-1 and the NC-4 were damaged in a fire in Rockaway. They're all fixed up, so I hear, but they had to cannibalize the NC-2 for parts ...'

There had been four Navy-Curtiss flying boats, or 'NCs' for short – the first of their kind. As Maggie had already heard, the second one had been taken apart and used to repair damage to two of the others. The flight of three aircraft was commanded by Commander John Towers. Nicknamed 'the Nancy boats', they were a statement of American ambition. They were *enormous*, each weighing eleven tons when empty, and with a wingspan of over a hundred feet. The plan was to fly each with a crew of seven, but in a test flight at Rockaway Beach, one of the aircraft had carried *fifty-one men*. Having seen the two thin-skinned British aeroplanes in St John's, Maggie couldn't grasp how that was possible. It was unbearable to think that she would have to go home tomorrow without having set eyes on these incredible machines.

'... just heard that a machinist's mate got his hand chopped off ...' Bob Lee was saying.

'Hang on ... what?' Maggie exclaimed. She'd only been half-listening, her attention on the baseball game. 'What was that?'

'Just happened today,' the sailor said. 'Guy name of Howard, on the crew of the NC-4, was working on one of the engines while the propellor was still spinning. Stuck his arm out into the prop by mistake and it chopped his hand right off. Poor guy. Won't be making the flight now, will he? Hell, that's the end of his career, I'd say. Hard to be a mechanic with only one hand.'

Maggie's eyes went wide, appalled and fascinated in equal measure. It seemed that the American operation had been plagued with mishaps – fires, storm damage, mechanical failures and radio problems. Everything about these machines was an experiment, and experiments could, and did, go wrong. The Americans were having to adapt and improvise as they went, but by all accounts, it wasn't holding them back. The operation was to proceed as planned, and the ships here in Trepassey were proof of that.

There were seven destroyers, including the ones Maggie had seen in the bay, along with a tanker called the *USS Hisko*, a repair ship called the *USS Prairie*, whose band would be playing in the village tonight, and Bob Lee's ship, the 3,000-ton *USS Aroostook*, which was serving as the base ship for the seaplanes.

Unlike the British aviators, the US Navy weren't trying to win Lord Northcliffe's prize of £10,000 for crossing the Atlantic in one journey. This was a matter of national pride; they intended to be first to fly across by any means necessary.

Maggie gazed out beyond the harbour, where the ships lay at anchor.

'It's some job you're doing,' she commented. 'All those ships just to help the aeroplanes.'

'"All those ships"?' Bob Lee repeated. He chuckled, thumped the shoulder of the sailor sitting beside him, and gestured out towards the vessels in the bay. 'D'you hear that, Mitch? "All those ships"! She thinks that's all of 'em!'

The other man laughed too, and Maggie sat up straighter, not happy at being mocked.

'What's so funny?'

Bob Lee buttoned down his smile and shot her one of those 'how–little–you–know' looks that Agnes was always giving her, which was both patronising and pleasingly conspiratorial.

'Maggie, you got no idea how big this is. There are nearly a *hundred* ships involved in this, all told. The NCs are flying to the Azores first, those tiny islands out in the middle of the Atlantic, then on to Lisbon in Portugal. You know how hard it is to find your way around out there? Those islands are like dots of dust on a rug.

'It's over 1,200 miles just to the Azores – another seven or eight hundred to Portugal. There'll be boats stationed out along the whole route, from New York to Halifax, Halifax to here, here to the Azores. Then from there to Lisbon … We'll have a ship about every fifty miles. We got some out there right now whose only job is to watch the weather in different parts of the sea. Weather reports are coming in from all around the Atlantic, three, four times a day.'

Maggie gaped at him. 'Are you havin' me on?'

'I don't know what means, sweetheart. Speak American.'

'Are you coddin' me?'

'What? For land's sake! *Speak. American.*'

'Are. You. Joking?'

'Why, no I am not, Maggie. Those three seaplane crews are risking their lives, and the Navy is gonna give them all the support it can. The ships'll have white numbers, eight feet long, painted on the decks for the flyboys to know what stage they're at. They'll be firing starshells and using searchlights during the night to help them find their way, and giving off smoke during the day. And it's not all just to help with navigation. If one of those flying boats gets in trouble and has to land in the water, we want to be in radio range, and close enough that we can go help 'em out.'

Maggie turned to look out at the ships in the harbour again. For the first time, she felt real fear for Hawker and Grieve, Raynham and Morgan, these men in Cochrane's that she had come to know and like. Even though she had sailed across the Atlantic to reach Newfoundland; and though she lived on the edge of the ocean and had experienced its tempestuous weather; even though she regularly talked to the sailors and fishermen she met around St John's; she hadn't really understood how dangerous the fliers' undertaking would be.

The extraordinary scale of the Americans' operation brought it home to her. The seaplane pilots would fly from one powerful warship to the next, all the way across the Atlantic, their path marked by lights and flares and trails of smoke, and still these men were risking their lives to make the flight.

The aviators in St John's had none of this support. Once they took off and set out over the ocean, that would be it. They had to reach land or join the long, long list of sailors whose lives had been claimed by the cold, deep water. Was it madness to even contemplate such a journey?

'They'll want to be picking up the pace, those flyboys,' Mitch said as the batter hit the ball far off into the corner of the field and the crowd cheered. 'I hear there's an airship going to try the crossing too.'

'An airship?' Maggie said. 'What airship?'

'The C-5, one of the Navy's,' he told her. He was the bass-voiced, square-faced black fellow who had bought one of the first sealskins. 'Buddy of mine serving at the Naval Air Station at Cape May in New Jersey said it was all hush-hush. He wasn't supposed to tell a soul, but they're takin' off from there, heading to St John's in the next few days. Flyin' to Ireland, like those British boys mean to. The *Chicago*'s gonna be in St John's for support.'

'What's that, Mitch?' asked one of the sailors sitting nearby.

'The C-5,' he called over to them. 'It's all hush-hush, I was tellin' them. Very secret.'

'Oh yeah, I'd heard about that.'

'There's an *airship* coming to *St John's*? For the love of God, I'm going to miss *everything*!' Maggie nearly jumped to her feet, her heart thumping. She had taken three days off work. Should she stay here another day? Should she head back now? 'Who's going to arrive first, the flying boats or the airship?'

'No way of tellin',' Bob Lee shrugged. 'They're like weather or women, these fliers. They work in mysterious ways, and come along in their own sweet time.'

Mitch laughed and Maggie scowled, and then the crowd cheered again as the bat cracked against the ball, sending it out towards the road, with sailors sprinting out after it.

16

The Cunard liner, the *Mauretania*, pitched back and forth in the heavy, rolling swell. As the deck swayed under his feet, Teddy was struggling to stay standing, and had to grip rails all the way from the ship's bridge to the bar. The waves were big enough to heave the 32,000-ton ship around with some violence, though the motion could not be compared to flying an aeroplane through the same weather. Would that even be possible?

When she launched in 1906, the *Mauretania* had been the largest moving structure ever built. Now, she was an aging but still impressive passenger liner, and still one of the fastest. Under the command of Captain Arthur Rostron, she did the regular Atlantic run between Britain and North America. The ship's officers were intrigued with the aviators and the challenge they were undertaking, and Teddy had been told he was welcome on the bridge at any time, to discuss navigation and weather fore-casting, an invitation he had enthusiastically accepted. Long-distance aerial navigation was still only being studied by a few pioneers, and though finding your way through the sky was very different to finding your path across the surface of the sea, there was much to be learned from these veteran sailors – not to mention the lively conversations they were having on the subjects of science, engineering and geography. Despite the bad weather, Teddy was having a grand old time.

Far behind him, the bow smashed through a particularly high wave and tipped forwards. For a few moments, Teddy was walking uphill, pummelled by the freezing wind, before the deck tilted back again and he reached the door that led into the bar. The bright light and smoky warmth of the wood-panelled room was comforting after the grim, grey scene outside. He was wet from rain and spray and smelled of the sea, but he was too worked up to notice. He could have made his way through the corridors, but in his excitement, he'd wanted to get outside where he could get the best view of what lay ahead before he went looking for his friends.

There were fewer than a dozen people in the bar that afternoon, most of the passengers having retired to their cabins for the duration of the storm, to ride out the nausea-inducing movement of the ship. Jack and Bob were there though, holding their pint glasses so they didn't slide around on the table. Despite having had a few beers at this point in the day, Jack wasn't looking the slightest bit bothered that the room was tilting this way and that. Bob was a touch paler, having lost some of his dinner over the side earlier. The two were deep in conversation.

'Boys, you have to come outside and see this!' Teddy called to them, staggering across to the table and clutching Jack's shoulder. 'You won't believe it!'

'What, out in that weather?' Jack said, wincing. 'It's perishin' out there. Can't it wait?'

'No, you have to come now,' Teddy insisted.

'Well, can't I finish my pint, at least?'

'No, look … Take it with you, if you must. I'll get a round in afterwards, but you have to –'

'We'll only be few minutes, Teddy,' Bob assured him. 'We're out in the middle of the sea, it can't be that urgent …'

'Boys, there's a ruddy *iceberg* out there!'

That got the attention of the whole bar, and in seconds, everyone was rushing for the door. They all remembered the sinking of the *Titanic,* which had collided with an iceberg seven years before, claiming more than 1,500 lives. That had happened in the area of the Atlantic they were travelling through now, at around the same time of year. Arthur Rostron, whom Teddy had been speaking to only minutes before, had been captain of the *Carpathia* at the time, the ship that had rescued hundreds of survivors from the famous disaster.

But ice was a common problem out here at this time of year. Despite the bad visibility in this storm, the *Mauretania*'s look-outs had spotted the iceberg in good time, though there would be smaller pieces of ice in the water around it. People chattered excitedly and pointed. Far out in the rain on the port side, a stark, pale slab of a shape could be seen against the overcast sky. That visible portion of the ice was much larger than the ship, which meant that the vast majority of it, hidden from sight beneath the water, was many times bigger. It didn't rise and fall with the waves – it was too immense for that. The rough movement of the ship added to the passengers' sense of vulnerability, making them painfully aware that despite the solidity of their vessel, they were floating over water that was miles deep.

'Think of it,' Teddy said, in a voice tinged with awe. 'We're on board one of the largest ships ever made, out in the middle of the ocean, and still dwarfed by one of nature's creations as it floats by. How terrifying it must have been to see one of those monstrosities bearing down on you out of the darkness and knowing you couldn't stop or steer away in time.'

Other passengers around them, realising they were standing near the madmen who hoped to cross the ocean in one of those flying machines, had gone quiet in an attempt to listen in to the conversation over the bluster of the wind.

'Yes, let's try not to tempt fate, old chum,' Bob said. 'Still, it's quite the sight, isn't it?'

'I'd rather be flying over it,' Jack grunted. 'Though maybe not in this wind, eh?'

'Everyone will, some day,' Teddy said. 'Somebody will do it first, and then another and another … Someday, flying over this ocean will be a routine matter. A journey that's taking us a week on this ship will take less than a day. Isn't it extraordinary, when you think about it? From the point where humans started using boats, it took thousands of years before they crossed an ocean. But look at the speed with which air travel is progressing! The Wright brothers made their first powered flight only *sixteen years ago* – they flew a hundred and twenty feet. And here we are, about to take on the Atlantic.'

'Not in weather like this, we're not,' Jack retorted. 'Still, there's nowt to be done for it. And I suppose this means Hawker and the other lads won't be going anywhere either, so it's something to be thankful for. Maybe we've a chance yet.'

'The Vimy's still in London, 'cos of the bloody strikes at the docks,' Bob reminded him. 'Even when we get there, you won't have a machine to fly in for at least two weeks.'

'Don't I know it! Everything's taking so bloomin' long!' Jack growled. He gestured out at the iceberg. 'We're like that thing – big and slow, crawling across the water. But you're right, Teddy. Someday flying will be how it's done. It may be that machines will even fly in storms like this.'

'Captain Rostron called this "a bit of a squall",' Teddy told him.

Some of the other passengers laughed at this, and Jack chuckled.

'And maybe it is, if you're safely wrapped in thousands of tons of iron. Imagine what those winds would do to the Vimy. She'd be tossed around like a kite up there.'

The other men nodded. The ship's bow dug into a deep trough and they all had to hang on to the rail as they felt the jarring impact in the deck, before the vessel tilted upwards again. As it did, something grated down the side and everyone peered over the rail to see a great chunk of ice breaking the surface of the water. It was only a fraction of the size of the iceberg, but still as big as a house.

It slid past, thumping against the hull. It took a few moments for those who saw it to assure themselves that it had done no damage to the thick steel skin of the vessel.

'It's not slow, Jack,' Teddy said, his gaze set on the distant island of ice. 'Things are moving *so fast* now, though it's difficult to see from where we are, inside it. The Wright boys' first flight, then all those early pioneers in their experimental, Jabberwock aircraft. Then the war, when aeroplanes became an industry and a new means of delivering destruction. And you know, soon there will be commercial flight, ferrying passengers to every point in the world. I'm thirty-three years old and this has all happened within my lifetime. It's moving faster and faster … And the world will move faster with it, the good and the bad; news, business, science, disease, war … It's tremendously exciting, but it's possible that we humans may not change quickly enough to adapt to it. One can only imagine how different things will be in twenty or thirty years. How different *we* might be!'

Nobody spoke for a few seconds, as they all considered this. Then Bob piped up:

'Bloomin' 'eck, you're not going to be like this for the whole trip, are you Teddy? I was hoping for a bit of a laugh.'

17

Maggie was having breakfast with some of the American sailors, in the weathered, whitewashed, two-storey wooden home of Gretchen's cousin, Judith. The sailors had come to know Judith as 'the ham-and-eggs lady', on account of the cooked breakfasts she served, making her house one of the most popular destinations in the village. Patrick would not come downstairs while the Americans were there, though whether it was because he was self-conscious about his ruined face or he did not want to sit with these foreigners, he wouldn't say. His one comment when she'd talked to him earlier, that they were 'as bad as the British', suggested that his tolerance for the military men was wearing thin.

Judith had met Maggie a couple of times before, when she had visited St John's. Narrow in face and frame, but a brighter, less formal woman than her cousin, she was a welcoming soul, and happy to have the two dozen eggs from Gretchen's hens, and Maggie's help cooking and serving that morning. Her husband was a fisherman, and had left before Maggie and Patrick woke up. When Bob Lee and Mitch came in with three of their shipmates,

Judith noticed that Maggie was on friendly terms with them and insisted she take a break and sit down to eat with the young men. Judith kept an eye on proceedings, however, to make sure the conversation stayed on appropriate topics. They were Navy sailors, after all.

They had just finished eating and were enjoying a leisurely coffee, when there came the high-pitched droning sound of an aeroplane flying over the house. Maggie nearly knocked her chair over in her haste to get out of the kitchen to the back door, searching the sky for the aircraft. There it was, soaring over the bay. It was a seaplane – she could tell by the lack of wheels, the boat-shaped hull and the floats under the ends of its wings. She couldn't believe it, they'd made it after all! The NCs were here!

'It's not a Nancy,' Mitch told her as he followed her out. 'That's a Curtiss Model F – a single-engined bird, about half the size of an NC. We've got two of 'em on the *Aroostook*. They're probably just taking her up to see what the flying is like out on the water.'

Mitch was a machinist's mate on the *Aroostook*, a mechanic, and though he shared Bob Lee's easy-going view of life, he spoke about half as much.

'Do you get to work on it?' she asked, watching the sleek shape circle above the ships.

'Naw, I'm down in the engine room. They got other guys just for looking after the aircraft.'

'Is there anyone on shore who works on it, d'you know? Any of the pilots?'

'Could be, I dunno. Why?'

'What about the ship's officers? Any of them on shore?'

'Prob'ly.' Mitch took his flat hat off to scratch his head. 'You could try lookin' in the church … or that railway coach the reporters are usin'. What's on your mind, Maggie? You got somethin' else to sell?'

'Oh … it's nothing really. Just an idea.'

She was excited to see the flying boat, even if it wasn't one of the stars of this show, the giant Navy-Curtiss machines. Still, it was a real aeroplane, and it made a very impressive roaring noise as it appeared and disappeared among the clouds.

Bob Lee and Mitch soon took their leave, borrowed fishing rods in hand, to try for some trout at a stream further inland. It was nearly noon, and Maggie had to accept that she needed to leave. The NCs would not be here for at least two days, and she couldn't wait that long. Perhaps she might still come back and catch them, though it hardly seemed likely; by the time she found out they were here, they'd be preparing to leave on their epic flight.

She went to call for Patrick, and found him in the room where they'd slept, drinking screech from a bottle and looking miserable. He belched rum-scented breath and gazed balefully at her.

'Are you all done?'

'What's up with you?' she asked in a cold voice.

'Don't take that tone with me, girl. I didn't sleep. My nerves are at me.'

'Well then, maybe you can sleep in the car.'

'On that road? I'd have a better chance of dozing off on a cow's back.'

'What an' ever. It's time to go.'

With her money safely stowed under the seat, Maggie got behind the wheel, while Patrick went up the front to crank it into life with the starter handle. In a moment of fantasy, she imagined this was her aeroplane and her uncle was spinning the propellor to fire it up. The old Buick, however, had ideas of its own. The motor wouldn't turn over. No matter how hard Patrick turned the handle, it wouldn't catch. Cursing, he walked around the back, pulled his toolbox out of the trunk, then lifted one side of the hood to expose the engine.

'It's carbon in the chambers again … or oil sludge in the crankcase,' he muttered. 'You might as well go in and have a tea. I'll be a while.'

He was still in a bad mood, and slightly drunk, but he was occupied with a mechanical problem now, so Maggie was confident he'd soon mellow out. It was turning into a bright, blustery afternoon, and Maggie sat on the steps of the back porch to watch the seaplane. It landed, and then took off and landed again, and she marvelled at how it could move about on the water like a boat, and then take to the sky. She didn't like to think less of the British fliers, but surely that made sense? If you were going to fly across the ocean, then using an aeroplane that was able to put down on the water was surely the smart way to do it.

Judith suggested she take a walk along the beach, which was at the bottom of the steeply sloping field at the back of the house.

Maggie strode over the dead, yellow grass and clumps of Canadian bunchberry, just starting to show signs of new life after the long winter. The beach was more stones than sand, but Maggie could see harp seals among the rocks out to her right, away from the docks. She smiled at their playfulness, already familiar with their dog-like social habits and intelligence. She felt a touch of shame about the furs she'd sold yesterday, the money she'd made off the skinning of beautiful animals like these. She lived on a farm; slaughtering animals was a normal part of life, but she decided then and there that this would be her last foray into the seal fur trade.

Walking on along the rugged coastline, losing track of time, Maggie was more content today than she had been for years. She had money and time to breathe, and new things to feed her mind. This place teemed with animal life. There were other seals further along the shore; harbour seals, she thought they might be. The seaplane's silhouette was lost among the birds wheeling about overhead – powerful, yellow-headed gannets, black and white razorbills, and of course, the puffins with their colourful beaks. Craggy cliffs rose up to the southwest, from which Judith had said that whales could be spotted breaching the surface.

Maggie could see that humans were already changing this place. The presence of the Americans filled the harbour, big and bold as they were. There were rainbow traces of oil in the water pooling around the rocks, and a faint whiff of smoke in the air from the Navy's coal-fired engines, idling to provide the vessels with power. But even the locals' modest lifestyles left their mark on the natural world. The ragged remains of a fishing net was caught in a gap between two boulders near the line of the surf. Trepassey was a wild place, slowly being tamed and tainted by mankind.

Perhaps, in a way, this was how Patrick felt, this distaste at how things were changing. But wasn't that just how it was? Life moved on. The world wasn't going to stay the same just because you wanted it to. And while Patrick tightened up and became angry with it all, it made Maggie curious, all the more keen to see new sights, to find places that had yet to be touched and changed by humans. For the moment, however, the world had come to her, thanks to all these aviators, and she was determined to make the most of it. She had more money right now than she'd ever seen in her life – even after giving Finch his cut, she had more than tripled her savings. And out in that bay, there was a real seaplane.

She strode off to find some Navy officers.

18

I t was a short walk from the coast to the train station, and Maggie found what she was looking for easily enough: the railway dining carriage, nicknamed the 'NC-5'. The reporters who had travelled from St John's had leased it as accommodation and a base for their work, as they crowbarred information out of any sailors that came ashore.

Mitch had told her that if there were any officers on shore, they would be found either at the church or in the journalists' carriage. Maggie knew that disturbing a person's worship was not a way to get on anyone's good side. The leased carriage stood just beyond the small wooden building that served as platform, ticket office and shelter, at the end of the narrow-gauge spur line. Someone had put a sign up on the door of the railway coach:

Nancy Five

American Press Correspondents

US Navy Transatlantic Flight

Trepassey, Newfoundland

Maggie did not know whether to knock or not, so she compromised, gave a quick rap of her knuckles and opened the door.

A number of people looked up when she stepped inside. The carriage was little more than a wide corridor with wooden seats in booths facing small tables, running down each wall. On one table, there were blankets and pillows folded up with the kind of carelessness that would have had Agnes Dooley rolling her eyes. The place smelled of stale food, tobacco smoke, sweat and unwashed socks.

There were groups of men in threes and fours at some of the tables. Two others were each sitting alone, tapping away on typewriters. Someone had obviously managed to acquire some beer from somewhere, despite the Prohibition law – and despite the fact it wasn't even lunchtime, a few of the men had glasses in front of them.

There were no other women in the carriage, but Maggie decided that if she could handle the mob of young sailors haggling with her yesterday, she could easily cope with a crowd of journalists. She cleared her throat, and then did it again, louder this time.

'Excuse me,' she said in a voice she hoped would reach the end of the coach. 'Are there any officers here from the *Aroostook*?'

'I'm Lieutenant James of the *Aroostook*, young lady,' one of the men said. 'What can I do for you?'

He looked the perfect image of a military man in his navy blue officer's uniform, a rangy fellow with a ruddy complexion, washed-out blue eyes and sandy blond hair in a stylish cut. He was sitting at one of the nearest tables, opposite a man who'd been scribbling shorthand in a notebook. The officer's accent was almost more English than American, like a Newfoundlander's, and his expression was one of amused interest. She worked up her nerve and put her offer to him.

'I'd like one of your pilots to take me up in that seaplane that's flying about out there. I'll pay the Navy for its time. Would twenty dollars be enough?'

There was a moment's silence, and then everyone burst out laughing. Lieutenant James, to his credit, did not, but he did give her a patronising smile.

'Miss, I'm afraid we don't allow civilian passengers on our aircraft. No adults, and certainly no little girls.'

'I'm not a *little girl*! I'm six– … I'm eighteen,' she blurted out. 'It's one passenger, one time. Who'd know or care? I'll give you thirty dollars!'

There was more chuckling, and the men at one table even started clapping and cheering.

'Miss, most sincerely,' the officer's smile got wider. 'I commend you on your initiative, but we can't take you up on your offer …'

The laughter started again, one man bursting into hysterical giggles.

'Fifty dollars! I'll give you *fifty dollars* if someone will take me flying in that machine!'

She was on the verge of tears now, desperate to be taken seriously, but growing more and more humiliated. Fifty dollars was a huge sum; how could they mock her like this? Lieutenant James shrugged and shook his head. Maggie wiped her eyes and scowled, looking around angrily at all these men who thought she was nothing but a fanciful child. They weren't being nasty, she understood that. She opened her mouth to deliver a few choice swearwords, but was interrupted by a voice barking from behind her.

'Maggie, come away from there! What are you doing? You shouldn't be in there!'

It was Patrick, who'd come along at the worst possible time. His cheeks were flushed and his eyes bleary; his breath smelled of rum. Her face contorted into a frustrated scowl. If he had no interest in being here, why could he not stay out of her way?

'And you, all of you blackguards!' he snarled, waving his hand in a floppy motion. 'Look at the lot of ye, crackin' up at a young girl just 'cos she's got an idea in her head and she has the neck to act on it. You're all a shower of swines!'

'You stay out of this!' she snapped at him. 'Just leave me alone!'

'Don't talk to me like that, you little whelp!' He grabbed her arm and shoved her towards the door. 'Get on back to the car now, it's time to go.'

'I'll go when I'm good and ready, and you won't tell me different!'

'Hey buddy, what's with the face mask?' One of the sailors sitting at the nearest table turned to gesture at Patrick's prosthesis. 'You in the theatre or what?'

A few of the others laughed, though most didn't. Maggie saw someone start to say something to caution the man, but Patrick spun around and swung his left fist into the side of the sailor's face.

It contacted with enough force to knock him sideways out of his seat. Landing on his hands and knees, he shook his head, stunned. As he struggled to his feet, the mood in the carriage changed instantly, and another half-dozen men were standing to join him.

The US Navy looked after their own.

Four of the sailors charged into Patrick, with others crowding in behind them, and Maggie was thrown backwards, smacking her head against the door before she hit the floor. Patrick was screaming like a wild man, throwing punches and kicks at everyone around him. The Americans clearly thought this disfigured Irishman had lost his mind, and though they were laying in digs, they weren't trying to do much damage – cursing and laughing at him as he lashed out at them. One even tried to pull Maggie out of the way and she gave him a good elbow in the crotch, folding him over. Patrick might be a bad-tempered swine, but he was her uncle, and you didn't let anyone mess with family. She started swinging kicks into the legs of the sailors surrounding Patrick, but another man pulled her away.

'That's enough!' the lieutenant said sharply, jumping from his seat. 'Stand down! You men, *stand down*!'

Once they heard the officer's command over their own noise, the sailors responded immediately, standing back in whatever space they could find, their eyes fixed ahead of them.

'Help him up!' Lieutenant James glowered at them, and they rushed to obey.

Patrick was bleeding from his nose and his lip, and he was going to come out in some nasty bruises, but he wasn't badly hurt. He shook off the support the men offered, and got to his feet. His mask was hanging from his ear by one arm of its spectacles, and his gruesome scarring was plainly visible. It struck the entire carriage into silence, broken only by some soft swearwords from near the back.

'I apologise, sir,' James said, trying not to stare. 'The men over-reacted. And though you delivered the first blow and I smell drink on your breath, their behaviour was unbecoming of Navy sailors. They will be disciplined. Will you please accept my apology for their assault?'

Patrick fumbled with his mask, straightening the wire frames of the glasses. He let them all have a good, long look at his sagging, hollowed-out flesh and his blind eye, taking a bitter satisfaction from their expressions.

'There is no need to discipline them,' he said hoarsely, before spitting some blood on the floor. 'They are decent enough men, I'm sure, just standing up for their friend. I'd have done the same, when I was in the service. As for the man I hit, he is merely ignorant, and I've dealt with that. But I'll thank you to stay away from my niece … you and all your countrymen. Get your business finished here, take your war machines and your big plans and be on your way. The sooner you're off this island, the better.'

He took Maggie's hand, gently this time, and pushed through the door to make his way outside and down the steps. She followed him without protest, still trembling from the violence only moments before. She had been more frightened than she'd like to admit, and now that the adrenaline was draining from her, it had left a chill of unease in its place.

'We need to go home, Maggie,' Patrick said, wiping more blood from his nose and mouth with his sleeve. 'You've got what you wanted, I think. Me, I've had all I can take of America.'

Shaken as she was, Maggie did not argue. Besides, with the NC flying boats still in New York, there was nothing to stay for. And if she did, she risked missing the departure of the British aviators and the arrival of the colossal airship in St John's. It was time to go home.

As they walked away, one of the American reporters was dashing towards the railway car. He barely nodded to Maggie and Patrick as he passed, crashing up the steps and into the carriage.

'Hey, guys! Guys! I just got word from New York! The Nancies left Rockaway a couple of hours ago, bound for Halifax. No confirmation from the Navy yet, but get this: one of 'em's disappeared! *They've lost the NC-4!*'

19

The Canadian state of Nova Scotia, lying southwest of Newfoundland, is almost an island, joined to the state of New Brunswick only by a thin bridge of land. Once famous for the quality of its wooden sailing ships, it was now serving as a brief stop-off point for three of the world's most advanced aircraft. Or at least, that had been the plan. After their three-hour flight from Rockaway Beach in New York, the NC-1 and the NC-3 had arrived at Halifax, on Nova Scotia's southeast coast. The NC-4 had not.

The Navy's newest seaplane had vanished.

Early on that morning, the 10th of May, when the *Mauretania* cruised into Halifax harbour, the six members of the Vickers Vimy team were standing on deck, as far forward on the bow as they could get. They wanted to get a good look at the huge flying boats, which they soon spotted, moored astern of a cruiser named the *Baltimore*. The *Mauretania*'s radio had picked up some US Navy transmissions the afternoon before, and Teddy, in another of his visits to the bridge, had heard the news of the missing seaplane. Now the Vickers crew were passing a pair of binoculars around so that everyone could cast a critical eye over the machines.

The Americans had lost one of their aircraft after a flight of only a few hundred miles – before they'd even started across the Atlantic, but the Vickers men took no satisfaction from the news. Though they might be competitors, they wished the Americans well, and hoped the NC-4's crew were still alive. They had seen too many friends die in similar circumstances.

Like most aircraft, the Navy-Curtiss machines were a biplane design, with a very wide, complicated tail assembly. They had four engines – one on each side, another mounted in a streamlined casing called a nacelle, over the fuselage, facing forwards. The fourth was in the same nacelle, with a 'pusher' propellor, facing backwards.

'The size of the bloody things!' Monty exclaimed. 'Whut's the span of them wings?'

'Well over a hundred feet, I think,' Teddy replied. 'And each one is about seventy feet long and twenty four feet high.'

The men climbing around on the structure of each seaplane looked like tiny ants. Apart from the red, white and blue roundels and tail stripes and the white numbers, each craft's fuselage was painted a no-nonsense grey enamel, with the aluminium sections left bare and the thickly lacquered wings a deep yellow.

'Those are Liberty V-12 engines,' Bob Lyons, the Rolls Royce engineer told them, chewing on the stem of his pipe. 'Four hundred horsepower each, with a ten-foot propellor. And a crew of six or seven, so they can carry out repairs floating or flying. Lads, the Americans have built themselves a flight of titans.'

'They're big, but they've got the weight that goes with it,' Teddy observed, as he took a turn with the binoculars. 'And they're *lame* titans, it looks like. Something's up.'

Men were swinging the propellors on the NC-1, but the engines weren't catching.

'Probably freezing cold from last night,' Jack guessed. 'Must be even worse if your machine's sitting out on the sea the whole time. The oil in the crankcases will be like treacle until it warms up.'

'Look up on the deck of the ship.' Teddy pointed. 'There are airscrews lying out. Used ones. Looks like they've changed out every propellor on both machines. Not a good sign.'

'They've a cruiser loaded with fuel and spare parts,' Bob Dicker grunted. 'One of many. I doubt they'll be stopped for long. I doubt *anything* will stop them for long.'

'So what do you think, Jack?' Teddy asked. 'Can they cross the Atlantic?'

'Those things? With ships as stepping stones the whole way?' Jack snorted, clearly trying to brush off the unease he felt. 'They could cross the bloody *Pacific*. But it's supposed to be a long jump, not a game of hopscotch, isn't it?'

The ship docked, and they hurriedly disembarked. Bob Dicker handed his bags to the others and went off to find the telegraph office, to let Percy in Vickers know they'd arrived, and to check on the Vimy's situation. They had a few hours to wait before their train to Sydney, on the northern coast of Nova Scotia. From there, they would take a ferry to Newfoundland

and then another train to St John's. The long, drawn-out journey was wearing to both their bodies and their nerves. To be so close to the starting point of their flight, and yet still have another two days of travelling ahead of them … and the sight of the American aircraft seemed to taunt them.

Apart from the disturbing note of the missing NC, it looked as if the Americans already had the race won.

'They're not competing with us,' Jack reminded the others. 'Even if they succeed, they won't have flown non-stop. They can't carry enough fuel to make the crossing in one go. That's what will count, boys. That's what people will remember. One flight, straight across the ocean.'

'Aye. Still though …' Monty muttered.

'I need a cup of tea and a biscuit,' Ernie said, and Teddy could see the carpenter was in a low mood.

They'd agreed to meet Bob at a café they'd spotted on the quays, one that had a good view of the harbour and the flying boats. Like many buildings here, it was wood-fronted with a pitched roof and large shop windows on the ground floor. It seemed like a working man's type of place; wharfies and sailors probably made up the bulk of its customers.

When they walked in, a bell chimed over the door. The warm room was a welcome shelter from the skin-tingling breeze out on the harbour, and smelled of bacon, toast and cigarette smoke. The café had that comfortable feel of an establishment that had been here a long time, well used but well maintained, with plain wooden chairs and sturdy tables covered with white tablecloths. It was Saturday, but there were already some customers in having breakfast, and a middle-aged Asian woman, Chinese perhaps, sat behind the cash register.

She was knitting, while reading a newspaper on the counter. She glanced up at them, then back at the newspaper, and then looked up more sharply, as if studying them, particularly Jack and Teddy. She was very thin with high cheekbones; her well-proportioned face was all lines, as if there was little flesh beneath, though it moved with lively expression.

'Captain John Alcock and Lieutenant Arthur Whitten Brown, from Britain,' she declared. 'You and your friends are very welcome to the Harbour Café.'

The men were amazed, and exchanged looks of surprise.

'You have us at an advantage, Madam,' Teddy said, leaning on his cane. 'How do you know who we are?'

'I am Madam Lin. I *know* all. I *see* all. I *remember* all,' she said, mysteriously.

'Is ... is that some kind of ... of Eastern power?' Ernie, the Vickers head carpenter, asked, with a touch of reverence.

'Ha ha – *No*. No, I read the news, all day. Every day.' She pointed a knitting needle at a stack of newspapers standing on the table behind her, a movement that did not seem to reduce the speed of her knitting. 'And what I don't see in the paper, I hear in my café. You are on your way to Newfoundland, to fly the Atlantic, like the Americans. You are the Vickers men.'

'That's right,' Jack grinned. 'We are the Vickers men.'

They ordered teas and coffees, and Madam Lin called out something in Mandarin to someone beyond the door in the back of the room. A younger woman with a chubby face and a harried expression hurried out, asked a question in the same language, and received some sharp instructions in return.

'You'll want the table by the window, to look at the aeroplanes,' Madam Lin told the men, gesturing to it.

They sat down, and the younger woman arrived promptly with the pots of tea and coffee, some biscuits and a clean ashtray. She did not speak; that seemed to be Madam Lin's role. The men lit cigarettes and pipes and continued to watch the work on the flying boats.

'Tell me, tell me now,' the woman asked them. 'The Vickers Vimy, is it a good aeroplane?'

'One of the very best!' Jack replied. 'Are you interested in flying, Madam Lin?'

'Not in the least,' she retorted. 'I am interested in *news*. I enjoy connecting the threads, you know. Like a detective? My husband's cousin works in the aerodrome in Nanyuan, for the Chinese Aeronautical Department. They are buying Vimy air-craft from Vickers, to set up an air service – and a Chinese Air Force. China is a big place, and they need to start flying. I hear of the Vickers aeroplanes there, and you with your aeroplane here … *threads*, you see. It is all connected.'

'Indeed it is, madam!' Teddy tapped the table in agreement. 'So China is taking to the skies, eh? And Britain will help make it happen.

You see, boys? She's quite right, it *is* all connected. See how fast the world is moving? These are the most exciting times, I tell you.'

'They'd be a damn sight more exciting if we had an aeroplane to fly,' Jack sighed, looking jealously at the NCs. 'Pardon my language, madam.'

'Most of my customers are sailors, Captain Alcock. You cannot shock me with language.'

'Have you heard anything about the missing American seaplane?' Ernie asked, an anxious crease to his eyes. He was a sensitive sort, was Ernie.

'Not yet, but I am still on the morning editions,' Madam Lin told him. 'We have had no sailors in the door today; they are all too busy. But I will tell you what I *have* heard. I have heard that an airship is to attempt the Atlantic crossing. Another Navy aircraft.'

'An airship?'

'Yes, it is very hush-hush … but I hear everything.'

'Bloomin' hell,' Monty groaned. 'If this keeps up, the skies'll be downright crowded by the time we get up there. *Everyone*'s ahead of us.'

'Speaking of which, it looks like they've got the NC-1 started,' Bob Lyons said, gesturing with his pipe. The raw throb of the engines could be heard even from where the men were sitting. 'You've got to love the sound of that. Pure American muscle.'

The engines were left to run for a while, warming up. When the crew started pulling in the mooring lines, the Vickers men took the binoculars and went outside to watch the first flying boat take off.

Moving slowly at first, ploughing through the water, the NC seemed to drag its weight, despite the power of its four engines. Turning into the northwest wind, however, it built up momentum, gaining speed and lift, skimming the waves, before finally breaking contact with the water altogether and soaring into the sky. Turning its nose to the northeast, it set off towards Trepassey and its chance to make history.

'Heavy belly on her, and awkward in the air,' Jack muttered, staring through the field glasses. 'Not handling that crosswind well, and she won't even have her full load of fuel yet. All that power comes at a price, I suppose. Still though, she's an impressive bird.'

Half an hour after the NC-1 departed, the NC-3 took off and followed it out over the sea. Again, they went outside to watch. Bob had returned now, and was able to watch it leave. He didn't say anything at first, just gazed at the disappearing seaplane, though his expression promised bad news.

They went back inside. Bob waited until he had a cup of tea in front of him, before he told them.

'The Vimy's still in London,' he said, and there was a chorus of curses from around the table. 'The strike's over, but everything's backed up. The *Glendevon* hasn't left. The telegraph clerk was a mine of information though. I had a good chat with him. The NC-4, the missing one? It turned up yesterday, at the Naval Air Station at Chatham, between here and New York. Get this – they had to shut one engine down not long after they took off, and then another one blew on them. The thing's hardly been flown, hardly tested, so these will be its shakedown flights, getting to Trepassey. They put down with two engines, and then they had to drive across the sea ... for *fourteen hours*! Couldn't find a ship, couldn't raise anyone on the radio, and nobody could find them.'

Jack shook his head, and the others threw anxious looks at their pilot and navigator. This was yet another chilling demonstration of the scale of their task. Despite all of the Navy's support and advanced equipment, the giant flying boat had found itself crippled and unable to call for help, within fifty miles of one of its ships.

'The air station was actually sending out two more seaplanes for the search when the NC arrived. But that forward engine of theirs was reduced to junk, so they'll be at Chatham for a few days yet. The press is already calling her "the lame duck". There's more news, though: the Handley Page team have arrived in St John's ... and *they* have their aeroplane.'

A chorus of groans greeted this news. Their competitors were lining up ahead of them.

'Well, that's just bloody brilliant,' Jack sighed, stubbing out his cigarette. 'Still, no point gettin' all mardy about it, eh? I'm gonna take a leak and then have another cuppa.'

It wasn't Jack's way to suffer much doubt, but they could all see it in him, despite his attempts to hide it. As the pilot, he was the leader of this team, and ultimately responsible for its success or failure. With no machine to give his attention to, he was becoming frustrated. And that set everyone else on edge too. When he came back, they tried to talk of other things – the football and the cricket they were missing; the racing at Brooklands. Anything to avoid facing the thought that all this travel, and all their work, might come to nothing. Eventually they fell quiet, and a dark mood settled over them as they sat there, each lost in his own thoughts.

'I think this is the first time I've ever wanted to pray for bad weather,' Bob said, breaking the silence. 'But that's where we are. We need a bit of luck, boys. Fate needs to play a hand here or we've no chance.'

They all cast their eyes out at the dull, overcast sky.

And out of that sky came an aircraft, from the northeast. As it drew closer, they saw it was one of the flying boats. The NC-3, Commander Towers' aircraft, was returning to the harbour. The American seaplane must have developed another mechanical problem, and had come back for repairs. Teddy gave a slight shake of his head and grim smile.

'It seems that nothing about this endeavour is going to be simple.'

20

Maggie was sitting behind the wheel of the Buick when she saw the police constable come into view on the dock at St John's. She cursed to herself and winced as she looked out at the rain, falling relentlessly over the town and its harbour. The police were out in numbers because there were American sailors in town, on shore leave from the *USS Chicago*, and because the Handley Page team had arrived. Maggie watched as the dock's cranes reached up over the ship, unloading crates containing sections of the team's aircraft.

The Handley Page V/1500 had been split into over 100 boxes, the largest of which was forty-five feet long and had to be fitted with its own wheels and axles for the journey along the road. Maggie had intended to follow the convoy of carts in the car, as they took their cargo to whatever site they'd chosen for their aerodrome. She had tried asking the carters where they were bound, but they'd been too busy to talk. Nobody wanted to be out in this rain. Let them get moving, and then she'd pull up alongside, have a chat, and then drive on ahead to their destination. If she could get past the policemen.

It was early afternoon on Saturday, the 10th of May, though it looked more like evening, it was already so dark. At times, the downpour reduced visibility to a few dozen yards of grey murk. Maggie didn't have a driver's licence, and there was no denying how young she looked, so she couldn't take the chance of driving past the policemen on the dock – and they were blocking her only way through. She could walk at the speed the heavyset dray horses moved, but she had to be back in time for the evening shift at the hotel. And besides, she did not want to leave the car. It was miserably cold and she was going to get drenched; she was already pretty wet from the rain blowing in the open sides of the vehicle. She felt sorry for the horses that had to pull their loads in these conditions.

A figure with the upright bearing of a career military man stood near the cab of one of the cranes. He was holding an umbrella, and calling out directions from time to time, and watched the proceedings with an air of authority. Maggie had already grilled Joey Smallwood, the young reporter from the *Evening Telegram*, on these new arrivals. Smallwood had established himself as a local guide, which included advising the fliers on likely sites for use as aerodromes, and though Maggie was not sure of his qualifications on that subject, he was a useful source of information. Huddled here behind the steering wheel, she felt a bit like a spy, closely watching the movements of these men.

The commanding figure was Admiral Mark Kerr, leader of the Handley Page team. At fifty-five, he was the oldest person so far involved in the challenge to cross the Atlantic. There was a woman standing near him, under her own umbrella, and Maggie recognised Assistant Principal Sulley, from the Women's Royal Naval Service, whom she'd met out on the hill with the American aerologist. This wasn't a Royal Navy operation, but Admiral Kerr appeared to have pulled some strings to get military support. The woman was in the same navy frock coat and pudding-basin style hat, and was saying something to the senior officer, and pointing to the *Chicago*.

Kerr was qualified as a pilot, though he would only serve as co-pilot of the Handley Page. The pilot was Major Herbert George Brackley, who was half the admiral's age. A former journalist for Reuters news agency, he had flown bombers in the war. He was now up on the deck of the ship, directing the removal of the crates from the cargo hold.

Not far from where the Buick was parked, the team's navigator was standing on the edge of the dock, staring out to sea, seemingly oblivious to the rain. This was the Norwegian, Tryggve Gran. A cross-country skier who had played football for his country, Gran was an explorer and an accomplished pilot in his own right. He'd been the first to find the dead bodies of the explorer Robert Falcon Scott and his companions, on the ill-fated *Terra Nova* expedition to the Antarctic in 1912. Gran was a willowy-framed man with a long, lean face and an intense gaze.

Maggie knew these men would not be coming to Cochrane's. All the rooms were taken, as were all the rooms in the smaller guesthouses in St John's. The race to cross the ocean had attracted so many reporters and other visitors that there was no accommodation to be had anywhere in town. She didn't know where Kerr had chosen to take his large team, and she wanted to find out.

The nearest police constable noticed someone was sitting in the Buick and started to walk towards her. Maggie's plan was to say that she was waiting for her uncle, but how long would that excuse work? Though the rules on driving weren't rigidly enforced across Newfoundland; given the small number of people on such a big island, and the even smaller number of cars, the police were stricter about it in the larger towns where there was more chance of an actual collision. Although Maggie wasn't doing anything wrong – she wasn't driving the car right at that moment – she didn't want to attract their attention. She had to be able to drive out of here at some point. Lowering her head, she tried to look as invisible as possible.

'Maggie, isn't it?' a voice called, giving her a start. 'Aren't you the curious one? You'll freeze to death sitting out in this!'

It was Assistant Principal Sulley, standing beside the passenger side door, smiling from under the brim of her umbrella. How had she appeared out of nowhere?

'Sorry for sneaking up on you. Permission to come aboard?'

'Yes, of course,' Maggie replied. 'It's … is it Miss or Mrs Sulley?'

'"Kate" will do fine,' the Wren said. She climbed in, and shook her umbrella before tossing it onto the floor behind her. She took off her hat, and dropped that behind her too. 'So, are you another one of these poor souls who's become obsessed with the fliers then?'

Maggie blinked slowly, then gave a reluctant shrug.

'A little bit,' she said quietly.

'There's a lot of it going round,' Kate laughed. It was an easy, friendly sound. 'A bit young to be driving, aren't you? And before you deny it, you little dervish, I spotted you arriving earlier, when the ship was docking. Before the *police* showed up. I must stay, this is *quite* the machine you have here. Did you find it roaming wild in the woods?'

'It's not finished … I'm still working on it,' Maggie replied defensively. 'And I'll get my licence soon. As soon as I can, I mean.'

'Oh, I'm not bothered with all that. Though this thing could do with a lick of paint,' Kate said, waving her hand in a dismissive gesture. She narrowed her eyes, looking sideways at the younger girl. 'So what's your interest? Is it the dashing men? The wondrous machines? The spirit of adventure …?'

'I want to be an explorer!' Maggie blurted out, before she'd realised she was going to.

And there it was, finally out there. She'd never said it to anyone before. Kate arched an eyebrow and turned to face her, elbow on the back of the seat, an earnest expression on her face.

'Good for you,' she said. 'Good for you. And why the hell not, eh? Can't let the men have all the fun, can we?'

Maggie was taken aback. It appeared that the Wren was being serious. She'd expected the older woman to laugh at her, or perhaps show pity at her innocence.

'You … you think I could do it?' she asked.

'Who knows? Is there any reason you shouldn't try?'

'No,' Maggie said firmly.

'Well then, why not?' Kate took out a compact and checked her hair, which was tied up in a bun, and needed binding up again. She did so with quick, efficient movements. 'I want to be a sailor, myself. In the Navy. But they won't let us, will they? I'll never serve on a submarine, or command a destroyer. They probably won't even keep the Wrens in service, now the war's over. Perhaps I'll become a *spy* instead. Wouldn't that be a hoot? They still need women spies, as they did in the war. But an explorer? I mean, anyone can be an explorer, if they want, can't they? You just have to go where nobody's been. Who's to say you can't do that?'

'That's exactly what I think!' Maggie exclaimed. 'Eh … em … speaking of going places … I saw you with Admiral Kerr. Are you working for him? Do you know where he's going?'

'I'm doing the liaison bit again, between him and the Navy this time,' Kate told her. 'He needs advice on the area, weather reports, that kind of thing. They're setting up their aerodrome at Harbour Grace.'

'Oh. Is that right?'

It was just as well Maggie hadn't tried to follow the carts on foot. Harbour Grace was more than sixty miles away, northwest of St John's, an even longer drive than Trepassey. The Handley Page team wouldn't be heading straight out there today – not with animals, not in this weather. Maggie felt deflated. She'd hoped to see them start assembling their aeroplane.

'There's a copper coming!' Kate said in a bright voice, as if this was good news. 'Let me handle this.'

As the constable came closer, Kate leaned out and waved at him.

'Is that Tommy Parsons? Oh Tommy, you're *just* the man we need! Thank God for the Royal Newfoundland Constabulary!'

'*What are you doing?!*' Maggie hissed at her. 'Tommy knows me! I sell eggs to his mother! Here, change places. You'll have to drive!'

'Not at all. You'll be fine, just follow my lead,' Kate whispered back.

'What can I do for you, Miss Sulley?' the young policeman called, obviously uncomfortable in his saturated uniform and coat, his peaked cap dripping with water.

'You wouldn't be an absolute darling and crank that starter for us, would you? It's a bit stiff for us girls, and with this rotten weather ...'

'Say no more, Miss! We'll soon get you on the road!'

From his eager manner, Maggie got the impression that there was a lot Tommy Parsons would be willing to do for Assistant Principal Sulley. He unclipped the starter handle from behind the fender and fitted it into the socket under the radiator grille. With a few sharp turns, Tommy had the engine coughing into life.

'You're a hero, Tommy. Thank you so much!' Kate called to him.

She blew him a kiss as he put the handle back in its clips, and Maggie saw him give her a ridiculously pleased grin in response. Putting the car in gear, Maggie pulled away, waving to him as she passed by. He looked momentarily suspicious, but then waved back, perhaps not recognising Maggie in her overcoat, with her cap pulled down low. She tried to stifle a fit of giggles, and didn't quite manage it.

'Oh yes, he did recognise you,' Kate said breezily, as if hearing her thoughts. She gave a whoop and laughed again, and it was infectious. 'And there he goes, suspecting only now that he has been complicit in a criminal act. Don't worry, he won't say anything – he'd only get himself in trouble. Mark my words, Maggie. You can get away with a lot in this life with the right attitude. But I like your style. I think you and I are going to be friends, Maggie McRory!'

'Where are we going?'

'Admiral Kerr has borrowed the Navy car I was driving, and I have a date at the Bioscope Theatre, so you're going to have to drop me there. I shall be dreadfully late, but that's all right. Keeps 'em keen.'

Their route took them past the convoy of heavily laden carts, now starting to snake away from the harbour and through the town. Maggie drove past the *Chicago*, looming like a great grey wall over the wharf. It was here to serve as support for the Navy's airship, the C-5 – another contender in the race to cross the ocean.

'Have they got the airship on board, do you know?' Maggie asked. 'I'm surprised it would fit on that ship.'

'What? Oh, no! I mean, you're right, it's a great big thing – much, much larger than any of those aeroplanes, but it's a blimp – what they call a "non-rigid" airship. The rigid ones, like the German zeppelins, have this ruddy great steel frame … if you pull back the envelope covering it, it looks like the hoops in one of those old-fashioned crinoline dresses. But the C-5, apart from its control car, is just an enormous balloon. It could deflate right down to an empty bag if they wanted it to; they could easily get it onto a ship, but no, it's flying here from Montauk, in New York. That said, I imagine they have the same problems with the weather that everyone else has, so who knows when it will get here?

'It's funny, you know. Newfoundland has become the centre of the world's attention, what with all the people coming here to fly the Atlantic ... and they're all discovering as soon as they arrive, that we have the *worst possible* weather for flying.'

Yes, thought Maggie. And that's before they even get out over the ocean.

21

Arthur Whitten Brown dreamed of fire. Once again, he was dimly aware that this was a dream, and a dream of a memory at that. He was flying over the battlefront at 6,300 feet, in a BE2c biplane, sitting in the forward cockpit as observer. They were soaring in a straight line, parallel to the German lines, taking reconnaissance photographs. Archie had found their range, and puffs of smoke burst around them. His pilot that day had been a nineteen-year-old lieutenant called William, but when Teddy looked behind him, it was *Jack* he saw at the controls, the same age as he was now.

The aeroplane jolted as it took a hit. Shrapnel tore through the engine, the pistons clattering and making a frightening ripping noise. As the nose dipped and they started to lose height, fire flared along one side, quickly catching on the plywood and the highly flammable doped fabric of the aircraft's body and wings. Fire – every flier's nightmare. As the blaze, accelerated by the wind, rushed along the fuselage, Teddy grabbed the spare magazines of ammunition and threw them overboard. Then he unbuckled his belt and lunged out of the cockpit. He felt the heat on his legs even as he slid down onto the lower wing and began inching back towards Jack. There was nowhere else for him to go.

Jack pointed the nose down, and Teddy clung on, the wind screaming past him, trying to wrench him away, as they plunged towards the ground at 120 miles per hour. Time was their only ally against the fire and their altitude. They had to land before the blaze consumed the aeroplane. He heard wood cracking, wires snapping, the flames roaring ... he and Jack could either hang on until the fire consumed them, or leap to their deaths from thousands of feet in the air ...

The train jerked abruptly, waking him, and he suffered that moment of confusion before he found himself slumped in his seat, head leaning against the window. He rubbed his eyes and peered out into the darkness. They had reached St John's. It was nearly midnight on Tuesday, the 13th of May, and they had finally completed the three-day journey from Halifax. He must have drifted off while reading his poetry, for the book lay open in his lap. He had found recently that he was more likely to dream of Kitty if he read some evocative verse last thing at night; clearly, it hadn't worked this time. He took a moment to gaze at the photograph of her that he used as a bookmark.

'I'll be home soon enough now, my darling,' he said softly.

Jack was already standing, taking down cases from the luggage racks above them. Monty, Ernie and the two Bobs had started down the aisle towards the door. Like Teddy, they were tired, but pleased to have finally reached the starting point of their great venture.

'Now all we need is an aeroplane!' Jack said to him, winking.

The man at the station directed them to Cochrane's, which was apparently the only proper hotel in town. It was a short walk from the station through a light fall of rain, but when they got there, the hotel was locked up for the night. Their knocking was eventually answered by a stout, no-nonsense woman in her late thirties or early forties, who told them there were no vacancies, what with all the aviators in town. However, when she learned they were the Vickers team, she introduced herself as Agnes Dooley, ushered them in and assured them she'd find somewhere for them to sleep. She insisted they call her Agnes, and asked if they'd like something to eat. They eagerly accepted.

Their host brought them into the smoking room, where four men were sitting at a table, playing poker.

'Well, I'll be damned!' Freddie Raynham exclaimed, throwing down his cards. 'Jack Alcock! And Bob! And the rest … hello, lads! So you Vickers laggards have finally dragged your backsides over to join us, have you?'

Freddie, Harry Hawker and Fax Morgan jumped to their feet to greet the newcomers. They introduced Kenneth MacKenzie Grieve, who had not been one of the Brooklands set, and there were enthusiastic handshakes all round. Flying created firm friends, and these were some of the best.

'I thought you'd have left by now!' Jack sniped back at Freddie. 'Getting cold feet, are we?'

'Literally, old sport,' Harry told him. 'This place is freezing. We've been ready to go for a *month*, and we haven't had a clear day that whole time. I tell you, this is the longest I've gone without flying in years.'

'Aye, I think you might have mentioned that once or twice,' Grieve grunted, and Freddie and Fax laughed.

'You still have the jump on us,' Jack told them. 'We'll be another week at least, waiting on our machine. And in the meantime, we need to find a field.'

'Good luck with that,' Freddie chuckled. 'We found a spot out by the lake, but it's shorter than we'd like. Have to back the machine right up to the bank of a river to get the distance to take off. It's a wild place, this one. This whole side of the island seems to be hills and rocks; there's hardly a flat surface on it.'

'Yes, we found our field had a great big depression in the middle of it when the snow cleared,' Harry added. He threw his hands up in exasperation. '*Snow*, in *April*! And it's over 400 feet above sea level. Seems to catch all sorts of winds we don't want. The Handley Page lot have gone sixty-five miles north to find somewhere they could use. You've got your work cut out for you, boys.'

'It's a fine state of affairs, this!' Jack said, laughing. 'No hotel rooms, booze is illegal, brutal weather, terrible terrain and the Americans are coming! Any *good* news for us, lads?'

'The locals are friendly, and the hotel does a fine breakfast,' Fax said, fingering his bushy moustache, of which he was so fond.

'Though you'll have to watch out for one of the girls who works here, Maggie. Give her a chance and she'll bombard you with questions. She's worse than the reporters. Frankly, I'm worried that if we're stuck here much longer, she's going to steal one of the aeroplanes. The girl's obsessed.'

'Yes, she reminds me of *Harry*, when he was starting out,' Freddie quipped, to more laughter. 'And pay no heed to Fax – he loves any excuse to tell his war stories.'

They all sat down and lit their cigarettes and pipes as Agnes brought in pots of tea and coffee and sandwiches. Teddy joined in the chat with the rest of them, but he was studying the other fliers as he sipped his tea. The strain was starting to show on them.

Despite the jolly front that Freddie, Fax, Harry and Grieve were putting up, they were under incredible pressure. Like Vickers, the manufacturers that were paying for them to be here would be expecting results, and would be growing impatient.

Every day spent here was a day lost, with more money down the drain and the increasing likelihood that more competitors would show up and challenge them for the prize. They had already spent a month here, with nothing to do but check and test their aircraft, over and over again, waiting for the weather to break. Telegrams were coming in from the money men, wanting to know what was happening, when they'd be leaving. The newspapers would lose interest too, if this inactivity went on much longer. They would pull their reporters, and the manufacturers would lose the publicity that they desperately craved.

The Vickers team were friends, but they were also a threat to the other aviators' attempts to write themselves into the history books. Jack and Teddy's arrival, and that of the Handley Page team, had piled still more pressure onto men who were fit to burst with impatience and frustration. That kind of frustration could affect a man's judgement, and make him take stupid risks.

Agnes had camp beds brought into the smoking room for the new arrivals. She promised to contact the other guesthouses tomorrow, to help the men find rooms, though she wasn't hopeful. Jack assured her that this would do them for the time being, and while Teddy agreed, he knew sleep would be difficult on one of these folding beds with his lame leg. Still, he was grateful to finally be here, with a great purpose and good men. Once the Martinsyde and Sopwith boys had left, he undressed and settled under the covers of the camp bed. It was surprisingly comfortable.

With the lights off, the other men soon drifted off, Ernie snoring loudly and Monty's pipe smoker's lungs making a strange wheezing sound. Teddy read some Shelley by the light of a torch until he felt himself drifting off … and this time, when he fell asleep, he dreamed of Kathleen.

22

On Thursday, the 15th of May, Maggie arrived at Cochrane's before dawn. She had persuaded Agnes to join her in a venture, to make some money out of the arrival of the US Navy's airship in the town. News of its imminent arrival had spread, and crowds were expected. Maggie had gambled some of her newly acquired cash on buying more candy, gum and bottles of soda. If Agnes agreed to make some of her renowned pies, a mix of sweet and savoury, Maggie would sell these too, by the slice, and split the takings.

The pies were almost cooked when she arrived, the smell of meat and pastry and baked fruit filling the kitchen with a delicious air. There was a man sitting at the kitchen table, writing a letter. Though he greeted her politely enough, he seemed a quiet type. Light and wiry, he was handsome, with fine-boned features, his face clean-shaven and his wavy, greying brown hair somewhat askew. He had the manner of a man holding a great deal of nervous energy under careful control, and his blue eyes were tired, with a touch of sadness to them. A cane was leaning against the wall beside him.

Agnes, who had now started on breakfast for the early risers, introduced Lieutenant Arthur Whitten Brown, navigator for the Vickers team. This explained the sea chart he had on the table in front of him, which he stopped and gazed at whenever he was not writing. He seemed to misinterpret her interest in the map.

'Pardon me,' he said, rolling up the chart. 'I don't mean to get in your way. I couldn't sleep and the kitchen was warm. Agnes kindly invited me to sit in.'

'Oh, that's all right,' Maggie told him. 'You should talk to some of the fishermen, if you're interested in what's out there on the sea. They know more than you'll find on any map. More than all those aerologists seem to.'

'You've been speaking to aerologists, have you?' he said with interest. 'I'd certainly like to talk with some of the local sailors. Do you know any?'

'Maggie makes it her business to know everyone, don't you pet?' Agnes said, with a smirk.

'You should talk to Alistair Finch or Jeremiah Smith,' Maggie told him, wrinkling her nose at Agnes. 'They'd see you right. I can introduce you, if you like.'

'I'd be very grateful, Miss.'

'Maggie. Everyone just calls me Maggie.'

'Then so shall I!'

'Who are you writing to there, Mister Brown?'

'Maggie!' Agnes scolded. 'Don't be nosey!'

Teddy replied nonetheless:

'That's all right. I'm writing to my fiancée, Kathleen.'

And he said the name with such genuine warmth, such obvious love, that Maggie decided there and then that she liked Arthur Whitten Brown. She would have liked to stay and talk, but he saw that they were busy, so he excused himself and moved out into the dining room. Agnes took the pies from the oven, cut them into slices, wrapped each slice in waxed paper, and labelled it with a pencil. Maggie packed them into cardboard boxes and took them out to the Buick, parked in the lane out the back. Her other stock was already loaded up.

She drove slowly and carefully through the streets. A thick fog had drifted in from the sea, though there was still a strong wind, and even with their lights on, it was hard to see other cars on the road. The buildings on either side were almost invisible.

The airship was due to arrive at the cricket ground in Pleasantville, on the north side of Quidi Vidi Lake, about half a mile from St John's, and not far from where Freddie Raynham's Martinsyde *Raymor* sat in its hangar. Some cars were already stopped along the road, with people hanging around gazing at the sky. Maggie parked in a prominent position, near to an open area where some sailors from the *Chicago* were driving great metal screws into the ground to anchor the airship to.

Thankfully, there were no police around. If one showed up, she would say that this was her uncle's car, and he was coming back for it later. She noticed other vendors were setting up nearby, but she thought she'd chosen her spot well.

She began to wonder if the C-5 would show up today, after all the money she'd spent. Could *anything* fly in this clammy, featureless grey murk, draped like a cloak over the land? She'd heard enough from the pilots to know that aeroplanes couldn't. If the airship *could* travel in fog, then it must surely have a huge advantage over the other aircraft taking on the Atlantic.

She imagined what it must be like flying through cloud, hoping you were high enough that you wouldn't crash into anything. How you could land an aircraft when you couldn't see the ground was beyond her.

Time passed, with no sign of any aircraft, and boredom proved a powerful incentive for people to eat and spend money. Many had brought their own picnics, but Maggie still sold out of pie slices within two hours, and most of the rest of her stock an hour or two after that. Alistair Finch showed up with his wife, grinning when he saw Maggie, and bought some gum. He had been delighted with his share of the seal skin money, and suggested they might do other business in the future.

As he unwrapped a piece of gum and popped it in his mouth, he told her that word had come from the other side of the island – the blimp was on its way. It had been seen at Placentia Junction. The crew had become lost in the fog, and were now flying low so that they could follow the railway tracks to St John's.

The mist eventually cleared, thinning out to reveal a blue sky, the air cool despite the bright sun. Maggie sat down on a blanket with Finch and his wife. By now, thousands of people had gathered on the cricket ground. Finch said that the Governor of Newfoundland himself was coming to greet the airmen.

At around 11am, people started calling out and pointing at the horizon to the southwest. A dot had appeared in the sky, in the direction of Placentia. Nobody was sitting any longer; a buzz of excitement vibrated through the crowd. The edges of the object were blurred in the hazy air, giving it the appearance of a silvery cloud, though it was too regular in form. As it drew closer, Maggie could hear the rhythmic drone of its engines, see the control car hanging beneath the oval shape of its envelope.

The people of St John's had been looking at aeroplanes being constructed for a month now, and the thrill had worn off somewhat. It didn't seem as if any of them would ever take off on their epic journey. The airship promised an entirely different level of spectacle.

Since her return from Trepassey, Maggie had been reading up about these aircraft, as well as grilling Kate Sulley on everything she knew, about the C-ships in particular. The rubberised cotton hull was bullet-shaped at the front and tapered towards the fins at the back. It was 196 feet long and forty-two feet at its maximum diameter, dwarfing any aeroplane. The envelope was filled with hydrogen gas. It had two engines, on either side of the control car, an aluminium body shaped much like an aeroplane fuselage, with three open cockpits on top that carried its six-man crew.

It blotted out the sun as it glided overhead, casting an enormous shadow on the ground. Then the engines were cut off. Once the clacking of the propellors had stopped, the airship made hardly any sound – just a soft creaking and the swish of the wind over its gas-filled skin. The men's voices were louder. Steel mooring cables were thrown down, and a team of 100 sailors from the *Chicago* pulled the craft down and secured the lines with the earth anchors screwed into the ground.

Maggie gaped up at it, her heart pounding. It was like a vision from a Jules Verne novel, like something from another world. No aeroplane could do this – hover motionless in the air. An aeroplane couldn't stay aloft without the constant pull of its engines to help the wings ride the wind. The airship might only fly at half the speed, but it floated effortlessly. Aeroplanes struggled into the air, while this incredible vehicle had to be *tied to the ground* to stop it from flying away on its own. She had read that an airship could refuel from a ship at sea, without having to touch down. She felt a moment of disloyalty to the fliers in Cochrane's as she thought that *this*, surely, was the craft that would conquer the Atlantic.

Once it was tied down, the crew of six men climbed out of the silver control car to a lively cheer from the crowd, to be greeted by Governor Harris himself. Dressed in leather flight suits, with hats and goggles, they looked every bit like adventurers. And yet they were clearly exhausted, drained by their journey. They had been flying for twenty-five hours straight, exposed to the elements, and the rough weather had taken its toll. A couple of them were rubbing their ears and shaking their heads, as if the engines had left them deaf. People crowded around them, and Maggie couldn't get close. She cursed in frustration, standing on tiptoes to try and see more.

A car was driven up, and the men climbed on board. Maggie heard someone say they were to be taken to the *Chicago* for dinner and some rest. Would she have to stay here all day now, for a chance to see them depart? She wished someone could tell her what would happen next.

Like Maggie, Finch had come forward with the crowd, though his attention was all on the bulging, silvery-grey envelope that shuddered in the gusts of wind, straining against the cables that held it, and the ground screws that anchored the cables. As the airship crew were driven away towards town, he frowned and gave one of the earth anchors a kick, looking unimpressed. His eyes followed the steel cable up to the nose of the airship, high above.

'Surely they're not going to leave it here like this?' he asked, almost to himself. 'This thing's like a bloody great sail. They do know there's a storm coming, don't they?'

23

And the storm came. If the Americans were aware of the rising wind, they didn't show it. This was a military operation and these sailors didn't spook easily – national pride was at stake. Navy mechanics started taking the engines apart for maintenance, while some other sailors added more anchor lines to the airship – hemp ropes this time, instead of the stout steel mooring cables. The crowd began to thin out now, but Maggie hung around, thinking that the aviators might come back. Finch was still there too. The trawler captain was watching the movements of the giant craft with an expert eye. He advised his wife to go back to their car; he'd spent enough of his life under sails to know the power of the wind against such a large surface.

By 2pm, it was clear to everyone that there was serious weather coming.

'That's a thirty-knot wind, man!' Finch called to the officer in charge of the ground crew, a Lieutenant Little. 'Gusting to forty or fifty, I'd say! And it's going to get worse! You have to let the gas out, pull this thing down!'

'It's not my decision to make!' the man cried back. 'If we rip the envelope, the whole thing collapses! We can't inflate it again without a hangar – and the nearest one big enough is back in the States! It'll be the end of the whole operation. We have to wait for Commander Coil to come back. Only he can make the call!'

There was no sign of the crew. Shattered as they were after their tumultuous flight from New York, Maggie presumed they were still relaxing aboard the *Chicago* in the sheltered harbour, unaware of how bad conditions were becoming up here. She supposed that ground crews were used to handling airships in heavy weather, but even with nearly 100 men holding the lines, the blimp was in danger of tearing free. The cables were snapping like whips, and the envelope was making creaking and booming sounds as the wind pushed against it, distorting its shape as it strained against the ropes and cables. By late afternoon, two ropes had torn loose and been carried away. Many of the remaining spectators were pitching in to help hold the lines.

Maggie joined in too, along with a couple of boys even younger than her – fourteen, fifteen? – clinging on behind a bunch of others, leaning all their weight back to hold it firm. The rope burned her hands, jerking and hauling away, only to be pulled back again. Before long, her arms were aching with the strain, her feet sliding along the damp, grassy ground, her heels trying to dig in and find purchase. It was frightening, but exhilarating, a battle against the elements themselves. For nearly another hour, she and the others fought the giant bag of gas as the winds tried to drag it away.

The mechanics, still intent on preparing the airship for its Atlantic journey, were hurriedly starting to reassemble the carburetors, which lay in pieces on tarpaulins stretched out on the ground near the blimp. With the way the control car was bucking around like an untamed horse, however, they wouldn't be getting the engines back in working order any time soon.

Without engines, there was no way of controlling the airship's movement if it broke free.

'There's nothing for it!' Little shouted to one of the men in the control car. 'Preston, we have to rip or we'll lose her! Pull the cord!'

Maggie had read about this. A cord ran up through the blimp's envelope to the 'ripping panel', a section of material glued over a vent at the top of the airship. The panel was to be torn off in only the most desperate circumstances, to quickly collapse the envelope.

Preston, the young man in the rear cockpit, grabbed the cord and pulled on it with all his strength. It broke off in his hands. The cord had snapped somewhere inside the envelope. Little swore at the top of his voice and rushed over, clambering into the rocking control car. There was another mechanic up there too, and the three men tried to cut through the tough rubberised cotton skin to reach the cord inside. One small hole wouldn't do it – they needed that whole panel at the top to come off.

The wind howled as the enormous airship thrashed against its restraints. A steel cable broke free from the finned tail of the blimp, and the whole craft swung violently to the side. Another cable was swinging loose, having pulled a ground screw out of the earth.

It was whipping dangerously over the heads of those holding the lines. Swooping down, it tore through the fabric roof of a nearby car and smashed the windscreen. A group clinging desperately to a rope were being hauled across the field as more ground screws came loose. People dropped away, losing their grip and falling to the grass.

Little and his two men were still in the cockpit, struggling to cut into the envelope. The airship was starting to lift, lines of people dragging along the ground below it. Maggie heard a warning shout. Finch was calling her name. She looked up as a cable swung its ground screw towards her. The iron bar, with its thick, sharp threads, smacked across the head of the boy behind her and spun, chopping against her right forearm hard enough to break the bone. The force of the blow knocked her to the ground and she screamed as she felt a pain like she'd never known, like jaws crushing her arm.

Rolling over, she saw the blond-haired boy lying motionless beside her, eyes closed, the side of his head split open. She wondered if he was dead. Agony blurred her vision, but the looming shadow of the envelope suddenly moved away, replaced by brighter, grey-white sky.

'Out!' Little bellowed. 'Out! Get out, now!'

The other two men jumped from the control car as it jerked away, and rose higher into the air, all the lines pulling free now. It was nearly thirty feet up when Lieutenant Little leapt from it, and he landed with a sharp cry as his leg folded awkwardly under him.

Still wailing and cradling her arm, Maggie watched the great airship wheel away. Its enormous bulk careened away sideways, carried towards the sea by the storm. It was quickly swallowed up in the mist.

The pain in her arm was immense, overwhelming, but she was still aware enough to see the blood on her hand. She went to pull up the sleeve of her thin jacket. It caught on something and another bolt of agony shot up her shoulder. Sobbing as she carefully peeled the sleeve up, she saw a piece of bloody bone sticking through the skin of her forearm. She nearly threw up in shock. She felt Finch's arms around her, his rough voice saying her name, and then she passed out.

24

Jack took a long drag of his cigarette and cast his eyes over the Martinsyde *Raymor*. It was a good machine, the fastest in the race, though he thought the Vimy was better, with its greater range and two engines. The two cockpits in the *Raymor* were only narrowly separated, with Freddie in the rear and Fax in the front, but it would still make communication and navigation that little bit more difficult. The Vimy's cockpit might be a tight squeeze for two, but Jack would be glad to have Teddy at his side for the long flight.

A brisk breeze still pushed against the canvas sides of the hangar, making the wooden frame creak. Jack carefully flicked his cigarette out the door, well away from the fuel and oil drums that stood outside, and regarded Freddie Raynham, who was checking over the engine one last time. Fax and a few of the others from the Martinsyde team were combing over the rest of the aircraft. There was no need; the machine was ready. It had been ready for nearly a month. The temporary building buzzed with nervous excitement.

'Seems a bit breezy still,' Jack commented, not wanting to needle his friend. 'More storms forecast for over the ocean too.'

'We're going, Jack,' Freddie replied tightly, his attention on the seals on one of the radiator pipes. 'You heard Harry, and I agree with him. If the Americans reach the Azores, we're going for it. As if you'd do any different, in my place.'

'Aye, I suppose I wouldn't.'

Yes, there was always risk, Jack thought. Balancing that was the nature of the game. Even so, he thought Freddie and Fax, and Harry and Kenneth, were rushing into this.

Freddie had a cap on his head, turned backwards, and was wearing fingerless gloves. It was cold, even in here, with an even colder wind that burrowed through you when you walked out-side. It was Friday, the 16th of May, and news had come through that the NC flying boats had departed from Trepassey. Their Atlantic flight was underway. They were ultimately bound for London, but they'd be crossing to Lisbon in Portugal first, stop-ping at the Azores along the way.

Freddie and Harry could still get to Britain before the Nancies reached Lisbon, if they both took off tomorrow. Though the weather was far from ideal, they could risk it, if it didn't deteriorate. But they would wait to hear if the Americans had made it the 1,200 miles to the Azores, which was still open to question. Jack was in two minds, himself; he'd flown in worse conditions, but to take off in this for such a long flight, with such a heavily loaded aircraft …

'It's funny, you know?' Freddie added. 'Harry and I made a deal. In the first few days after we were both ready to go, we were all keeping tabs on each other – Fax and Grieve too. It was like some bally spy operation. It got ridiculous; we'd see them getting up for something and think they were making a move … We started pranking each other, to goad one another into a false start. It was exhausting! We were all as jumpy as scared cats, and getting right huffed. In the end, we made a deal, that if one team was going to leave, they'd give the other an hour's notice. Stopped us all going gaga. Meant we could relax, you understand. And now, here we are, with the Americans goading us on instead.'

He couldn't hide the tension in his voice. Everyone had been in a bit of a funk after the disaster with the airship the day before. None of the crew had been hurt, of course, which was a mercy, but a local boy had nearly been killed, struck across the head by one of the steel cables. Another boy had had his collar bone fractured, and that girl from the hotel, Maggie, had suffered a broken arm. She was a card, that girl, Jack thought. Full of questions, and desperate to make more of her life than what she'd been dealt. He'd been much the same at her age, and he hoped this brush with danger didn't dent her spirit.

But the injured children had taken much of the glow from this great adventure of theirs, and shone a very different light on it for the locals. There was nothing glamorous about a child nearly being killed, or seeing your aircraft carried away like a rag on the wind.

'Still though,' Jack said, shaking off the morbid thought. 'That's a narrow runway you've got there, Freddie. One direction only … you'll need the wind on your side.'

'Best we could do. You've seen the place,' Freddie said, scowling. 'Try finding a flat bit of land, I tell you! What about you? Any luck yet?'

'Not yet. Like you and Harry said, there's thin pickings,' Jack replied. 'Been driving around since we got here. And what *is* flat has already been planted with crops. The farmers aren't inclined to let us flatten 'em – not without paying a bloody fortune, anyhow. Even the car hire's costing us more than we want to spend, if we're going to be at this for more than a week or two. And we'll be a while yet, I'd say.'

'You can have this place when we've left, if you want,' Freddie told him, finishing his examination of the engine. 'Would it do you?'

Jack had already considered that. He had paced the longest stretch of the field the previous morning, when he'd come down to see the airship, though he hadn't stayed around long enough to see it tear free. The *Raymor* was smaller and lighter than the Vimy, and with its single engine, it would be carrying less fuel. It needed less room to take off.

'That's decent of you, old chum, but it's too short a run for us, fully loaded,' he said, shrugging. 'You've got about three hundred yards before you hit those trees at the end, and we need close to five, into the wind. We could probably make it out of here with near-empty tanks, but not loaded up.'

'Well, the offer stands, Jack. Even if we don't get off tomorrow, you can set up here until you've found your own base.'

'That's awfully good of you, Freddie. Thanks.'

There was little else to do now but wait. The aviators and their crews, the reporters and some of the local men and women, including a few musicians, gathered in the lounge of Cochrane's Hotel that evening. Word had got around that the fliers might make a go of it, and spirits were high. Everyone was looking forward to what they hoped would be a historic day.

For Jack, who liked a good party as much as anyone, it had a somewhat eerie feel to it. It brought him back to nights during the war, with the lads from the squadrons he'd served in, particularly the nights ahead of a major mission. As the musicians struck up their tunes, hands banged on tables, feet stamped and voices roared the lyrics, or did their best to at least.

There were other veterans here, and some of the songs the musicians played were rousing numbers men would have sung in billets and mess halls and bars across Europe, saying goodbye to lost friends or avoiding thoughts of tomorrow. There was 'Mademoiselle from Armentières', 'Keep the Home Fires Burning' and, of course, 'It's a Long Way to Tipperary'. People got up and started dancing jigs and reels and whatever else took their fancy.

Glasses of beer were quietly served as the evening drew on, and some of that local rum they called 'screech', though the fliers did not partake of much. Harry was a teetotaller, and the rest were intent on keeping their heads clear. Jack, with no aeroplane to fly, felt no such reluctance, however, and he hammered the table in time to 'Pack Up Your Troubles in Your Old Kit-Bag' as he knocked back one glass of beer after another. The booze was alright, but he'd have killed for a pint of proper Manchester bitter. As far as Jack could see, Teddy seemed to be having a right old time too, though he might be in for a rough night of it later, haunted by his memories – alcohol tended to have that affect.

Collapsing into an armchair, Jack felt the urge to sleep, though it was only just past ten and he didn't want to leave until Harry, Freddie and Fax had retired. Grieve, that little bit older and wiser, had already headed up to his room. This was their night. It could well be their very *last* night – a thought Jack quickly pushed from his mind. After all, he'd be going himself if he could. For all their revelry tonight, tomorrow would not be a good day for Captain John Alcock. He closed his eyes and rubbed a hand over his face. Either his pals would succeed, in which case there would be no place in the record books for himself and Teddy, or they would fail, and he might see four more friends lose their lives. Truth be told, he was in a right funk and the drink was not helping.

Teddy flopped into a chair beside him, grinning and sweating, stretching out his bad left leg so that he could knead the flesh of his thigh. He gestured at Fax, whose normally coiffed hair was wildly askew. He had beer foam on his thick moustache and was cavorting to some Irish fiddle music.

'Tell me,' Teddy said, 'how is it that I can barely walk on this ruddy thing, when Fax can dance around like a damn fool with that false leg of his?'

'Thinks he's got pirate's blood,' Jack slurred. 'Reckons he can do anythin', dun' he?'

'And maybe he will,' Teddy said, in a quieter voice. 'You're still on to make the flight ourselves, even if they succeed?'

'Abso-bloody-lutely,' Jack grunted. 'You?'

'Well, it is the quickest way back to Kathleen,' Teddy said, shrugging.

Jack gurgled a laugh. That would be true enough – if they had an aeroplane and a place to take off from.

25

Maggie sat in a chair in Dr Gerszel's cluttered office and listened to his advice with a sinking soul. Her emotions had been dulled along with the pain, by the dose of morphine he had given her. On the day of the airship disaster, he had reset the bone and stitched the wound up and encased the arm in a plaster cast. The memory of it sent shudders through her. It was the 18th of May, a Sunday, so most of the people of St John's were observing the Sabbath, but as the doctor was Jewish, his surgery was open. He'd told her to come back that day so he could check the movement in her fingers. The kindly, dapper old man with the sympathetic face and the soft hands, told her the break was serious. However, she was young and healthy and he was confident it would heal completely. It would take time. She'd need to keep the arm in a sling for a couple of weeks. The cast would have to stay on for at least six weeks.

Maggie silently ticked off all the things she could not do: She could not work at her job, washing dishes in Cochrane's. She could do only the simplest tasks on the farm – collecting the eggs perhaps, or feeding buckets of vegetable scraps to the goats and pigs.

She could not *drive*. And there was no question of anyone allowing her to fly in an aeroplane, her secret wish.

The thought of being stuck in the house for weeks was deeply depressing. And with *Patrick* too, still bitter, still not sleeping, getting drunk and angry almost every evening … she might well go out of her mind if she couldn't get away from the farm. It was unbearable knowing that she would miss everything that happened with the aviators. She had already missed the Americans flying out of Trepassey, and it was looking as if the British fliers would leave soon too.

There had been talk of them taking off today, now that the Americans were on their way, but though there was hardly a cloud in the sky, the morning had proved too windy, and their flights had been postponed once more. Alcock and Brown had gone off for the afternoon, searching for a suitable field for their aeroplane. Still, Hawker and Grieve, and Raynham and Morgan, could be taking off any day now. If either team succeeded, it would all be over for this wonderful excitement St John's was experiencing. Life would go back to small and boring normality. She wanted to cry, but she'd already done so much of it over the last two days, she felt emptied out.

Gretchen stopped to pay the receptionist as Maggie and Patrick walked out of the doctor's office onto the street, a few yards down from Cochrane's. The Navy had given them some money in compensation, at least. Now, Maggie had to go to the hotel to pick up her last pay packet; she wouldn't be working there for a while.

Patrick had been surprisingly sensitive through the whole process, and he put a tender hand on her shoulder now.

'An injury like this … it makes you feel vulnerable,' he said to her. 'That'll pass, but this is a lesson, Maggie. It's life's way of telling you to keep yourself safe. It's part of growing up. Maybe you'll see all these "adventurers" for what they are now. Their ambition always comes at a cost – and it's usually other people who pay it.'

She writhed away from his hand.

'So I should never try anything?' she said sharply. 'Never take a chance, is that what you're saying? That would make for a fine life altogether, wouldn't it? Those fliers came to do something … something that could change the world! And if it went wrong, well … that's just what happens if you take a risk.'

'Tell that to the Kavanagh boy, who got his head split open,' Patrick growled. 'Or the Clearys' lad, with his broken collar bone. What would you say to their parents if one of them was killed?'

Across the road, Harry Hawker and Kenneth Mackenzie Grieve were getting into their car. Hawker spotted Maggie and waved. Hurrying over, he frowned at the cast on her arm, then gave her a sympathetic smile.

'Looks like you took a right knock there, Maggie!' the Australian said. 'I don't think you'll let a broken wing keep you down for long though, am I right? Listen, could you do something for me? I need you to go over to the hotel and give Freddie a message.'

'She won't be doing anything for –' Patrick started to say.

'Mr Raynham?' Maggie cut him off. 'What is it?'

'Tell him I'll greet him in Brooklands,' Hawker winked at her.

'You're flying today? You're going *now*?!' Maggie called after him, for he was striding away, already halfway to his car.

'The Americans have reached the Azores!' he shouted back. 'We'll still beat them across, if we have half a chance!'

So the Americans had completed the first stage of their flight, and the longest stretch – 1,200 miles. An incredible distance. Gretchen came out of the doctor's to see Maggie shuffling towards the hotel as fast as her injury would allow her, holding her injured arm with her other hand. She looked back at her aunt and pointed at their Model T, which was parked nearby.

'Get the car started! They're doing it! *They're going for it!*'

Once Maggie had delivered her message at the hotel, and witnessed the frantic reaction it provoked, she quickly returned to the street, where Gretchen and Patrick were waiting with the car running. Maggie jumped into the back seat and urged her aunt to get moving. Patrick was being a curmudgeon about it all, but Gretchen appeared almost as excited as Maggie. That was, until she started driving. Careful by nature, and now also concerned for her niece's injury, she navigated her way out of town towards Glendenning's farm with excruciating care.

'Oh my God, could you drive any slower?!' Maggie exclaimed, as they were overtaken by a little girl on a bicycle. 'We're going to miss it!'

'I won't have any blasphemy in this car, young lady!' Gretchen scolded her, before reluctantly giving the accelerator another nudge.

The word was spreading about Hawker and Grieve, and other cars were now on their way to the Sopwith aerodrome. Maggie was gritting her teeth as they found themselves stuck in a queue along the road, with nearly a mile to go. A flock of sheep was blocking the way. After some irritated beeping of horns, the farmer eventually moved his animals off the road. At this point, however, Maggie could hear a buzzing sound coming towards them from beyond the hill to her right. She stood up and leaned out of the side of the car just as the buff-coloured Sopwith *Atlantic* came over the crest of the hill, flying low and heavy towards the coast.

Maggie whooped and, with only one working arm, she nearly fell out of the car as she waved at the fliers, who passed almost directly overhead. The engine was roaring at maximum power as the aircraft slowly climbed, hauling its full load of fuel. All along the road, people jumped from their cars and cheered the adventurers. Grieve leaned out of his cockpit and waved back at them. Once the Sopwith was over the coast, a few hundred yards to the left of the car, Maggie saw the undercarriage, with its oversized wheels, drop from the machine and fall into the sea.

'Dear God, they've lost a piece of their aeroplane!' Gretchen cried.

'No, they meant to do that,' Maggie said, her chest heaving with emotion. 'Less weight, less drag. It gives them another seven miles per hour. They've got landing skids on the belly of the plane for when they want to land. It's a clever design, actually.'

'Oh, quite,' Gretchen replied, glancing in surprise at her niece. 'Of course. Silly me.'

'Can we go home now?' Patrick muttered, still sitting in the passenger seat with his arms folded.

'Are you mad?' Maggie retorted in disbelief. 'Raynham and Morgan will be leaving too! Gretchen, turn the car around. We have to get to the lake!'

And as her aunt turned the car around on the road with painstaking caution, Maggie felt herself bursting with pent up passion. This might be it. This might be the day of one of mankind's greatest achievements, started *right here* in her adopted home. It made her feel so overwhelmed with exhilaration, and yet so insignificant. These men were *giants*. What else in her life would ever compare with this?

'Oh, Gretchen, please! The *sheep* are moving faster than us – put your foot down!'

26

There was a scattering of cars and people at Quidi Vidi Lake to watch the *Raymor* preparing for take off, though it was nothing compared to the crowd that had greeted the airship three days before. Most people still got their news from the papers and few houses had a telephone. The sudden urgency of the aviators had caught the Newfoundlanders by surprise.

Gretchen stopped the car as close to the canvas hangar as she could get. The ground crew were pulling the aeroplane into position, right back to the bank of the river to give it as long a run as possible. Maggie had spent the last month soaking in as much information as she could about flying, and what she was seeing and feeling struck a discordant note. Hawker's runway had been wider, and faced a different way; it had allowed him to take off directly into the east-northeast wind, whose gusts were tossing Maggie's hair across her face. The narrower area here meant that Raynham could only take off in one direction – with a stiff crosswind.

The aircraft looked magnificent, shining in its crimson and silver, with bright yellow wings. The pilot and navigator strode out to their machine, lifting their hands to acknowledge the enthusiastic spectators. Morgan spotted Maggie and gave her a wink and a salute with his famously rakish smile.

Then it was down to business. Climbing into their cockpits, Morgan began double-checking his navigation kit as Raynham directed the man at the propellor to swing away. The engine caught immediately, despite the cold; they must have warmed up before they moved the aeroplane back. The sudden noise caused a flock of tufted ducks to take flight from the lake, a way off behind them.

Maggie felt shaky, caught up in the moment, and as they ran up the engine, she turned to Gretchen. 'Can we drive further up the field, closer to where they'll lift off?'

Gretchen had been watching her niece, taken with how intensely the girl was experiencing all this. The car was still running, so she nodded, slid back behind the wheel, and they set off parallel to the runway. It was rough going; unlike the runway itself, this field of yellowed grass had not been levelled out, but it was a sturdy car and Maggie endured the bumps and jolts, cradling her injured arm. She wanted this time to last as long as possible, to soak in all that she could.

Halfway along the runway, the terrain became too much for the car and Gretchen had to stop. They all got out in time to hear the *Raymor*'s engine begin to rise in pitch. The chocks were pulled away from the wheels. Slowly, very slowly at first, it started to move.

As it crawled along, the Martinsyde machine, with its Rolls Royce Falcon engine, looked as if it couldn't possibly make it up into the sky. Then, as if it was finally taking a grip of the air, its tail lifted off the ground and the aircraft surged forward. There was a lightness to its movement now, though it was rolling and bouncing, the weight of its oversized fuel tanks holding it down as it passed by, the pitch of the sound dropping again as the machine rushed away from them. The crosswind was catching it now, shunting it sideways, lifting the left wing, throwing it off balance. The aircraft bounced again, juddering, a more jarring motion this time, and Patrick went tense, swearing under his breath.

'No, no!' he rasped. 'The ground's too soft. God help them!'

The *Raymor* bounced again, came down, and this time the wheels dug into the flattened earth. With a sound like an animal's screech, the undercarriage was torn off, the aeroplane pivoted to the side, crashed onto the ground, smashing its propellor and slid, ripping metal, wood and fabric from its underside.

'Come on, come on!' Patrick bellowed, leaping into the driver's seat. 'We have to get them out before the damned thing catches fire!'

With no thought for the damage he might do to the car, or Maggie's arm, Patrick stamped on the accelerator as soon as the other two were on board, sending the vehicle scrambling across the rough ground and onto the runway, heading for the crashed aeroplane. Maggie was nearly crying in fear. The aeroplane was carrying hundreds of gallons of petrol. A tiny split in one of its tanks or fuel lines, one leak, one spark and the entire thing would become an inferno.

As they drew closer, they could see both men were injured. Raynham was struggling to climb out of his cockpit, while Morgan was unconscious, half his face covered in blood. Patrick brought the car to a skidding halt twenty yards back and was first out, with Gretchen and Maggie clambering out behind him. Others were coming too, cars pulling up and men sprinting down the runway.

There was no sign of flames, but the engine was still chugging, spinning the stumps of the propellor. Maggie could smell petrol and she saw sparks coming from the exhaust pipes. Patrick reached into the pilot's cockpit to cut off the magnetos and kill the motor. Turning to the other men approaching, he saw that a couple of them were smoking and he roared at them:

'Put those cigarettes out, you fools! She's leaking fuel!'

Raynham was helped out and though he was dazed and in shock, he was able to walk with the support of two other men. Patrick, Gretchen and two more men gently lifted Morgan out and carried him a safe distance from the aeroplane to rest him on the ground.

Maggie gasped as she saw shards of glass from the cockpit's windscreen embedded in the navigator's forehead and scalp. With his head resting on the ground, blood was pooling in the hollow around his right eye.

'Maggie, don't look!' Gretchen warned her.

But how could she not look? When Gretchen dabbed at the largest wound on Morgan's brow with her handkerchief, Maggie saw bare bone. Dr Gerszel had pulled up in his car, and already had his bag in his hand as he rushed forward. He took one look at Morgan's scalp and drew a breath through his teeth.

'It's a grievous wound, and there could be an injury to the brain. We have to get him to the hospital if he's to have any chance!'

Maggie had to get out of the way of the men who surrounded the navigator and bore him over to the doctor's car, laying him down on the back seat. She saw Raynham being helped towards another car.

Turning around, she watched some of the ground crew already backing a flatbed truck over to the aeroplane with some barrels on the back. They had to draw the fuel out of the aircraft to prevent a fire, before it could be examined to see if it too could be saved. There was urgency, but no sense of panic. They had immediately set to doing their jobs once more. One of the men went over to speak to Raynham, who was sitting on the running board of a car. As his head was being bandaged, he issued instructions to the men, pointing to the crashed machine.

It was a moment that would stay with Maggie for the rest of her life. Fax Morgan was on his way to hospital, and Freddie Raynham would be following. It seemed almost cold-blooded. Morgan might die, and yet even now, someone was seeing to the aeroplane. Perhaps they even intended to try to fly again at a later date. Crashes like this were just part of life for these men. Just as it had been with the boy who was nearly killed by the airship cable; people might get hurt, but these adventurers would carry on regardless.

She clutched her broken arm, feeling its fragility and recalling the agony in the moment it had been struck, remembering the injection the doctor had given her later, how she could still sense the grinding together of the edges as he'd reset the pieces of bone. She could feel the morphine-dulled pain even now, and wondered how anyone could get back into one of these machines after a crash like this, as many of these aviators had.

And for the first time, she understood the power of Patrick's fear. She found Gretchen standing behind her and she turned to embrace her aunt, clinging tightly to her.

27

Teddy turned his face to the sea breeze, taking a deep breath of the sharp, clear air as the bank of fog approached from the ocean. It carried none of the dangerous pollution of London's famous 'pea soup' smogs, of course, but it was every bit as thick. The harbour would soon be invisible, and much of the town after that. He was up on a flat section of the roof of Cochrane's Hotel, attaching a radio aerial to a chimney. Lieutenant Clement, the Meteorology Officer at the Admiralty Wireless Station in Mount Pearl, had lent the fliers a radio for the hotel, so that he could pass on weather reports more quickly, and they could pick up some of the other signals out there in the ether. When he'd finished hammering in the last of the nails holding the wire to the chimney, Teddy sat down on the tiles of the roof that sloped up behind him.

He was tired. It was Monday morning, the 19th of May, the day after Harry and Kenneth had departed in the Sopwith. Everyone was waiting for word of their arrival in Brooklands, or news of progress from the fliers themselves. They had a radio in their aircraft, and though its Morse Code transmissions could not reach as far back as Newfoundland, it could send messages to ships it passed, which might relay them back to the Wireless Station, from where Lieutenant Clement would then radio, or telephone, the hotel.

So far, no message had been received.

Tension was building now. The crowd in the hotel had been up most of the night. Once fourteen or fifteen hours had passed since take off, Teddy, Jack, Freddie and their crews had begun to expect news of the Sopwith, though it might still be hours before it arrived in Ireland. At the aircraft's cruising speed, the flight might take up to about twenty hours.

Freddie Raynham, now wearing a bandage on his head, was in a low mood. Fax had been badly injured in the crash – he was out of the game now. Thanks to emergency surgery, he would live, but the doctor had been forced to remove Morgan's eye. The poor soul, Teddy thought to himself; one leg, and now only one eye. Some people had the damnedest luck.

Jack had been hit hard by it too. He, Freddie, Fax and Harry had all been friends before the war, part of the original Brooklands set of fliers. Though Teddy had long been a fan of cars and motorcycles, he'd only started flying during the war, and had been a latecomer to the famous aerodrome and race course. Even so, bonds formed quickly in such a dangerous occupation. Nothing cemented friendship like the threat of sudden death.

They all expected Harry and Kenneth to make the crossing. Though he'd been prevented from flying in the war because of old injuries, Hawker was arguably the best of the pilots taking on this challenge. The Australian was a hero to many of his fellow fliers – good-natured, intelligent, daring and forward-looking. Freddie had been the first person to successfully pull an aeroplane out of a spin, the pilot's nightmare, once considered certain death if it happened to you. But Harry was the man who'd worked out the *technique* for escaping one, and taught it to others. Harry Hawker was a man to make history.

'Lieutenant Brown!' a cheery voice called through the hatch leading up from the attic. 'I come bearing wireless!'

It was Kate Sulley, the Wren from Mount Pearl.

'You are a most welcome sight, Miss Sulley!' he replied. 'I'll be down in a moment.'

Gathering up the tools he'd borrowed, and the spare length of wire, he climbed down into the attic, where Jack and Bob Dicker were placing the radio set on a stout table. Weighing over a hundred pounds, it took some strength to move it around.

'Miss Sulley has news of the Americans,' Jack said, with a grim smile.

'Oh?'

'Yes,' Sulley said, clearly making an effort not to appear too pleased. 'The early reports that they'd all reached the Azores were … overly positive. In fact, two of the seaplanes got lost in fog. They were low on fuel, and couldn't find any support ship, so they had to land on the sea to get their bearings. They mis-judged the conditions, which were pretty rough by all accounts, and they were unable to take off again. The machines ended up being smashed up by the sea. The NC-1 sank after the crew were rescued. The NC-3 made it to Ponta Delgada, but the aircraft is a wreck. Only the NC-4 landed safely, but now it's stuck there … because of the weather.'

'The *NC-4* made it? The one that went missing before? The one they called "the lame duck"?'

'Yes, it seems it has resurrected its reputation.'

Teddy raised his eyebrows at Jack. A flight of 1,200 miles – it was a tremendous achievement. But despite the colossal support they'd provided, the US Navy had already lost two of their three aircraft, and had only made it to the middle of the Atlantic. It was unnerving to think of what Harry and Kenneth might be facing out there, alone in the sky.

'They relied too much on those ships,' Jack said firmly. 'And on being able to land on the water. Kenneth is old-school; he'll find the way – and Harry will keep them flying straight. If their machine doesn't fail them, they'll make it. You'll see.'

Their conversation was interrupted by the hotel's receptionist, who was calling up that someone was looking for them. They came downstairs to find a burly, wide-featured man with oiled hair, dressed in an expensive-looking black pin-striped suit. He introduced himself as Carl K Bellamy, and said he'd heard they were looking for an aerodrome.

'I have the perfect piece of land for you, sirs, near Harbour Grace,' he said, with the practised pitch of a professional salesman.

'A meadow, one hundred yards by three hundred, and flat as this floor. As God is my witness, you will find no plot more ideal for your purposes!'

'And how much are you asking for this perfect piece of land?' Jack asked, flicking a glance towards Teddy.

'Why, I can lease it to you – and I'm happy to take British money – for five thousand pounds, plus the cost of getting it ready, and an indemnity for all damage,' the businessman said, with a confident smirk. 'What do you think of that?'

It was well above what they had to spend, and Teddy was about to say so, when another voice cut in:

'I think you're chancin' your arm, Crocker Bellamy, and I think you know it!'

It was the girl, Maggie, who'd stayed here all night, with the assent of her aunt and Agnes Dooley, waiting for news of Harry and Kenneth. She was sitting in the lobby, cradling a cup of tea, and now she rose from her seat and came over to Bellamy. He stood a head taller than she did, but she glared into his eyes with the air of someone facing a familiar opponent.

'Captain Alcock, land *sells* in Newfoundland for about one shilling and fivepence an acre,' she said. 'And *Mister* Bellamy here knows that well.'

'You mind your own business, little girl!' Bellamy growled, instantly losing his smooth manner and now sounding more like a low grifter putting on an act. 'This is grown-up talk. Go back to selling your eggs and chewing gum.'

'It's too rich a sum for us, nonetheless,' Teddy told him, giving Maggie an appreciative wink. 'And too small a space, I fear – but thank you for your offer.'

Bellamy gave them a greasy smile and slid away. Jack watched him go, shaking his head.

'We couldn't even pay half that, Teddy,' he muttered. 'And hiring the car is eating up our budget too. Every day we're delayed here means less money to spend on the site. If this goes on much longer, we'll have no money for a field by the time we have our aeroplane.'

Teddy nodded, then noticed the girl was still standing a few feet from them.

'Thank you for that, Maggie,' he said, 'but we had it well in hand. Do you have an interest in property?'

'I have an interest in aeroplanes, and in making money, Lieutenant Brown,' Maggie replied. 'And I have an offer for you.'

'Oh, really?'

'I heard you say you can't find a field, and your car's costing you too much money. Whatever you're paying for that Oldsmobile is too much, I'd wager. The shocks are going on it, for a start.'

'The shocks *are* going,' Jack agreed with a chuckle. 'All right then, lay out your stall there, young lady.'

'I have a car I can hire out to you.'

'You … have a car?' Jack sounded sceptical.

'A 1912 Buick tourer – it's outside. Come on, I'll show you.'

Teddy looked to Jack, who gave a 'worth-a-look' shrug, and gestured to Maggie to lead the way. The patchy, dull blue motor car that stood outside the hotel looked as if it had served in the war, and come back more traumatised than Teddy from the experience. It was hard to believe it had been driven here; it seemed more likely it had been delivered on the back of a cart.

'Looks like it was dragged up out of the harbour,' Jack commented, paying little heed to the girl's feelings. He paused to light up a cigarette. 'Not sure what you're offering us here, Maggie.'

'This car, for a dollar a day,' she said. If Jack's remark had stung her, she didn't let it show. 'And my knowledge of the area, which is substantial. But there's another cost too.'

'Is there indeed?'

'If I give you this car, you have to … to *put up with me*. I want to learn about flying. I'll be coming to the hotel every day, and I'll have questions. And I want to see you put your aeroplane together … if it ever gets here …'

'That hurts,' Teddy murmured.

'Well, that's the deal.'

Looking at the Jabberwock of a car, Teddy prodded a rusty fender with his cane. He was reminded of the mechanical components and simple machines his father had given him to play with when he was young. Those experiments had led to model- and kite-building, days riding a motorcycle across the Lancashire countryside and, eventually, his early career in engineering. He felt an odd kinship for this wilful, unusual girl. Jack was about to turn her down, when Teddy pulled him aside.

'Let's do it, Jack. If the car runs all right. Why not?'

'We're not here to entertain children, Teddy,' Jack said in a low voice.

'But we should inspire them, shouldn't we? As *we* were inspired?'

Jack gave a grimace … and then agreed with a reluctant grunt.

'All right, but we're not paying for a work in progress. The brute has to start.'

'So, you want to charge us a dollar a day?' he said, turning back to Maggie. 'For the use of *this* car?'

'It needs painting, I'll grant you that, but the engine's good,' she assured him. 'My uncle's a mechanic.'

'I tell you what: if it starts first time, you've got a deal,' Jack told her. 'Otherwise, we stick with our saggy-bottomed Oldsmobile.'

Maggie pulled the starter handle from its clips and handed it to him, trying to look confident, and not quite managing it. Jack slid the handle into the socket in the front and cranked it twice, three times … He pulled the handle free as the engine coughed into life, caught and began rumbling healthily. Jack listened closely for about half a minute, then looked over at Maggie.

'Looks like we're in business,' he said, grinning around his cigarette.

28

By early evening, it was becoming clear that there would be no message from Hawker and Grieve. Over twenty-four hours had passed since their departure. Their fuel had run out. Whatever had happened, they were no longer in the air. Maggie watched the spirits of the other aviators sink as the evening wore on. Raynham sat motionless in an armchair in the lounge, a hand to his face. Alcock had sought refuge in the kitchen, where he was baking. Brown said he liked to cook when he had things on his mind, and was particularly fond of making desserts. He was making something called 'baklava', a recipe he'd picked up while in prison in Turkey.

Brown went out to the hotel reception to telephone the wireless station. He spoke to Lieutenant Clement, who informed him that no news had come from England. The crowds that had gathered at Brooklands to greet the arrivals had dispersed in disappointment.

Nor had the fliers landed in Ireland. No message had been received from there either. Harry Hawker and Kenneth Mackenzie Grieve were either dead or adrift, somewhere out in the North Atlantic Ocean. They had survival suits, and a section of the aeroplane's fuselage could be detached as an emergency raft, but there was little chance that anyone could survive for long out on the water at these latitudes. Even so, Alcock, Brown, Raynham and the others still held out hope that their friends might make it.

When Kate Sulley had arrived, she'd been accompanied by Admiral Mark Kerr, the commander of the Handley Page team. They were not staying in Cochrane's, like the other aviators, but were house guests of a wealthy builder in Harbour Grace, to the north.

Kerr was ramrod straight, proud-faced and balding. He had come to the hotel to hear news of Hawker and Grieve, but also to make Alcock and Brown an offer. Consumed as they were with concern for their friends, neither was in the mood for discussing business, but Kerr was insistent, inviting them to sit at his table with Kate Sulley. He had to head back to Harbour Grace soon, and needed to make his proposition. Maggie was sitting close enough to their table to overhear.

'Like you, we've had a devil of a time finding a suitable site,' he was saying, his upper-class English accent clipped and cultured, and hardened by authority. 'But we've got one now. Not a single stretch, but a series of gardens and fields. We've leased the lot, knocked all the walls between, and flattened the ground with a tractor and roller. We had to take down three houses and a farm building too, but it's large enough for our machine – and yours. One thousand two hundred yards of clear ground. If you agree to share the cost, you can use it, on the condition that we take off first.'

'That sounds extraordinary,' Brown said, amazed at the scale of the Navy officer's operation. 'How much did it all cost?'

'Four thousand pounds, all told,' the admiral replied. 'Split the cost, and you'll share the runway.'

'But we have to let you take off first?' Jack grunted, his tone less impressed. 'Thank you for the offer, Admiral. We'll give it serious consideration.'

The older man did not appear happy with this answer, but they were interrupted by the sudden appearance of Patrick, who seemed to come from nowhere. Patrick had driven Maggie back into town the previous night, so she could wait to hear news of Hawker and Grieve. Maggie had wondered where he'd gone to. Clearly he'd found his way to one of the speakeasies in town, and had been there all this time.

'This is how it starts,' he declared, his voice slurred by drink, his one living eye dull and bloodshot. 'I know *your* type, all right. You bring your war machines here, and your ... your ... corrupting money. You buy up land, move people out of their homes ... Knock the houses and ... and ...'

'Patrick, please,' Maggie hissed up at him. 'Don't be doing this here. Not *now*.'

'This is how it was in *Ireland* too!' Patrick shouted, looking round, for he had an audience now, the rest of the room going quiet to listen to this rant. 'You know my countrymen, my family, are at *war* with the Brits now, trying to get them out? How long will it ... will it be before they're ... they're sending their bombers out over Ireland? How long before ... before they're flying over our towns *here*, eh?'

'Don't be absurd! Nothing untoward has occurred here,' Kerr growled, still in his seat, working his jaw and making a show of stirring his tea as he stared down at the table. 'Agreements were signed, and the locals were well paid for their land and for their inconvenience. What is this nonsense?'

'How long before these swines start another one of their bloody wars *right here?*' Patrick bellowed. 'Wars that everybody else fights for them, eh? How ... how many good men did *we* lose? Yes, I fought for the British ... *and look at me now!*' He pointed to his masked face, his features twisted in grief. 'Cuh ... cuh ... cannon fodder, that's what we were. And here ... here ... here they are again, with the last war barely over, and they're already building their aerodromes, knocking down our homes and flattening our farmland. Look at them all! Buh ... buh ... buying our loyalty, extending their reach, *seizing our territory* ...'

'Patrick, will you ever pipe down!' Maggie said through gritted teeth, cringing with embarrassment. 'Please!'

'Sir, I can see that the war has left its mark on you,' Kerr said, standing up to meet Patrick's glare. 'Can I ask where you served?'

'New ... Newfoundland Regiment, in France, then the ... the Royal Flying Corps,' Patrick answered automatically, his face going slack, as if he was relieved to respond without thinking. 'Finished up in Num ... Number Three Squadron, flying the Morane Parasol mostly, and the SE5.'

'Then I thank you for your service. But if you were a pilot, then you, sir, were an *officer*,' the admiral said firmly. 'And every British officer is expected to show the kind of moral fibre that is appropriate to that position. This is no way for one to behave, even if you are Irish. Stop talking rot and have some pride, man! It's British mettle that has imposed order across half the world.'

'It's British *pride* that has imposed *misery* across half the world, you mean!'

'You are *drunk*, sir!'

'Aye, and you're *British*. But tomorrow *I'll* be sober!'

That got a bit of a laugh, even from some of the other Brits, though Maggie could barely listen, she was so embarrassed. The men here had lost friends today. They should have been left in peace to mourn their dead; instead, they had to listen to this Irish-man, drunk on rum, ranting about their country. She wanted to curl up and sink through the floor. Everyone was staring at them.

'Maggie, go and get in the car,' Patrick said, the words sliding clumsily out of his mouth. 'We're leaving.'

'I can't,' she replied quietly. 'I've done a deal with Captain Alcock and Lieutenant Brown. They've leased the car.'

He swivelled round to regard her with a livid expression. She had never been so frightened of him as she was now. He sucked back some spit and swallowed, his face wrinkling in disgust as he stared at his niece.

'Of course they did. So you've taken the shilling too, girl?'

'I can drop you both home,' Brown said quickly. 'It's no bother at all.'

'Thank you, but I'd rather walk,' Patrick said, coughing and turning away.

'Mr McRory, you're in no state to –'

'*I said I'll walk!*'

'I'm so sorry,' Maggie said to everyone gathered there, as her uncle staggered out of the hotel. 'Oh my God, I'm so sorry. He gets like this sometimes. He doesn't mean any harm, really …'

'I understand more than you know,' Brown said softly to her, putting a hand on her shoulder. 'Many of us do, who served on the front. Come along now.'

Maggie was surprised to see Freddie Raynham hurry out after her uncle. Brown tilted his head towards the door and led her out too. Further down the street, she could see Raynham talking to Patrick, and she wondered what business the pilot would have with a drunken lout.

As she climbed into the passenger seat, Brown cranked the engine into life and then pulled himself up behind the steering wheel, the movement made awkward by his lame leg.

'Believe me, Maggie, I understand your uncle very well. In fact, much of what he said is true,' the navigator told her, shifting the car into gear and pulling out into the street. 'Aeroplanes are reshaping the world, even as they revolutionise warfare. And when you understand this, it is easy to be overwhelmed, as your uncle is, by the way things are changing. He has been hurt, and he's still hurting. It can make a person feel frightened and vulnerable.'

Brown gestured towards her broken arm, and she was suddenly conscious of how she cradled it against the movement of the car. It was true, the pain made her defensive.

'And people in pain can sometimes lash out, because of that fear,' he added. 'It is easy to hate too, when you think other people are responsible for what you're feeling. I know the kind of darkness your uncle has gazed into. There can be a shallow kind of comfort in hate. I've tried not to let myself succumb to it.'

'I heard that you served in the trenches too, like Patrick did, Lieutenant Brown,' Maggie said. 'And you've been hurt in aeroplane crashes, like he was. So how can you still want to fly? Why would you want to fly over the *ocean*?'

Brown gave a gentle laugh.

'Because my sense of wonder is greater than my sense of fear, I suppose. Does that make sense?'

Maggie thought about this, and found it to be a very satisfying answer.

'Yes, sir, it does.'

'Then I think we might be cut from the same cloth, you and I,' he said. 'And from now on, you must call me Teddy.'

29

The time seemed to fly for Maggie, while for Jack and Teddy it dragged. She relished the hours she got to spend with them, while they were condemned to wait for their aircraft to arrive. And as they waited, Kerr, Brackley and Gran and their large team were busily constructing the Handley Page machine up in Harbour Grace. Jack and Teddy were out in the car every day, trying to find their own aerodrome site, and had still had no luck. If they were forced to accept the admiral's offer, they would be granting him the right to take off first, which grated on them no end.

It was Monday, the 26th of May, and Maggie was sitting behind the wheel of the Buick, down at the harbour. She had introduced Teddy to Alistair Finch and Jeremiah Smith, to discuss navigation. Maggie had sat with them for a while, in the wheelhouse of Finch's trawler, but in the end she'd grown bored of all the talk of bearings and prevailing winds, and had returned to the car.

Looking out across the sea, she was imagining herself in an aeroplane. Teddy and Jack had told her about women aviators such as Katherine Stinson, Ruth Law and Harriet Quimby, the first woman to fly across the English Channel to France.

She chewed over Teddy's words: 'Aeroplanes are reshaping the world.' Maggie's mind soared out across the sea, wisps of cloud beneath her, the horizon ahead lost in a haze. Ships blew their whistles as she passed above them.

The wreckage of the Sopwith *Atlantic* had been spotted a couple of days earlier by a passing vessel. There had been no sign of the crew. It was estimated that they'd flown nearly 900 miles before something terrible had gone wrong. Maggie pictured herself flying over the wreck, looking down at the ragged remains – the wings sagging in the water like a dead gull's, the broken plywood of the fuselage, the leaking fuel tanks.

Maggie's arm was still in a cast, but she could use it now and no longer needed the sling. She gently gripped the steering wheel and made engine sounds to herself, imagining the controls of the car were those of her aircraft.

The rudder bar in an aeroplane was like the steering wheel in a motor car. Controlled with the feet, like pedals, it worked the rudder on the tail, which turned the nose right or left, without tilting the craft.

You could tilt the aeroplane to one side or the other by turning the wheel, or yoke, moving the ailerons in the wings. Pulling the wheel backwards or pushing it forwards worked the elevator in the tail, which pointed the nose up or down.

She pretended the gearstick was the throttle. An aeroplane had no gears and no brakes, just the throttle controlling the forward thrust of the propellor. Banking hard to the right, Maggie levelled out and then began climbing up and up to do a loop, mimicking the sound of an engine at full power. She gazed through the blur of the propellor, the nose pointed at the blue sky, pushing upwards until the machine began to tilt backwards …

A sideways glance caught Teddy and Finch standing by the side of the car, grinning at her. Maggie immediately dropped her hands into her lap and frowned at them.

'Are you finished then?' she asked, as if she had been sitting like that the whole time. 'Took you long enough.'

'Look,' Teddy said, pointing out to sea, his voice shaky with emotion. 'She's here. *She's finally here.*'

Cruising into the harbour was the *SS Glendevon*, the freighter carrying the Vickers Vimy. Alcock and Brown's aircraft had arrived at last.

Eight more of the Vickers ground crew were also travelling with the aeroplane, which was packed into twenty-two separate crates. As the stevedores and cranes began their work, unloading the ship, there were high spirits as the two halves of the team were reunited.

'Stone the crows!' Jack exclaimed as he greeted the new arrivals. 'You lads are a sight for sore eyes! We thought the day would never come. Let's get stuck in, eh?'

A local carter, Charles Lester, had been hired to haul the crates to Quidi Vidi. Jack and Teddy were taking Freddie Raynham up on the offer of his site until they could find their own field. The Vickers lads were loathe to play second fiddle to Admiral Kerr and his team. Raynham's crew were also hard at work, repairing their own aircraft, though they now had no navigator. The Vimy could be built at the lake, and then flown from there to another site with a runway long enough to take off from with a full load.

Constant heavy rain did not make transportation easy. The newcomers were now introduced to Newfoundland's weather, and the muddy gravel roads of its countryside, having left a balmy summer behind in Brooklands. Hauling all the crates to the site by horse and cart took a day-and-a-half, and every hour that passed made the aviators more conscious that the Handley Page team had a two-week head start. They took some comfort in the fact that Maggie told them the V/1500 had been broken into many more pieces – it had arrived in more than a hundred crates – and had to be transported much further.

The morning after the *Glendevon* docked, Lester and his carters and teams of hulking dray horses were bringing the last of the crates up to the lake, when they were passed at speed by a Royal Navy staff car, spraying mud and honking its horn. It was Kate Sulley, and she skidded to a halt near to where parts of the Vimy were laid out on the ground.

'They're alive! They're alive!' she called to Jack and his team, waving frantically as she jumped from the car. 'Harry and Kenneth – *they're alive!*'

30

In breathless tones, Kate told them how Hawker and Grieve had survived their landing in the Atlantic, and how they'd been rescued by an old Danish tramp steamer. The ship had no radio, and so they could not send word to anyone until they arrived in Scotland. This fantastic news lifted the mood no end, and gave a huge boost to the day's labours.

However, Kate was back later that evening, after dusk had ended work for the day, and the men were in Cochrane's, tucking into a well-earned dinner. This time, she brought news of a very different nature, picked up from radio transmissions from the US Navy.

The Americans had crossed the Atlantic.

Word was already spreading around the world. The NC-4, the machine reporters had once nicknamed 'the lame duck', had finally taken off from Ponta Delgada in the Azores. It had flown the remaining 750 miles without further incident, landing in Lisbon at 8pm local time.

They had done it; the Americans were first to fly across the Atlantic Ocean. Lieutenant Commander Albert C Read had navigated; the flying boat had been piloted by Lieutenants Elmer

Stone and Walter Hinton, accompanied by radio officer Ensign Herbert C Rodd, and engineers Lieutenant James L Breese and Chief Machinist's Mate Eugene S Rhoads.

The British men ordered drinks and, with the reporters and everybody else there in the hotel dining room, they stood to offer a toast to Lieutenant Commander Read and his crew. It was a solemn moment, all of them acknowledging that the Americans had made history that day. They had succeeded where Harry and Kenneth had failed.

'My hat's off to them. It's an incredible feat,' Jack said, after they'd all sat down again. 'A crackin' piece of flying.'

He knew, after all the waiting and hold-ups, that his lads were disheartened by this news. Leaning in, he waited until he had everyone's attention, then he continued:

'... But this thing's not done yet. It took them *eleven days* to make the crossing – they'd have been faster by *ship*. And who flies with *an entire navy* beneath them, ready to catch them if they fall? And even then, only *one* of the three aircraft made it. What confidence will that give anyone that *this* is the way of the future? The US Navy were proving a point, lads, crossing the ocean with all of America's might to help carry them ... but it showed that they don't really trust their own aircraft, or their navigation. Now ... let's show them how it's *supposed* to be done, eh? One machine, one flight, non-stop. Are you with me?'

And they were, with all their hearts, every last man there.

Over the next week, the Vimy took shape. In its early stages, propped on supports and hanging from hoists, it looked like a cross between a complicated tent and a giant insect. They had no hangar; the only shelter was from tarpaulin screens around the scaffolds, but the weather spared them its worst, and they made good time. Maggie watched in fascination. Bob Dicker, who was in charge of the flight controls, and Monty, who was responsible for the rest of the structure, saved time travelling back and forth to the hotel by living in a couple of the crates the wings had been packed in. Jack or Teddy, both keen cooks, would make them breakfast on site in the morning – anything at all, they would say, as long as it's bacon and eggs. The midday meal for the crew was sausages and fried toast.

Jack was a skilled organiser. In his lively, good-humoured way, he worked them hard, and they responded well to him, putting in fourteen-hour days. If any reporter came too close, they'd be pulled in to help as well. There were plenty of spectators too, and the crew had to regularly stop people from poking and prodding at the aircraft's delicate skin.

One day, Maggie arrived with a gift for Jack, one she'd made with Gretchen's help: A stuffed toy – a black cat with a huge head and a tartan ribbon around his neck.

'The lads said you needed another mascot, as a partner for Teddy's,' she said shyly. 'It's to say thank you. And … I wanted to give you something to take with you, to remember me by.'

Jack was delighted. Twinkletoe finally had a worthy companion to bring good fortune to the journey. Jack named him Lucky Jim.

A young flier named AB Ford arrived from San Diego, offering to act as navigator for Raynham. He had little experience, however, and when Teddy wasn't busy with the construction, he began tutoring the younger man, the pair studying books and charts together. Maggie marvelled again at how these fiercely competitive men could have such a spirit of cooperation.

'Why is finding your way over the ocean so complicated?' she asked Teddy one day, as he was taking a break. 'I mean, Ireland's pretty big, isn't it? It should be easy enough to find. It's not like you're in a ship that's fighting the currents. An aeroplane can fly in a straight line. Why can't you just look at your compass, figure out which way you're going, and just keep flying in that direction until you get there?'

Teddy gave the question serious consideration. Of course, this was part of their deal for the use of the Buick – that he would answer her questions. But he was a man who generally took questions seriously anyway. He was sitting on a pile of rocks, and now he rose stiffly to his feet, leaning on his cane, and waved her towards a nearby tree, where she'd hung a rope as a swing.

'Come along, and I'll show you,' he said as they started walking. 'To begin with, for these kinds of distances, you're never travelling in a straight line – you're following the curve of the Earth. Fortunately, the mathematics for this has been established for a long time, so others have done many of the calculations for us.'

He ushered her up onto the short plank of wood that served as a seat for the rope, and pushing her shoulder gently, he started her swinging from side to side.

'You're riding on the wind,' he told her. 'The very air around you is moving constantly, pushing you back and forth, knocking you off your course. Out over the ocean, you have no landmarks to follow, but you *do* have the sun, moon and stars. These move in very set arcs across the sky, more reliable than any clock, and these arcs have been recorded for you on charts. Once you know the date and time, you can use a sextant to measure the angle of the sun or a star above the horizon, and use your chart and a map to calculate your position on the Earth's surface. This technique has been used by sailors for hundreds of years. Now, point at the Vimy for me.'

Maggie pointed at the aircraft, which by this time was almost complete, still half-hidden behind the screens. She could see Bob Lyons up on the lower left wing, pipe in his mouth, tuning the engine.

'It's easy enough when you can *see* where you're going,' Teddy told her. Gripping the rope over her head, he began swinging her wider and wider. 'Now close your eyes. You're halfway across the Atlantic, in dense cloud, you can't see past the nose of your machine. There's no sun and no stars, no horizon off which to take a sight. Your compass gives you a *general* direction, but every time your aeroplane hits an air pocket, or twists in the wind, the compass needle moves. Keep pointing at the Vimy.'

This was much harder with her eyes closed, but she was reasonably sure she was still pointing in the right direction. He started to turn her now, rotating her slowly, one way and then the other.

'You're caught in strong winds,' he told her. 'They're pulling you all over the place. Every motion sets your compass spinning, so you lose your sense of direction. Your altimeter and air speed indicator are unreliable in these conditions too. You're not sure what height you're at.

'This is not the slow plodding of a ship. You're flying at nearly a hundred miles an hour. With each hour that passes, every degree you go in the wrong direction is taking you miles off your course. You have a spirit level for when you can't see the horizon, but if the movement of the aircraft is violent enough, that's useless too. You can become completely disorientated. You're not even sure what angle you're flying at, which way gravity is pulling you. You could end up turned *on your side* and not even realise it.' He stopped her moving. 'Keep your eyes closed and point again at the Vimy.'

She did as she was told, arm raised, trying her best to judge where the aircraft was.

'You come out of the cloud and finally, you can see the horizon and take a sight of the sun,' he said. 'Open your eyes and look where you're pointing.'

She was facing the wrong way, out towards the lake, past the Martinsyde hangar. The Vimy was to her left, nearly ninety degrees off where she had thought it was.

'Instead of heading east towards Ireland, you're now flying south, towards *Morocco*,' Teddy said. 'You'd run out of fuel and fall into the sea before you got close. No one would even search for you here, you're so far off your planned course.'

'So what do you do, if you can't see the sun or stars?' Maggie asked.

'We call it "dead reckoning",' he replied. 'If we know the aircraft's speed, the speed and direction of the wind, the length of time we've been flying and our direction, we can calculate our position.'

'You mean … you can *guess*?'

'*Calculate*,' he said firmly. 'But the less information you have, the less accurate you'll be. On a journey of this length, you'd need to take as many sights as possible during the flight, to keep you on course. It's only possible to …'

His voice drifted off as he looked past her, and Maggie turned to see Jack running up to them, pointing towards the hills to the north. They heard the sound then. A low hum, growing steadily louder and more piercing. From over the hilltops, an aircraft appeared. It flew straight for Quidi Vidi, straight for the two aircraft being prepared to compete with it. It bellowed past overhead, low and fast like a giant bird of prey, banking to swing around in a wide curve. Jack trotted up to them, and he and Teddy watched the Handley Page V/1500 with grim faces.

Maggie had heard it was a behemoth, but it was quite a different thing to see it in real life. Built on the same scale as the American Navy-Curtiss flying boats, its wingspan was over 125 feet, its fuselage close to sixty-five feet long. Like the Vimy, it had been designed as a long-range bomber, capable of flying from Britain to Berlin. It had *four* engines to the Vimy's two – in the 'push-pull' configuration, one facing backwards and one forwards on either side. And they were the same engines: powerful, reliable Rolls Royce Eagle VIIIs, each one packing 375 horsepower. Of course, this was only a test flight, but Admiral Kerr and his team had done it. It was Sunday, the 8th of June, and they were in the air ahead of the Vickers team, nearly ready to challenge the Atlantic. She saw Jack wince as the huge aircraft came back around again. It soared over them, then headed northwest over the hills.

'That's about torn it,' he said.

31

Freddie Raynham drove like a man who would prefer to be flying. Maggie was delighted to see what the Buick could do at the hands of a professional racing driver, even if she did cringe with unease as she felt the springs crunch and creak over the hostile surface of the narrow country roads, the car leaning precariously as he threw it around corners coated dangerously with gravel and mud. Patrick sat beside Freddie, hanging on to the door and cursing from time to time, but otherwise unmoved by the thrill of the ride. He and the Martinsyde pilot had become unlikely friends after Patrick's drunken outburst in Cochrane's, which mystified Maggie. She still felt embarrassed every time she thought about it.

Sitting with her in the back seat was Charles Lester, the carter whose teams of horses had hauled the Vimy in its crates to Quidi Vidi. A mellow, spry middle-aged man, slow of word and movement, Lester was visibly alarmed to find himself travelling at such high speed. They were all on their way to Lester's farm in a state of excitement.

The Vimy was in the air, on its first test flight. And thanks to Lester, Jack and Teddy now had a field long enough for the craft to take off fully loaded with fuel for the Atlantic crossing. Maggie and the others had watched the aircraft lift off from Freddie's aerodrome and do a few circles before flying out to sea. Now, they watched it coming back, the low sun picking out its pale, utilitarian grey. The British aviators were bound for Monday's Pool, on Lester's property, about three miles from Quidi Vidi, and not far from Gretchen and Patrick's farm. A bonfire had been lit to guide them in through the dull evening light.

This large meadow, where Lester usually kept some of his horses, was half on a hill, with a swamp at the bottom. They would have 300 yards of reasonably level ground, which Lester had offered for free, as long as they covered the costs of thirty men to do the levelling and the blasting that was required to clear protruding rocks and hillocks. After striking a deal with Lester's neighbours, the Symonds, they were able to take down a few walls and fences and extend it out to 500 yards. It was soon christened 'Lester's Field', and Maggie was keen to share her passion for aeroplanes with this new member of their growing fliers' family. So now, while they careened along at high speed, she was telling him all about Hawker and Grieve's ill-fated flight, the details of which had now reached Newfoundland.

'... and then, after they'd flown about eight hundred miles, the engine started to overheat again,' she said breathlessly. 'That can crack the head gasket or warp the cylinders, you know? It was the *radiator*, you see – it was getting clogged, so the water wasn't getting through. The engine wasn't being cooled, and it started to cut out. Imagine how scary that would be, out over the ocean and you're going to fall out of the sky because your engine's broken down!'

'Yes, it must have been a terrible thing.' Lester looked a little pale, gripping the edge of the door to hold himself steady.

'They knew they weren't going to make it much further, so they zig-zagged back and forth until they found a ship, and then, in *gale force winds*, Hawker landed safely on the sea! What a pilot! It was so rough, the ship still took an hour and a half to get them out of that freezing cold water.'

'Who'd want to go up in one of those things, eh?' Lester sighed, shaking his head.

'*I would*,' Maggie said, her tone a little more surly. 'But Jack and Teddy won't let me.'

'We simply can't take passengers, Maggie,' Freddie called back to her. 'For a start, it's a bit iffy, legally speaking. And even if we could, there's too much riding on these flights for us to be taking people for jaunts around the sky. You understand, don't you?'

Maggie grunted her acceptance, but she couldn't pretend to be happy about it. Freddie swerved off the road, through a gate and onto Lester's Field, pulling up not far from the bonfire. They were just in time; the Vimy's engines went quiet and it glided down towards them. It landed smoothly, trundling to the near end of the field, Jack gunning the starboard engine to swing the aircraft around before they hit a wall at the end of the runway. Taxiing to the lowest, most sheltered corner of the field, he cut the engines.

There were dozens of spectators there to meet them, and the crowd hurried forward. The people of St John's had taken Alcock and Brown into their hearts, these underdogs who had become a familiar sight over the past few weeks. Like Lester, they appreciated Jack's hearty and open nature, and Teddy's thoughtful, enthusiastic curiosity. They wished the two men well against the Handley Page's mighty Goliath, up there in Harbour Grace.

There was nothing like a bit of local rivalry to motivate a community.

Jack dropped down with athletic ease while Teddy took things a little slower. Monty and Ernie kicked chocks under the wheels to prevent it from rolling in the wind, and a couple of the other lads pegged ropes down. The pilot cast his eyes around at the spectators, conscious of the reporters with their notebooks and cameras.

'Machine's absolutely top-hole!' he declared, clapping his hands together. 'One or two more trial runs, I think, to shake her down, and that's it. I hope to be in London by the weekend!'

There was a rousing cheer, and Jack shook Lester's hand as he walked away. Taking Teddy's cane from the car, Maggie strode over to him as he lowered himself to the ground.

'We saw Kerr and his boys out while we were up there,' he said to her, nodding his thanks for the cane. 'That's their fourth test flight. They must be having some sort of problems. You'd think they'd be keen to leave.'

'Kate says they've been having radiator problems,' Maggie told him. 'Their engines are running too hot. A bit like Harry and Kenneth's was.'

Teddy turned and frowned at her.

'Is that right?' he murmured. 'I say … would you be so good as to go and fetch Jack?'

Much of the Vickers equipment had already been moved to the new site, and Teddy limped over to some crates stacked nearby. Instead of looking for some tool or piece of equipment, however, he picked up the blackened kettle the men used to make their tea, and looked inside. Maggie did as she was asked, and ran over to get Jack, who was chatting to the two Bobs as he lit a cigarette. When they came back, Teddy was holding up the kettle so they could see inside. There was a hardened coating of white powder at the bottom.

'Sediment!' he said excitedly. 'Maggie says Kerr's having problems with his radiators. The water in this area must be thick with mineral sediment – lime perhaps! Certainly thick enough to block the pipes, give it long enough. This could be causing the Handley Page's engines to overheat – and it would explain Harry's problems too.'

Jack took the kettle and wiped his finger along the bottom.

'Stone me, it's much worse than the water in England,' he said. 'This would choke up the radiators in no time. We'll need to distil our water, boil it out, and improve the filters on the pipes. Good girl, Maggie. This could have blown our engines halfway across and we'd never have known why! But Kerr's lot will work this out too, soon enough. I want to be out of here while those boys are still scratching their heads. One more flight I think, Teddy, and then we're off.'

32

U p against a competitor with a superior aeroplane and superior facilities, Jack and Teddy were determined to get a head start – they would take off at the first chance they got. Once again, however, they were held up by the weather, a strong westerly wind.

On Saturday, the 14th of June, they sheltered from the driving rain, huddling under the wing of the Vimy, dressed in their dun-coloured Burberry flying suits. They drank coffee from a vacuum flask, ate Agnes Dooley's sandwiches and waited for the sky to clear.

Most of the rest of the team were in their tent. They had been up since before dawn, transferring the last of the fuel and examining the aircraft. Their preparations had been meticulous. All the last-minute jobs had been completed; everything had been checked and checked again ... and then checked one more time, down to the last split-pin. If the worst happened, and the aviators had to ditch in the sea, one of the extra petrol tanks, the first one to be emptied, had quick release mounts and could serve as a life-raft. There was a compartment in the tail stocked with emergency rations.

They had been presented with a small sack of post, each letter bearing Newfoundland's first airmail stamps. A cupboard behind the seats held sandwiches, bars of Fry's chocolate, flasks of hot Oxo, Horlicks malted milk, bottles of water and packs of cigarettes. Jack often smoked while flying, but he would refrain this time, what with all that extra fuel on board. Teddy had Twinkletoe and his photograph of Kathleen in his pocket, and had tied Lucky Jim, with his oversized head and tartan ribbon, to the strut behind the cockpit.

About 150 people had gathered despite the weather, and the British and American reporters were out in force. By late morning, the rain stopped and the wind began to ease. The sky cleared. A group of girls laid out a rug on the ground and had a picnic. As he would have done during the war, Jack pulled a handful of grass from the ground, tossed it into the breeze, and watched it blow away.

'Not yet,' he said.

The fliers consulted with the ground crew, arguing over the strength of the wind. They didn't want to make Raynham's mistake, but they were afraid Kerr's team would get off first. Eventually, Jack made the decision: They were going for it.

'Teddy will aim us for Galway,' Jack declared. 'We shall hang our hats on the aerials of the Clifden wireless station as we go by!'

It was an emotional moment. Whether the flight was successful or not, most of these people were unlikely ever to see the two aviators again. Maggie was standing nearby, and when Jack and Teddy were finished talking to Bob and the others, she rushed over and hugged each of them, her expression caught somewhere between feverishly excited and distraught.

'Chin up, girl,' Teddy told her softly. 'It's been a treat knowing you. And I do believe your day will come, before long.'

Then they pulled on their leather flying caps and climbed aboard, settling themselves into the four-foot-wide seat they shared in the small cockpit and securing their safety belts. They connected their electrically heated vests up to the wire running to the battery under the seat. This would also power the throat microphones of their intercom, and the earpieces in their fur caps, so they could communicate over the noise of the engines.

It was 1.20pm local time, on the 14th of June, when Jack called out 'Contact!' and Bob Dicker swung the starting handle on the port engine; it coughed into life with a burst of smoke. Then Bob Lyons cranked the starboard engine and stepped back from the whirlwind it produced. Teddy breathed in the familiar scent of warming oil, petrol and fresh lacquer. Jack gave them the thumbs-up, the chocks were yanked free, and he pushed the throttles forward. The engines roared and the aircraft pulled away. Teddy gave the spectators a wave, and then fixed his eyes on the end of the field.

It was a bumpy ride, the engines going all out, the overloaded aeroplane slowly building up speed. Too slowly. The machine was feeling damned heavy with its hundreds of gallons of petrol, oil and water; it lumbered like a truck. Three hundred yards, and Jack made no attempt to pull back on the yoke. Three hundred and fifty. Teddy could feel some lift now as their speed increased, but not enough. Strong, sudden gusts of wind were knocking the machine around now. Jack sat rigid, hands gripping the wheel.

He pulled it back slightly. The wheels lifted, then struck the ground again. Not enough speed, not enough lift. Four hundred yards, rattling, juddering along the rough surface. Four hundred and fifty yards. They were running out of space. Teddy licked his lips and gave Jack a sidelong glance. There was a boundary dyke ahead, and a house beyond it. Their flight could come to a very premature end against that stone wall.

At the last moment, Jack eased the wheel back and Teddy felt that lurch in his stomach as the Vimy responded to the pilot's deft touch, climbing, climbing, its undercarriage passing over the wall and skimming over the roof of the building with only a few yards to spare. Teddy resisted the urge to lift his feet. Jack seemed as cool as the breeze, except for the sweat that streamed down his face. He flicked his eyes to Teddy's, blew his cheeks out and gave a grin.

'That's the hard part done!' he called.

Before they lost sight of the spectators behind the tree-lined hills, Teddy gave them another wave. Then Jack turned the machine inland, straight into the wind, climbing slowly and carefully until they were at 800 feet. The wind whistled through the struts and wires, though they were protected from the worst of it by their low windscreen. Jack throttled down the engines and turned the Vimy towards the sea, continuing to climb at a slow pace. They had a thirty-five-knot wind at their backs, and the aircraft lurched and swayed as they passed over the forests, hills and fields, then the steeply sloping streets and square-patterned roof mosaic of St John's.

The aeroplane's clock was set to Greenwich mean time – Irish time. It was twenty-eight minutes past four as they crossed the coast, and set out over the blue-grey Atlantic. Teddy twisted around to check the crucial petrol overflow gauge on the strut behind him, where Lucky Jim was attached. He would also have to watch their air speed, engine revs and temperatures, oil pressure and altitude. Most of Jack's attention would be given over to enduring the physical challenge of holding the aeroplane on course, without rest, for the entire flight. It was a heavy machine to fly. The Vimy's cruising speed was ninety miles per hour, but with the wind behind them, they were travelling at close to 150 miles per hour. Teddy cranked the handle that wound out the radio's aerial beneath them and tapped out a message to Mount Pearl Naval Station.

'*ALL WELL AND STARTED.*'

Below them, they could see sailors and fishermen waving, see the spurts of steam from boats as their whistles blew, though the fliers could not hear them, wishing them well on their journey. Watching the trawlers cutting their Vs of white foam into the sea's surface, Teddy thought of Maggie and the fishermen, and the other friends he and Jack had made, and he felt a moment of sadness to be leaving this place where, on his short stay, he had gathered so many memories. Then he turned his attention to his navigation instruments and charts. His work was only beginning.

I'll see you soon, Kitty, he thought. Just a bit of ocean to cross, and we'll be together again.

33

Maggie experienced a tumult of emotions as she watched the Vimy disappear over the wooded hills on the horizon. Excitement boiled within her; with every fibre of her being, she wished them success, and yet she was almost grief-stricken at their departure. She felt Gretchen's hand on her shoulder and she clutched it with her own, glad of the contact. Everyone there had been affected by the Vimy's take-off; all across the field, people looked around them, as if recovering from a daze and unsure what to do with themselves.

'Patrick's coming with me,' her aunt said. 'Mr Raynham has said he can drive you back to the hotel. We thought you might like to talk aeroplanes with him.'

Maggie was able to drive now, though it was still a strain on her arm, and she couldn't do it for long. She nodded gratefully to Gretchen, eyes still fixed on the sky.

'We'll see you later,' Patrick called to her. 'Assuming your head ever comes down out of those clouds! Enjoy yourself, Maggie.'

It sounded odd, the way he said it, but when she turned to look at him, he was already walking away.

'Come on then, girl,' Freddie said from the Buick's driving seat. 'What to do you say we really put this old banger through its paces, eh?'

If the last drive with Freddie had been thrilling, this one was positively hair-raising. They were charging down a narrow stretch of road when they came to a T-junction, and he brought the car to a skidding halt. Turning right would take them to St John's, while the left turn led to Quidi Vidi.

'There's just something I have to do before we go back to Cochrane's,' he said, turning left. 'It'll be hours before we hear anything from the boys anyway. It'll just be more damned waiting. No rush getting there.'

As they continued down the road, now at a more sedate pace, the Martinsyde aerodrome came into view, and the lake itself. Maggie was surprised to see the *Raymor* had been taken out of its hangar. She'd thought it wasn't ready to fly yet, after its crash, though it looked all right now.

'You may not have realised it,' Freddie told her, 'but your uncle's actions probably prevented a fire after we crashed, switching off the motor and keeping those men back, with their cigarettes. What with the fuel leak, it was a disaster in the making. He might well have saved our lives, and I am deeply in his debt.'

They came to a trail that led off the road onto the open area, and he made a beeline for the aeroplane along the bumpy track.

'He wants nothing to do with us, of course,' the pilot continued. 'You know what he's like. I think he's only hanging about for your sake.

He's quite mad about you, and *very* protective. But he has asked me for one thing, and I find myself quite unable to refuse him.'

Freddie stopped the car by the hangar, cut the engine, and turned to look at her, an earnest look on his long, youthful face.

'Maggie, my girl, would you care to come flying with me?'

His question caused her breath to catch in her chest, and she found she couldn't speak. She answered instead with a vigorous nod. He smiled and waved to one of his lads, who pulled some spare flying leathers from a box and brought them over. Freddie got the *Raymor*'s engine warming up while Maggie pulled on the warm, fur-lined boots, oversized jacket and leather helmet and goggles. They didn't have a pair of trousers to fit her, but Freddie assured her she wouldn't get very cold. They were only going for a quick spin.

'Is it all right to fly?' she asked nervously, remembering the crash and the damage that had been done.

'Oh, I do hope so,' he replied, arching an eyebrow. Then he gave her a playful grin. 'Don't worry. She's not ready to take on the Atlantic yet, but she'll do for our little jaunt!'

As she used the short step-ladder the ground crew provided to climb over the crimson-painted wall into the observer's cockpit, she could feel the vibration of the engine through the body of the aeroplane, and remembered that the Martinsyde machine was the fastest of all the aircraft taking on the Atlantic. Sitting down, it felt as if all of this light structure was simply a trailer for the mighty engine at the front, its bellow so loud it was hard to hear Freddie as he reached in to buckle her belt.

'Leave the goggles up unless your eyes start to water,' he told her. 'You'll see better without them.'

His cockpit was right behind and to the right of hers, close enough for him to be able to touch her shoulder. As soon as he was in his seat, he gave the ground crew a wave. They pulled the chocks away from the wheels and he opened up the throttle. Maggie swallowed hard as the engine noise rose and they set off. The ride was bumpier than a car, the machine ill-suited for travelling along the ground. The windscreen, now replaced after the last one had been shattered, protected her from most of the blast of the propellor, but not all of it. Clutching the leather rim of the cockpit, up at the height of her face, she tried not to think about the day of the crash, how the wind had thrown the *Raymor* around, even as it was starting to do now, how the machine had smashed down onto the ground and driven a glass spike into the head of the last person to ride in this seat.

But even with the crosswind shunting the aeroplane to the side, this was an ordinary day for Freddie Raynham, one of Britain's crack test pilots. The aeroplane went light and the tail lifted up. The wings cut into the wind, the air rushing beneath them to lift them off the ground. Maggie felt her whole body quiver as the machine now took on a different motion, the bumps long and soft instead of short and hard, and every sense she had screamed at her that she had lost contact with solid ground. She was flying. She cried out with pleasure.

She was flying.

34

Teddy knelt up on his seat to take as many observations as he could of the sun and the horizon with his sextant, and bent over the side of the cockpit to peer at the sea through the eye-piece of the drift-bearing plate, which was otherwise kept under his seat with his cane. It was difficult to lean forward to sight on the sea, with his bulky flight suit in the confines of the small cockpit. He could use his Abney spirit level to line up the sextant if he couldn't see the horizon, though it wasn't as reliable, especially with the aircraft bouncing around in the fierce gusts.

On his lap, Teddy had his Baker navigation machine, a device that allowed maps to be spooled between two rolls, with transparent charts of the celestial bodies to lay over them. An aeroplane's cockpit was not a practical space for folding and unfolding large sheets of paper. He was glad to have taken the observations when he did, for after less than an hour of flying, they entered an immense bank of fog, which cut off their view of the ocean. The forecast had been for clear weather. Instead, the shifting blue turned a hazy purple, then a dull grey, until they were surrounded on every side by the same featureless murk. His skills were about to be put to the toughest test.

From now on, he could only hope that the speed and direction of the wind wouldn't change until he could sight on the sun again. For now, they were flying by dead reckoning.

Sandwiched between fog below and cloud above, the Vimy pitched and rolled in the rough air, dropping suddenly in down-draughts that would have lifted the men from their seats if not for their safety belts. Teddy fed Jack adjustments to their course, knowing they could trust neither their senses, nor the compass alone, to tell them which direction they were going in.

Little more than an hour-and-a-half into the flight, Jack yanked the intercom earpieces out of his helmet, finding them too uncomfortable. From that point on, they communicated by shout-ing and passing notes. So it was only when Teddy pulled the radio out to send another message, that he found they were getting no power from the Vimy's wind-driven generator. He leaned over the side of the cockpit to look at the small cylindrical device attached to the wing strut beside him. The little propellor that drove it was gone. Somehow, it had broken off and been swept way. The battery under the seat would provide enough power to receive messages, but they no longer had the means to call for help if something went wrong. Jack threw him an 'I told you so' look.

Teddy could remember, back at Brooklands, when Bob Dicker had asked Jack where he wanted the radio. 'Overboard,' had been his reply. Many pilots did not like the devices, which were heavy, fiddly and unreliable. Well, at least he'll see this failure as a positive thing, Teddy thought. However, their heated flying suits also ran off the generator, and would quickly drain the battery. It was going to start getting very cold.

Just after six in the evening, they were startled by a burst of deafening noise from the starboard engine, not unlike a machine gun being fired at close quarters, and Teddy had a sudden flashback: being hit by anti-aircraft fire; seeing for a moment, holes being torn in the thin skin of their aircraft. It wasn't Archie, however, but a chunk of exhaust pipe that had split along the side of the engine. It was now shuddering in the slipstream, still attached to the engine, but threatening to tear loose, flames flickering around it. They watched in suppressed horror as it glowed orange, then a burning white. The flames were heating up one of the cross-bracing wires, turning it red-hot. If it snapped, it would weaken the structure of the aircraft, and they had no idea if its burning touch could ignite the lacquer on the wing.

A minute or two later, the pipe broke loose and whirled away into the mist without hitting any other part of the aeroplane. The bracing wire cooled back to its normal colour. With the engine's noise no longer muffled by the exhaust, it was almost unbearably loud, but both men were relieved that the damage had not been greater. Listening carefully, they detected no interruption in its rhythm, no warning vibration. The engine was still running smoothly. They would just have to endure the racket.

The fog grew thicker, until they couldn't see much beyond their cockpit. Moisture condensed on dial glasses and wires as Jack pulled back on the wheel and they rose through the clouds to 2,000 feet. They would have to watch that. If condensation on the aircraft's skin started turning to ice, it would add drag, and could interfere with the machine's control surfaces.

Jack rarely wore his goggles; Teddy only used his when he had to kneel up into the slipstream to take observations. Even on a good day, they could get fogged with moisture and oil spray. Now, they were coated with condensation. The Vimy was rising into clearer air, but another layer of clouds at around 5,000 feet blocked their view of the sky. Teddy wrote in his notepad, advising Jack to keep climbing, but slowly, until they could take a sight on the sun. They didn't want to put too much strain on the engines. They ascended, 3,000 feet, 4,000 … but there was still no sun to be seen.

At around half-past seven, Teddy opened the cupboard behind his head and took out a couple of sandwiches for Jack, some chocolate and one of the flasks. Jack had to keep one hand on the wheel, so Teddy passed him one piece of sandwich at a time, and then a cup of Horlicks.

The jolting motion of the aeroplane was still setting the compass spinning on regular occasions, but Jack did his best to keep them level. At half eight, Teddy glanced down and spotted the Vimy's shadow behind them on their right, dancing over the uneven surface of the clouds below. Looking up to the left, he saw the sun, just visible through a gap in the grey blanket that stretched overhead.

Grabbing his sextant, he took a quick sight, aiming between the port wings before the clouds closed in again. His chart showed they were still on course, though they were further east than he'd calculated, which meant the wind had increased, instead of decreasing as he'd expected from the forecasts. A little while later, he was able to get a sight on a large iceberg on the sea's surface, and calculate their drift. He found they were too far south, and passed a note to Jack to adjust their course.

Any time he had to raise himself above the level of the windshield, Teddy was hit by a freezing blast of wind, which almost immediately started to numb his hands and arms. He had to take his gloves off to use the sextant, a precision instrument that was difficult to operate with freezing fingers. With no space to move around or work the cold out of his limbs once the chill set in, it took some minutes to get his coordination back every time he sat back down and buckled up again.

Checking the fuel overflow gauge a while later, Teddy noticed it was close to full. He nudged Jack, drawing his attention to the gauge, and the pilot turned both pump taps to reduce the flow. This control of the fuel was vital. With the extra fuel tanks, pumps were needed to regulate the feed of petrol to the engines, and it was a delicate business. If the service tank was overflowing, fuel could flood the engines, drowning the ignition, causing them to misfire or stall completely. On the other hand, if the supply started failing, the engines would run out of fuel and cut out. Jack had to keep the flow just right to keep the motors running.

Hours passed. The engine noise pounded on their ears, though its droning power was a comfort. The cloud blocked out the world around them. The two men sat together in a small cockpit, in a bewildering, colourless limbo. It gave them a strange feeling of loneliness, but also freedom. There might be no one around them for hundreds of miles. They felt as if they'd been removed from the world, separated and forgotten. They knew that those they had left behind would be wondering why they had not sent any radio messages.

Around them, the light was fading.

As darkness fell, they climbed higher, close to 6,000 feet, trying to escape the cloud, but with no success. Most of the instruments had lights, but Teddy needed his torch to check the overflow gauge on the strut behind them, where Lucky Jim was tied. The toy cat made him think of Maggie, and he imagined her back in Cochrane's with the others, waiting for news, as he had done after Harry and Kenneth had left. It already seemed a lifetime away. Beyond the orange glow of the broken exhaust and a faint glow of moonlight on the wings, there was no trace of the sky.

Then, not long after midnight, Teddy spotted the pole star. Unbuckling himself to kneel up on his seat, he used the sextant to measure its angle above where he judged the horizon to be. Sitting back down, he pulled the navigation machine onto his lap. He spooled out the map and slid the transparent star chart over it, working out their position. They had flown 850 nautical miles, nearly halfway. Again, they were drifting south.

It was cold in the cockpit, though nothing like as cold as the air beyond, thanks to their heavy clothing and the closeness of the engines' radiators. The two men ate again, and had some coffee. The moon appeared at their starboard side. In this weird landscape of silvery cloud, Teddy imagined himself in a Jules Verne or HG Wells story. It seemed that the solid ground had disappeared, and they might find themselves soaring up here forever.

At around three o'clock in the morning, a thick bank of dense, dark storm cloud loomed up ahead and rushed in to swallow them. Within moments, the Vimy was seized by fierce turbulence, winds clawing it off its course. Under normal circumstances, weather like this would have forced them to land. That was not an option now. They braced themselves in the cockpit as the world whirled around them and, in minutes, Jack and Teddy lost all sense of where they were – including their sense of balance. Teddy looked over at Jack, who grimaced as he fought with the wheel. The aeroplane was tossed around in the sky, and the pilot was increasingly unsure of where his horizon was out in that dark, churning grey. He no longer even knew which way was up.

Jack had lost control of the aircraft.

35

It was impossible to make any sense of the turbulence. The needles of the instrument dials shook and spun uselessly as the machine was thrown around like a toy. The aeroplane could be standing on its ear and they might not know. The banging, jolting violence of the winds reminded Jack of flying through a deafening barrage of anti-aircraft shells. Suddenly, the Vimy's forward motion stalled. They hung in space for a moment … and then they started falling. The spinning plunge of the aeroplane was so powerful that they couldn't feel gravity, just a sickening swing that pinned them to their seats. Jack couldn't correct the spin if he didn't know *which way he needed to steer*. Any movement of the yoke just seemed to make things worse. He could barely tell what position the wheel was in.

The compass was all over the place. Their air speed indicator was stuck at ninety knots, and yet Jack was sure they were accelerating. He could hear the revs of the engines rising, the propellors spinning faster because they were no longer pulling at the air … because the machine was falling, damn it! *They were falling.* He eased off the throttles to bring the revs back under control. The aircraft was either in a full-on nose-dive or a steep, steep spiral.

The altimeter. His eyes fixed on it. That needle, at least, was making some sense. They were dropping fast – 3,000 feet … 2,000 … 1,000 … 500 feet … He needed to set eyes on the ocean … anything, just to get his bearings, even for a moment. If the cloud stretched all the way down to the sea, they were done for. They'd smash straight down into the water.

Suddenly, the air cleared. Jack's addled senses struggled to orientate themselves. The ocean, almost black in the darkness, was standing up vertically, looming like a wall on his left side. The aircraft was in a steep bank, as if balancing on its wingtips. It took precious moments for him to adjust to their position, but the machine was his again.

They were less than 100 feet above the sea and still falling fast.

A less experienced pilot, in a panic, might have wrenched the controls in the opposite direction to try and right the aeroplane. That would have killed them outright. The Vimy was a fine machine, but it was no nimble scout, able to flip over at the touch of the stick. Some thought it impossible for a machine this size to pull out of a spin. Jack, however, knew it just needed to find its balance – if it could be done before they hit the sea.

He brought the wheel and the rudder bar back to the centre, opened up the throttle and let the aircraft pull itself upright. They levelled out at fifty feet, close enough to believe they could hear the swells, the crests breaking white in the wind. They could taste salt from the ocean's spray. Jack cursed with relief and patted the wall of the cockpit, grateful to his well-built machine. His eyes fell instinctively on the compass as it stabilised itself and settled into position. He looked over at Teddy and laughed. The fall had turned them completely around. They were heading west, back to North America.

Pulling back on the yoke, Jack climbed, did a wide, banking turn and got them on course again. The wind was still rocky, but they were through the worst of it. Now they needed to gain altitude. Teddy, meanwhile, took the opportunity to peer through the eye-piece beside him to check how much the wind was causing them to drift in relation to the sea. It was the first piece of solid information he'd been able to get in hours.

36

Dawn came as a dull glow in the cloud, with no sight of the sun. Three hours passed, as they flew through one mountain of heaped vapour little better or worse than the next … endless, featureless. Moisture dripped from the instruments. Then the weather turned again, the sky darkened and a heavy rain began to fall, soon turning to snow. At the speed they were travelling, it came at them almost horizontal. They tried to climb above it, to find the sun again, reaching an altitude of 8,800 feet. The snow gave way to hail and sleet, though they were still comfortable enough in the relative warmth of the cockpit. If they raised their face or hands up above the level of the windshield for any reason, however, the particles of ice lashed painfully against their skin, and the cold stung them to the bone in seconds.

They had gone far too long without a sight of the sun, and Teddy was becoming anxious about his constant estimates of their speed and drift. Then he looked back at the fuel overflow gauge on the central strut behind him, with Maggie's cat, Lucky Jim, dangling behind it. The gauge was covered in ice. Jack wouldn't be able to regulate the fuel to the engines if he couldn't read it.

The gauge wasn't within reach of the cockpit; Teddy was going to have to climb up and clear it. The aeroplane was still rocking around when he unbuckled his safety belt and stood up on the seat. The wind hit him like a blast of ice, slamming his thighs against the seat back, its ferocity causing his chest to tighten, making him gasp. It seemed to burn his exposed nose and cheeks.

Climbing up onto the back of the fuselage was made all the more awkward by his bad leg. He leaned one hand on the icy surface, steadying himself against the juddering motion of the aircraft, and reached out with the other to wipe the snow from the gauge. It was low; Jack would need to open the pumps up a bit.

The aeroplane jolted and Teddy only just caught himself, hands splayed to stop him from sliding sideways off the flat, lacquered wood of the fuselage. From the moment he'd stood up to when he slid back into his seat, the whole manoeuvre took no more than thirty or forty seconds, and yet he was shivering violently. For several minutes, his hands were too numb to buckle his belt. Jack patted his arm in appreciation.

The snowstorm continued, and before long, Teddy was forced to go out and clear the gauge again. And again. But they were still airborne; the fuel kept flowing, the engines kept roaring. By Teddy's reckoning, they had crossed four-fifths of the distance, though his climbs up onto the fuselage had brought a new threat to his attention. The sleet was freezing on the aircraft's horizontal surfaces, thickening into ice. They desperately needed to climb, to find the sun and get a fix on their position, but the higher they flew, the colder it became, and the greater the risk of ice.

The sleet was becoming packed around the hinges of the ailerons, interfering with Jack's ability to tilt the aircraft from side to side. For the moment, though, they were stable enough. They would be all right … so long as the wind didn't start throwing them around again. Teddy couldn't see how the tail was faring, but if the twin rudders and the elevators got jammed up, they'd be in real trouble. The sheer weight of the ice could start giving them problems too …

Once again, Teddy was forced to climb out and clear the gauge. When he came back in, he could not get warm again. His gammy leg was in agony. The Vimy too, was feeling the cold, the creeping ice starting to jam up its controls. Jack kept a tight grip on the wheel. The muscles of his arms, shoulders and back were aching now, the strain of all those hours starting to tell on him.

At around five o'clock in the morning, flying at nearly 11,000 feet, Teddy caught the tiniest glimmer of the sun through the cloud. He fumbled with the sextant, aiming it without a horizon. He struggled to get a clear reading, but by 7.20, he had confirmed their position. They were close to the Irish coast.

Even as Teddy started to write a note to pass on this information, the starboard engine began backfiring, a threatening popping noise that sent a shiver of fear through the two men. With the aircraft in its iced-up state, any problem with the engine would be disastrous. Jack throttled back and let the Vimy glide slowly downwards into warmer air. The wind began to gust again, but the ice was clearing off and the aeroplane, lightened by the consumption of most of its fuel, was much easier to handle.

Now, they were faced with a new problem. As they came close to land, the world around them was still obscured by cloud. They couldn't be sure where along the coast they would arrive. The altimeter measured air pressure from sea level upwards. They couldn't know what height the land ahead of them would be. It might be a beach or a mountain. If the fog extended all the way to the ground when they began descending further, they could fly straight into a cliff or a tree.

Fate was kind, however, and as they descended to 500 feet, they flew down out of the cloud to see the rough, steel-grey sea beneath them. Teddy checked their drift and decided they were a little too far north. The wind had changed direction at some point, but not so much as to push them away from Ireland. He gave Jack the course adjustment, and Jack nodded and brought the machine around, keeping them just below the cloud cover.

They had just finished a half-hearted breakfast and Teddy was turned around, putting the food back in the cupboard behind him, when Jack seized his shoulder and started shouting over the clamour of the engines. The navigator turned and looked where his friend was pointing: in the distance were two tiny specks of land, with a blur of the mainland above them.

Ireland.

The specks were the tiny islands of Eeshal and Turbot, off the coast of Galway, not far from Clifden. In an extraordinary feat of navigation, Teddy had guided them over more than 1,800 miles of ocean and placed them almost exactly where they had intended to arrive.

At 8.25 on that Sunday morning, they passed over the white breakers that surged into shore, and found themselves crossing a landscape that was eerily similar to the one they'd left behind in Newfoundland – a rocky terrain of green and grey, with stone walls, silvery pools and patches of woodland. Ahead of them was a wall of mist-shrouded mountains. Jack's careful tending of the engines meant they had over ten hours of fuel left – nearly a third of their full load, and certainly enough to reach London or Brooklands. But they had already succeeded, and were keen to free themselves from the cloud that had plagued them all the way across the Atlantic, and get down onto solid ground again.

Teddy was about to ask Jack to circle around so he could work out their exact position when he spotted the Marconi wireless station at Derrygimla. Its huge condenser building and power station, and its array of eight steel masts, each over 200 feet high, extended eastwards over the hill for about a quarter of a mile. It looked so out of place in this rural landscape that it seemed to be a from another world. It confirmed that the small town nearby was indeed Clifden, though when they circled over it at a mere 250 feet, they could see no one about, apart from one boy out on the street, who waved at them in amazement.

It was twenty to nine on a Sunday morning, and everyone was either in bed or at Mass. Swinging back around towards the wireless station, the two men saw a field nearby that looked perfect for a landing – a flat, green carpet with plenty of space, free of boulders or any other obvious hazards. Instinctively, both men loosened their seatbelts, in case they had to make a quick exit from the aeroplane. Teddy took out the Very pistol and fired off two red flares to alert those below. Jack wasted no more time, lining up to land into the west wind. Cutting the engines, he brought them gliding down.

As they passed over the condenser house, staff from the wireless station were running out, waving their arms at the aircraft. There were soldiers too; Ireland was in the middle of a revolutionary war, of course, and the troops were no doubt here to protect the strategically valuable radio station. Teddy waved back at the running figures below. As the Vimy descended, the people waved more frantically, and Teddy frowned. Looking around for any possible dangers to the aircraft, he still saw nothing to alarm him.

Jack pulled back on the wheel, flattening them out and bringing the wheels down with masterful skill, settling onto the ground with no more than a soft bump. They even seemed to be decelerating quickly, perhaps slowed by the wind.

They had rolled less than fifty yards when the Vimy came a sudden, shuddering halt. The tail tipped up and, with a sickening, brittle crunching sound and a massive squelch of mud, the nose punched down into the earth, hurling both men forward. Jack saved himself by slamming his feet against the rudder bar with enough force to bend it. Teddy's face hit the windshield. Apart from a bloody nose, he came away relatively unhurt, though he was stunned, his head reeling.

The 'field' was in fact a bog – they had landed on a surface that had all the solidity of thick porridge. The Vimy's body was buckled, its nose, propellors and the leading edges of its lower wings embedded in the muck. It took Teddy a few moments to realise that, though the engines had stopped, his ears were still ringing from the hours of noise. He wondered if it had left him deaf forever.

The crash must have ruptured some of the fuel lines. Petrol was gushing down the sloped floor of the cockpit. They needed to get out, fast. Jack had already switched off the current on the magnetos to prevent any sparks. Teddy grabbed his cane, his instruments and logbook and Jack took the sack of mail, and they both clambered out and dropped down to the spongey ground. Staggering on shaky legs that had not walked for nearly a full day, they could see the people from the wireless station running up, their mouths moving as they called out. Teddy could barely hear them.

Was anybody hurt? Who were they? What were they doing here? Where had they come from?

'America!' Jack yelled back, equally deafened, his voice strange, even though he was standing right next to Teddy.

There were laughs and expressions of disbelief. The crash had obviously rattled the fliers' brains.

'We're Alcock and Brown,' Jack told them. 'Yesterday, we were in America!'

Nobody would believe them until Jack showed them the sack full of letters, each one with its airmail stamp and the Newfoundland postmark. Then there were cheers and congratulations and vigorous handshakes, excitement spreading as more people began to arrive. The aviators had been in the air for sixteen-and-a-half hours, and the exhaustion was finally starting to settle over them. Jack was stretching out his limbs, pain evident on his face as his body released the hours of tension he'd maintained to keep the aircraft under control.

Teddy put a hand on his shoulder, and they turned to look at their Vickers Vimy. It was a sombre sight, a somewhat bitter end to their journey, and they wondered if the wrecked aircraft would ever fly again. The realisation of what they had done was still only starting to seep through them. It had been a flight, that was all; a very challenging one, but with passionate support from the many people at Vickers, their ground crew and the people of St John's. They had been lifted by the ingenuity and daring of the pioneer fliers who had come before them, who had helped lay the path to this moment. They had been lucky where others had not. But this moment was theirs, and would always remain theirs.

Captain John Alcock and Lieutenant Arthur Whitten Brown, the first people to fly non-stop across the Atlantic Ocean.

37

I t was the middle of January, deep in the Newfoundland winter, when the letter arrived. And though Maggie felt a flush of excitement at the sight of Teddy's handwriting, she dreaded opening the envelope. She took it out to the garage, where it was cold, but she could be alone.

There was a workbench under the window, next to the noticeboard, and she glanced at the kite sitting on its surface. It was the shape of an aeroplane, about the length of her arm, with oversized wings, and made of balsa wood and linen. It needed another coat of lacquer. This was her third attempt at designing a kite, and she was determined that this one wouldn't end up as a broken wreck on the beach.

Standing in the light from the window, she gazed at the envelope for a long minute. She had soaked up every word of news she could find about the aviators after they'd landed in Ireland, from their first interview with Tom Kenny of the *Connacht Tribune*, and the heroes' welcome they'd received in Connemara, to their triumphant trip home, on a train from Galway to Dublin, where crowds had greeted them at every station. Their hands must have ached from signing autographs.

Everything about their story was now contributing to a legend. Even she had been asked to write an article for the *Evening Telegram*, after Joey Smallwood heard that Freddie Raynham had taken her flying.

After Dublin came the boat to Holyhead and the train journey to London, where the crowds dwarfed those in Ireland, and where Teddy was finally reunited with his beloved Kathleen. A celebratory luncheon was thrown by the *Daily Mail* at the Savoy Hotel, with dishes whose names were inspired by the two aviators – 'Sole à la Brown'; 'Chicken Vickers Vimy'. They were presented with Lord Northcliffe's £10,000 prize, and they announced that their ground crew, back in Newfoundland, would receive £2,000 of the award. The Secretary of State for War, Winston Churchill, gave a rousing speech, describing their journey in suitably dramatic fashion. He also announced that the King of England had agreed that both men should be knighted for their achievement.

After London, they travelled to Manchester, and then to Brooklands, their spiritual home, where the Vickers workers and the rest of the Brooklands set were ready and waiting for them. Teddy and Kathleen began planning their wedding. Jack was keen to use his share of the money to set up a garage and car dealership, and he was intent on getting back into the air as soon as possible.

Maggie's chest shuddered with a sob. She leaned back against the workbench, and wiped her eyes before finally reaching for a knife to open the letter.

My dear Maggie,

I hope this letter finds you well. I am sure too, that with your curious nature, you will have kept abreast of all the outlandish goings-on that followed our arrival home. I felt compelled to sit down and write to you, given all that has happened, for there are some thoughts I needed to share.

As you will no doubt have heard, our friend Jack has died. It has enveloped this whole adventure in a most depressing cloud and now, for me, every mention of the flight's success is another reminder of our loss. On the 18th of December, Jack was flying a prototype Vickers aircraft, a Viking Mark I, over to France for an aeronautical exhibition in Paris. Flying the Channel was a mere jaunt compared to our journey over the Atlantic, and he knew the territory, so he went without a navigator. He flew into thick fog, battling bad winds as he approached Rouen, and it's thought he tried to make an emergency landing. The aeroplane struck a tree and he lost control. He suffered a head injury in the crash, and died before he could be taken to a hospital.

We were such close friends over such an intense period in our lives, it seems hard to believe that I only knew him for nine brief months. The loss is difficult to bear.

When we first made our plans after the war, Kathleen and I had intended to move to America, but given my change in circumstances, we will stay here now, and I shall take up a position that has been offered to me in Vickers. This episode of my life has been quite the experience. I am relieved that it has all calmed down and things can return to some semblance of normality.

The time Jack and I spent with you, and the people of St John's, was an intimate part of that experience, and I can tell you, young lady, that you made quite an impression on us, in the short time we knew you. I can only guess what you're feeling right now, but I urge you to dwell on Jack's life, rather than his death. It's what he did, when faced with the death of a friend. You have, as he had, an irrepressible spirit, and a hunger for adventure, and nothing would ever keep him down for long. Your generation will know a different world to ours, and I urge you to embrace it, to harness that hunger of yours and look to the horizon. Fly, Maggie. Explore. Seize life, and shake everything you can out of it.

Jack would have expected no less from you, and nor would I.

Sincerely, your friend,
Teddy

John Alcock and Arthur Whitten Brown with their Vickers Vimy aeroplane, 1919.

ACKNOWLEDGEMENTS

I am very conscious, in writing this, how influenced we are by our families, and by our environment growing up. No one develops in a vacuum. The way I write now, and the topics I choose to write about, are almost as much a product of my environment as they are of my work. I am grateful for my family; the parents and siblings I grew up with, and for my wife and children and the families that have grown up around us. They are, and always will be, a source of inspiration, imagination and wisdom.

I used a wide range of reference materials in the writing of this book, but there were four books that I kept coming back to and, towards the end of the writing, occupied a near-permanent place on the desk beside my keyboard. The first was Arthur Whitten Brown's personal account of the flight, *Flying the Atlantic in Sixteen Hours*. It is a characteristically modest and concise telling of their epic experience, and seems to have been written almost as an excuse for him to discuss afterwards his passion for navigation and research, and to ponder the future of commercial flight. His thoughtful curiosity and intelligence shines out of it. Cecil Lewis's memoir, *Sagittarius Rising*, has detailed and evocative descriptions of flying in the First World War and gives a firsthand taste of the lives of aviators in that era.

For anyone interested in the monumental operation carried out by the US Navy and the NC flying boats, *First Across* by Richard K. Smith records the events in meticulous and exhaustive detail.

It was a great help as an overview of the race to cross the Atlantic and is a fantastic story in its own right. Finally, for anyone looking for what must be the definitive account of Alcock and Brown's historic flight, Brendan Lynch's *Yesterday We Were in America* is engaging, immersive and packed with facts and character detail. I urge you to read it.

The team at O'Brien Press have, as ever, been a pleasure to work with. My thanks to my editor, Eoin O'Brien, to designer Emma Byrne and to Jon Berkeley for the excellent cover illustration, and to everyone who has helped to turn this story into a book.

Oisín McGann, 2019.